CITRON PRESS

IN THE LONG RUN

Made redundant aged 47, George Stratford was sure he would get another job. A year later he was still unemployed, struggling to survive on £40 a week benefit. The only thing which kept him going was his commitment to writing 1000 words a day, every day. Now a successful copy writer at Saatchi & Saatchi, George is on his third novel. *In the Long Run* is the first to be published.

Fresh ideas from
NEW AUTHORS
CO-OPERATIVE

Published by Citron Press
Connors Corp. Ltd., Suite 155, Business Design Centre,
52 Upper Street, Islington Green, London N1 0QH, Great Britain
www.citronpress.co.uk

This Book is a Work of Fiction. Names, Characters, Places and Incidents are either products of the author's imagination or are used fictitiously. Any resemblance to actual events or locales or persons, living or dead, is entirely coincidental.

Copyright © George Stratford 1999

The Author has asserted his moral right to be identified as the author of this work.

ISBN 075440126X

Printed and bound in Great Britain by The Basingstoke Press 75 Ltd.

All rights reserved. No part of this publication may be reproduced, stored in a retrieval system, or transmitted in any form or by means, electronic, mechanical, photocopying, recording, or otherwise, without the prior permission of the publishers.

A copy of this book is held at the British Library.

*To Mike.
With best wishes,
George Stratford*

■ **IN THE** LONG RUN

GEORGE **STRATFORD** ■

This novel is dedicated to the memory of my dear mother. How I wish that you could have lived long enough to see it published.

NOTE

Whilst this is primarily a work of fiction, the Comrades Marathon is an actual event which has been run annually since 1921. All performances regarding real-life competitors from the 1990 race have been accurately recorded.

I would like to thank Bruce Fordyce, Steve Cram and Linda Barron of the Comrades Association in Pietermaritzburg for her help and co-operation. Also thanks to John Stoodley, Mike Olsen, the Shuttleworth brothers and the great number of competitors, past and present, who gave me their time at home, in bars, in restaurants and just about anywhere else I could pin them down.

Finally, there has to be an extra special vote of gratitude to Chris and Jill Besson of Mandene Park Sports Club. Without the kindness and assistance that they and many of their fellow club members gave to a total stranger, this novel would probably never have been written.

FOREWORD

When Nelson Mandela gave the Rugby World Cup to the captain of the South African rugby team, François Pienaar, in 1995 it created a lasting image of the amazing power of sport in South Africa to dissolve race barriers and help the healing process within a famously divided country. Another example is the awesome 55-mile Comrades Marathon in Kwazulu-Natal — arguably South Africa's single most popular annual sporting event. The sheer number of people, of all shapes, sizes, ages and colours, who attempt the tortuous 55 miles over mountainous terrain each year has to be seen to be believed. The tension-filled atmosphere, the camaraderie and the sense of achievement at the finish make the Comrades stand out as one of the best road races in the world. Physical strength is important but it's mental strength that is paramount when tackling this arduous challenge.

I first encountered the Comrades Marathon through one of its champions, Bruce Fordyce, in Bosnia, where a replica of the Comrades was being run by a small British group to raise funds for children in the Balkans. That small group is now called COCO, Comrades of Children Overseas, and it was for them that I ran my first real Comrades in 1999. There are new lessons to be learned in every race, but, as the brilliantly-drawn characters in *In the Long Run* demonstrate so well, the specific challenges of the awesome Comrades Marathon — twice as long as any other marathon — allow the ordinary people taking part to achieve something truly extraordinary.

Steve Cram
Six-time gold medallist at Commonwealth, European and World Championships, Olympic silver medallist and world record holder

GEORGE **STRATFORD**

PROLOGUE

During the last ten minutes the pain had grown noticeably less. Still running at a fairly brisk pace, Steve Ryan followed the marker flags and bore left, finally leaving the quiet rural road he had pounded along for so many miles. The dirt track he now found himself on soon led into a large field, the cut down grass here a brilliant green after much recent rain.

As he entered this lush area Ryan was only vaguely aware of the applause and shouts of encouragement from waiting spectators. A wide, roped-off pathway covered in brown matting stretched ahead. It was at the end of this pathway, some hundred metres further on, that his attention was now focused. After twenty-six miles, the finish line and victory beckoned. A huge overhead banner bearing the sponsor's name proclaimed that this was the 1985 East Hampshire Marathon.

Ryan did not waste time looking behind. A quick glance shortly before leaving the road had already assured him that his lead was unassailable. And this in only his third marathon. After several disappointing seasons in far shorter track events, it seemed that he had finally found his athletic forte.

Moments later, as he ecstatically breasted the winning tape, he knew for certain that he had.

There was a steady stream of people eager to shake Ryan's hand and offer congratulations. Many were total strangers to him, but all who approached were dealt with politely.

IN THE LONG RUN

'Well done Steve. Your official time was two hours, sixteen minutes exactly. Pretty good for a twenty-year-old I'd say.'

The speaker this time was Stan Cox, a well-known and forthright sports reporter from one of the largest south coast newspapers. Ryan recognised the middle-aged man and grinned in his direction.

'Thanks.'

'You beat some good runners today,' the journalist continued. 'There'll be a few noses put out of joint.'

There was a pause before Cox added: 'I wonder though, was this just a flash in the pan? Tell me honestly Steve, have you really got the commitment to work hard enough to go all the way?'

This was typical of Cox's abrasive style. It provoked a heated response.

'I'll work hard enough,' Ryan assured the man, his eyes narrowing. 'Don't you worry yourself about that.'

His interrogator grinned and held up a hand in mock defence. 'OK, I believe you. Honest I do.'

Cox then consulted a small notepad. 'I've got down here that you're from Sussex University. Is that right?'

There remained a challenging tone in the man's voice that Ryan did not like. He gave a curt nod. 'That's right. So what?'

As he spoke he glanced across at his friend and fellow student, Ronnie Tyler, who was stood alongside. The look Ryan received in return urged caution.

Cox shrugged. 'Well Sussex *has* got a reputation for being a bit...' He paused to select the right word.

'Radical,' he said finally.

The supplementary nudge from Tyler had little effect on Ryan. As Tyler knew only too well, there were just two ways in which his normally easy-going friend could be provoked into rapid anger. One was to question his athletic dedication, the other was to mock or doubt his political beliefs. This man Cox seemed determined to start something.

Ryan took a pace forward, his right index finger extended. 'If by radical you mean supporting the principle of basic human rights, then yes, we are radical. A lot of people at Sussex, including myself, care very passionately about what's going on in the world.'

Cox's reputation had not been gained by backing away from an argument. He thrived on such confrontations. The passion they generated had proved the basis for many of his best articles. Several of these had centred on the separation of sport from politics.

He allowed a faint look of derision to spread across his face. 'Spare me the philanthropist bit. You're hardly a bunch of missionaries, are you? Look at the way you lot go about things. Take that anti-apartheid campaign for instance — the one involving broken glass being scattered over rugby pitches. That's really caring, isn't it? Full of human kindness. Never mind the fact that some poor sod could have been maimed for life.'

'That was never the intention and you bloody well know it!' The words sprang from Ryan. 'All we wanted to do was stop the South African tour. That was achieved.'

'By violent means,' Cox retorted. 'And hasn't it ever occurred to you that there were a huge number of people in this country who actually wanted to see the Springboks play rugby? What about their rights? Sportsmen aren't politicians, and they shouldn't be made scapegoats for what others do.'

The thin elastic thread separating Ryan's temper from reason was on the verge of snapping. 'How the hell can you say that?' he demanded. 'Talk about burying you head in the sand. You'll be telling me next that—'

'Leave it Steve!'

It was Tyler's voice that suddenly barked out. He grasped Ryan's wrist in a firm, controlling grip. Once again the two students' eyes met. This time however Tyler was not offering advice. He was issuing an order.

Ryan glowered back at the reporter as he was hustled away

For a moment it seemed that Cox would attempt to follow them. He then paused and smiled to himself. There would be other opportunities. Putting away his notebook, he instead headed for the refreshment tent nearby.

The pair drove back to campus in Tyler's battered Ford Capri.

Tyler had been a good friend, Ryan reflected during a lull in their conversation. He knew that his fellow student had very little interest in athletics. Nevertheless, he had always been willing whenever asked to provide transport and a supportive presence. Still on a success induced high, Ryan felt that, despite Tyler's general indifference to sport, his victory might just have gone some way towards repaying his friend's efforts.

There was of course another reason for their close friendship. A binding link forged by mutual enthusiasm and objectives. Even within the militant Sussex

IN THE LONG RUN

campus it was accepted that Tyler was an outstanding member of the regional anti-apartheid movement. A natural leader. Ryan, who within days of joining the university had been attracted by the moral issues at stake, quickly became one of Tyler's most vigorous supporters. Together they had been involved in just about every major demonstration of the last eighteen months.

The memory of these prompted Ryan to speak again. 'I can't believe I let that bloody reporter wind me up so much,' he said.

Tyler nodded. 'Sure, I know how hard it is to keep your mouth shut sometimes. But having a go at that guy isn't the answer Steve. It's the cause we need to draw attention to, not ourselves as individuals. Not yet anyway. Perhaps when we've won the fight.'

Ryan said nothing as he dwelled on this point. Some traffic lights ahead showed red. As they came to a halt, Tyler turned his head to gaze directly into Ryan's eyes.

'Besides,' he continued, 'there might come a time when we can do something really big for the cause. And I mean *really big*. If it does, that's when it will pay not to have had your past activities splashed all over the papers.'

There was now a powerful intensity to Tyler's voice. Briefly his eyes shone with the commitment of a true visionary. Then suddenly they didn't any more. It was if someone had flicked off a switch. In the space of one short breath his tone and expression became almost lighthearted. 'And don't forget your ambition to run in the Olympics. After today's performance I reckon you'll make it.'

For several seconds Ryan found his mind turning to the other great preoccupation of his life. To win an Olympic gold medal had been his ambition for as long as he could remember. Now it was beginning to become more than a dream. It *was* possible. Briefly he pictured himself on the victory rostrum, bowing low to receive the coveted gold medal.

A little guilty that he should be dwelling on this self-indulgent aspect, he hastily switched his mind back to more principled matters. Tyler's implication intrigued him.

'What do you mean by really big?' he asked. Have you got something lined up?'

Tyler's gaze remained steady. 'No, not yet. But you never know what's around the corner. Remember, I'm making new contacts all the time.'

The traffic lights changed to green, taking his attention back to the road. Ryan started to say something, but a flick of his friend's hand indicated quite forcibly that he did not wish to be pressed any further.

As the car pulled away, Tyler's face was expressionless.

GEORGE STRATFORD

CHAPTER ONE

June 1989

Although early winter and only eight o'clock in the morning, the South African sun was already warm on this section of the Natal coast. Blythdale Beach, a small holiday resort nestled comfortably at the foot of a hill approximately eighty kilometres north of Durban.

Three-quarters of the way down this hill lay Piet du Toit's recently built bungalow. He had lived in Blythdale for close on a year now, and still found his new home a pleasing contrast to the rush and tear of big city life in Johannesburg. As an employee of the nearby SAPPI paper mill it was an undemanding drive to work each day, a fact that he was eternally grateful for.

This morning however he was anticipating a much lengthier drive. Today was Saturday. This was the weekend he had promised the family a special day out in Durban. Piet knew for certain that his two daughters, Michelle and Claudine, had spent days eagerly anticipating the event. Both girls had been christened as such in deference to his French born wife, Cecile.

There was just one annoying hold up to their carefully planned early start. The non-appearance of Piet's gardener, Armstrong.

Armstrong, a seventeen year-old Zulu boy, came every weekend to tend the large garden. He was habitually punctual and a very hard worker. Monday to Friday the youth attended a school close to his home in the township of Shakaville. Early every Saturday morning he would cycle the twelve or so kilometres from his home to Piet's, arriving without fail at a quarter to eight. Piet

IN THE LONG RUN

would then set out his tasks for the day, and by eight o'clock the boy would be hard at work.

But not today. A little irritated, Piet paced around his front lawn, constantly gazing up the hill for the familiar sight of a beaming Armstrong racing down the slope astride his aged, creaking bicycle. Piet glanced at his watch. It was ten past eight and there was still no sign of him.

More as a deviation than anything else, Piet paused to look at the thermometer hanging from a low branch of his one and only mango tree. It showed twenty degrees and rising. It would be warm today for the time of year he reflected. This agreeable climate was just one more aspect of life here on the Natal coast that was so different from the much higher situated Johannesburg. There it could get distinctly cold during winter.

Michelle, dark-haired, pretty, and advanced beyond her fourteen years, joined her father in the garden. She wore just shorts and a tee shirt.

'What time are we leaving Dad?' she asked. There was a note of petulance in her voice. Along with other treats, she had been promised money to buy clothes of her own choice and was eager to get to the big city stores.

'We can't leave until Armstrong gets here,' Piet told her. 'I need to explain very carefully what I want him to do today.'

The teenager flicked a strand of long hair over her shoulder in a gesture of impatience. 'He's always here by now,' she said unnecessarily before poking at the grass with a bare foot and then wandering off again.

As she spoke Piet glanced once more up the hill. There was still no sign of Armstrong's bicycle, but he could make out the shape of a young African running rapidly towards the bungalow. As the figure drew nearer Piet took a deep breath. It was Armstrong, minus his usual means of transport.

A few moments later a heavily perspiring Armstrong arrived at the gate.

'Morning Boss,' he said between deep breaths. He stood where he was, as if uncertain about the reception he might get. Within just a few seconds his breathing was close to normal.

Piet waited for this to happen before looking pointedly at his watch.

'What happened?' he asked. His irritation was now gone. It was obvious that the boy had made every effort to be on time.

Armstrong sensed that he was not in trouble and relaxed a touch. His face clouded over. 'Some *sgebengu* stole my bike.' *Sgebengu* was the Zulu term for rascal or villain.

Piet looked suitably sympathetic. 'So how did you get here? Did someone drive you to the top of the hill? You couldn't have run all the way.'

The Zulu boy nodded his head vigorously, his teeth flashing in a broad smile. 'Yes, I ran all the way. I didn't want to let you down Boss.'

Piet stared at his for several seconds. The youngster by now appeared almost fully recovered from his recent exertion. It was simply not possible for him to have run all the way from Shakaville and then recuperate so rapidly.

'No Armstrong,' he explained. 'I didn't mean all the way down the hill. I meant from home.'

Armstrong continued to nod. 'That's what I mean too. Like I said, I didn't want to let you down. You say last week that you go to Durban today. Be early you told me.' He shrugged. 'With no bike, it was the only way I could get here.'

He began to run energetically on the spot in an effort to convince Piet of the truth.

As far as Piet knew, the boy had never lied to him. So why doubt him now? Even so, Armstrong must be incredibly fit, and much stronger than his wiry frame suggested, to have managed what he claimed.

Piet was impressed and it showed in his voice. 'I'm very pleased you made such a big effort for me,' he said. Scratching around in his back pocket he found a five rand note which he handed to Armstrong. 'Here's something extra for your trouble.'

The boy's expression was usually cheerful. This unexpected bonus however made his grin even wider than normal. He accepted the note in traditional Zulu manner, both arms extended with palms open upward to show that he was not holding a concealed weapon.

'I run for you every week Boss,' he suggested with a gleam in his eyes.

Piet smiled to himself. 'Surely you wouldn't want to do that run regularly?'

Armstrong shrugged. 'Why not? It's easy.'

The offhand way in which the youth dismissed his feat intrigued the Afrikaner. 'You'd have to get up very early,' he pointed out.

'Not so much.'

Piet's curiosity rose. 'So how long did it take you then?'

A couple of months ago he had given the boy an old watch. One that he himself had worn when at school. Although fairly cheap, it had kept going for years, and was now proudly worn by Armstrong at all times. The youngster turned his wrist to see the face.

IN THE LONG RUN

'Forty minutes,' he declared after some hesitation.

Piet did a quick mental calculation. That was less than three and a half minutes per kilometre. And then there was the undulating road and heat to consider.

He glanced at the boy's feet. He wore ageing tackies that looked a shade too big for him. They were probably handed down by an older member of the family. Whatever, they were hardly ideal footwear for such a run.

No, it was not possible, he decided. Surely the boy had made a mistake. A trained athlete would not be ashamed of a time like that, especially under such conditions.

'Are you sure Armstrong?' he asked, the scepticism evident in his voice. 'What time did you leave home?'

This time the Zulu youth did not even consult his watch. 'Same time as always Boss. Half past seven. My bike was gone, so I ran instead.' The casual manner of his words suggested that he could have been referring to a gentle jog around the block.

Again Piet studied Armstrong's face. There was no trace of deviousness there. He knew that the boy went to school regularly and was of above average intelligence. It was unlikely that he could be mistaken. All the same, what he was claiming was hard to believe. If the facts were correct then the youngster was a natural athlete. With the correct training and equipment, who could say what he might achieve?

Don't get carried away, Piet told himself. The first thing to do was see for himself how well the boy could perform. By now, amazingly, he appeared as fresh as could be. Full of all his usual energy.

'Do you feel like showing me how well you can run?' he asked.

'When Boss?'

'Why not right now if you feel fit enough?'

Armstrong frowned. 'What about my work? I need the money.'

Piet waved his hand in reassurance. 'Don't worry, I'll still pay you. You can start work when we get back.'

The youth's happy smile immediately returned. Clearly the idea of being paid for time spent running was a proposition too good to turn down. He laughed. 'Anything you say Boss. Where you want me to run to?'

Suddenly he was keen to show off. He could see that Piet doubted the time of his run. Well he knew that what he'd said was right. Now was his chance to prove it.

Piet thought for a moment. 'How far do you think you can go?'

'All the way back home if you like.'

Slowly Piet shook his head in amazement. It was clear that Armstrong was not joking.

'I'll tell you what,' he said. 'I'll drive along the Stanger road for six kilometres. That's near enough half way. I'll wait for you there and then bring you back. That will be enough for today.'

As he spoke Michelle returned, this time accompanied by her younger sister. 'Are you ready yet Dad?' they asked almost in unison.

So engrossed had Piet been with Armstrong that he had temporarily forgotten all other considerations. Now, slightly shamefaced, he turned towards his daughters.

'I'm sorry girls,' he said, 'I've got to go out with Armstrong for a short while. I won't be very long.'

Michelle all but stamped her foot. 'What for?' she demanded.

Piet regarded her sharply. 'If you take that tone with me, you won't be going anywhere young lady.'

Sensibly her younger sister kept quiet. Michelle however appeared determined to press matters. 'Where are you going,' she asked, her voice changing to a whine.

Piet sighed. Lately his eldest daughter had become increasingly difficult. She had been such a sweet girl until moving up a class at school. Now she had formed a new circle of friends, many of who came from rich families and who were spoiled beyond belief. Although never denied whatever Piet could afford, when Michelle compared her lot with that of the others, he had seen dissatisfaction rapidly set in. She had begun to mimic their over-indulged antics.

'Where are you going Dad?' she repeated.

Considering matters, Piet supposed that he did owe her some sort of explanation. She had, after all, been promised a special day out and an early start.

'I'm going to see how well Armstrong can run.'

Even as he spoke, he realised how stupid and inadequate the words must sound to a fourteen year-old girl impatiently anticipating her treat.

'I think he might be very good indeed,' he added in an attempt to explain himself.

Michelle could not believe her ears. 'What!' she howled. This time she did stamp her foot. 'You're going to watch *him* run instead of keeping your promise to me.'

She placed a heavy emphasis on the word 'him', at the same time fixing Armstrong with a contemptuous stare.

IN THE LONG RUN

The youth stared back at her for a moment before looking away. His face gave no indication of his feelings.

'That's enough,' Piet reprimanded angrily. 'One more word from you and you won't be going anywhere.'

Michelle's bottom lip jutted out. She gazed at the ground by her feet. Softly she mumbled something.

'What was that?' Piet demanded, moving closer. 'I didn't hear you properly.'

Michelle raised her face and glared at her father defiantly before shouting her answer.

'I said he's only a garden boy!'

With that she turned and ran into the house, tears streaming down her face.

Claudine, who had listened silently to this exchange, looked pleadingly at her father. It was nothing to do with me, the look said.

Although angry, Piet reassured her with a quick smile. At least she was still a good kid. Quickly though he reminded himself that, at the age of twelve, Michelle too had been a daughter to be proud of. He offered a quick prayer that history would not repeat itself.

He then turned to Armstrong, his embarrassment evident.

Before he could say a word the youth cut in. 'We run some other time eh Boss.' If he was upset or angry, he did not allow it to show.

'No,' Piet insisted, 'we go this morning. Just give me a few minutes to sort things out indoors.'

He turned back to Claudine. 'Come on,' he said. 'Let's go and see your Mum.'

*

Piet drove his Toyota Estate along the Stanger road until he had clocked up exactly six kilometres. He then pulled over beside a sugar cane field and prepared to wait.

He had left home at precisely nine o'clock. As he'd driven up the hill Armstrong had been clearly visible in the rear view mirror, sprinting after the car for all he was worth. His style was ungainly and energy sapping — arms waving and the body rolling from side to side. It seemed highly unlikely that he could keep up that sort of pace for very long. Nonetheless, as Piet turned the first bend, the boy had given him a cheerful wave.

Even with the windows open it was still uncomfortably hot inside the car. Getting out, Piet pondered on things. If the boy was accurate in his claims then he could be an exciting prospect. Although no athlete himself, Piet was a keen armchair sportsman. He had smoked too much in the past, and at forty-five years old it was a bit late in the day to fulfil any personal dreams of glory. If though he could be instrumental in helping someone younger attain success, that in itself would give him a large degree of satisfaction. A sense of achievement even. It would be as if he were using someone else's body to attain his own lost dreams of sporting glory.

The minutes passed. It was now nine-fifteen. If Armstrong was really capable of still running at the pace he claimed to, he should appear soon.

It was in fact less than a minute later when the boy appeared in the distance, arms still flailing. Piet felt a huge surge of satisfaction. There could be no doubting his ability now. None at all.

'Come on,' he found himself muttering. 'Can you do it in under twenty minutes? Try Armstrong — try hard.'

Closer and closer the Zulu came as Piet stared at his watch, all the time trying to equate the time and distance remaining.

'One last effort,' he shouted as the youth neared.

Armstrong responded with a huge grin and a confident wave. Despite the increasing heat he was enjoying himself immensely. Ducking his head lower, he lengthened his stride.

Even with this final burst, Piet quickly realised that the boy was not going to make it inside the set target. In fact it was close to a minute over when Armstrong reached him.

Even so, Piet told himself, it was still a hugely impressive performance, especially when he considered Armstrong's earlier efforts. His raw talent was there for anyone to see. His potential was unlimited.

Then, in a morning of surprises, Armstrong produced one more. Instead of pulling up alongside Piet, the youth ran straight past him. For a moment he was speechless. He watched as the boy ran around his car some twenty metres further on. Without breaking stride the youngster then headed back in his direction.

For a second time he ran straight past Piet, sweating profusely but plainly still full of running. It was clear that he intended to continue all the way back to Blythdale.

Regaining his speech, Piet called after him. 'That's enough Armstrong. Come back.'

The youth did not hear him, or perhaps did not choose to. Either way, he kept going.

IN THE LONG RUN

Piet hurried back to his car and set off in pursuit. Overhauling his runaway gardener, he sounded his horn several times, at the same time waving his other hand in a signal to pull up. Reluctantly Armstrong finally did so.

Reaching out to open the passenger door, Piet regarded the perspiring youngster. 'That's enough,' he repeated. 'Come on, get in.'

Armstrong, in his enthusiasm to show off his ability, had allowed himself to become carried away. The stern note in which he was now being addressed bought him sharply back to earth. His face clouded over.

'Sorry Boss,' he said.

Piet could not contain a smile. Even when Armstrong did something wrong, it was impossible to remain annoyed for any length of time.

As they drove back to Blythdale, Piet did some thinking. There were several excellent athletic coaches in the area that he knew socially. Neil Douglas, a hard little Scot who had lived in Natal for the last ten years, was probably the best. If anyone could get the full potential out of Armstrong it was him. As an ex-physical training instructor with the parachute regiment he was uncompromising in his attitude towards fitness.

Excited though he was, there were still several doubts in Piet's mind. How would the easy going Armstrong react to a strict training schedule? Come to that, did the boy have any real ambition to become involved in competitive running? These were just some of the matters that would have to be considered before too many plans were made. Now was not the time though. Later, when he returned from Durban, would be far better.

By four o'clock that afternoon Armstrong had nearly completed his work in the garden. The Boss had been very careful with his instructions. These orders had been followed exactly. He should be pleased.

The boy's thoughts then returned to that morning. He knew that he had made a big impression with his running, even though little had been said on their return journey.

After giving him directions for the day, the Boss had left for Durban with his wife and Miss Claudine. Miss Michelle, he knew, had been left behind as punishment for her bad behaviour. He did not feel any great malice towards her for her outburst, but at the same time her loss of privilege did give him a small satisfaction. Not once in the ten months he had worked here had she so much as smiled at him. In fact her presence made him feel slightly uncomfortable. The rest of the family, including her younger sister, treated him well. Often Miss Claudine would chat to him while he was working. She was a nice girl.

As Armstrong's thoughts wandered, Michelle watched him at work through the net curtains of her bedroom window. She was angry, humiliated, and mortified at the loss of her promised shopping spree.

In an effort to keep pace with her more affluent friends she had spent most of the previous week telling them of the many things she planned to buy today. She could well imagine their cruel comments when she had nothing to show them at school next week.

She glared furiously at Armstrong. It was all his fault. What if he could run a bit? That wasn't important. But her standing at school was vital.

Her eyes that used to be so innocent narrowed into slits. Well boy, she thought to herself, just you watch out. If I get a chance to get even with you, I will. Make no mistake about that.

*

In the week that followed, Armstrong was introduced to Neil Douglas and put through his paces. The Scot was a hard taskmaster, but the youngster had proved a willing pupil. His energy appeared to be almost limitless. Equipped with the brand new running shoes Piet had bought him, he trained religiously every afternoon as soon as school was finished. Even the dour Scot was impressed.

It was now evening with another tough training session completed. The coach was seated in the du Toit's comfortable lounge reporting to Piet.

'There's no doubt about it,' he stated, 'the lad shows a fair bit of promise.'

'You told me that after the first couple of days,' Piet pointed out. 'Can you be more specific now?'

Douglas was not a man to commit himself too early. Privately though, he had never felt quite so excited about any youngster who had passed through his hands.

'Specific about what?' he replied, ever the canny Scot.

'Well how about distances for a start? What is likely to be his best event? Five thousand metres? Ten? The marathon?' Piet raised an enquiring eyebrow.

Douglas thought for a short while. 'Well I've timed him over both the five and ten thousand metres. He's quite good at both. The strange thing is though, he almost appears to get stronger the further he goes. I'm sure a marathon would

IN THE LONG RUN

be no trouble at all. He's a natural for it. If I have him long enough I reckon I could even get him into the frame for the next Comrades.'

'The Comrades,' Piet echoed. 'Now that would be something special.'

He lapsed into a brief reverie. The Comrades was the ultimate test for any runner. South Africa's greatest race. Quite probably the most gruelling annual test for runners staged anywhere in the world. The prospect of having a personal interest in someone with a genuine chance of winning fascinated Piet beyond belief. Many times he had dreamed of competing successfully himself. Like for most South Africans, that was all it would remain. An impossible dream. But to do it through Armstrong would be the next best thing.

'I can see that the idea appeals to you,' Douglas observed.

'Do you really think that he could be up there with the likes of Fordyce?'

Douglas let out a short laugh and held up a restraining hand. 'Hang on a minute. Don't get too excited. You're talking about possibly the greatest ultra-distance runner the world has ever seen. Fordyce is a running machine. To get Armstrong anywhere near his level would take years. Believe me, the kid won't peak for years yet. No, what I'm saying is that we should be able to get him in the silver medal range. He might even sneak a gold if he continues to work as hard. He's that good.'

Douglas laughed again. 'But to seriously challenge Fordyce next year, no way. No way at all.'

Silently Piet chastised himself. Douglas was right. For an instant he had become completely carried away with his expectations of the boy. All the same, he could not entirely erase the vision of Armstrong battling it out with Fordyce up the notorious Polly Shorts. What a sight that would be.

More realistically, he began to dwell on what Douglas had said. Silver, perhaps even gold. Gold meant finishing in the first ten. That in itself was an achievement beyond the dreams of all but a few. Just to complete the torturous eighty-nine kilometre course was a feat any person could be justifiably proud of. For those not familiar with the race it was a challenge almost impossible to comprehend.

Piet looked at the Scot, noting with only mild surprise that his hands had turned into tight fists.

'If you think Armstrong's capable of the Comrades, then let's go for it,' he said.

*

GEORGE STRATFORD

Only the affluent own homes in the Johannesburg suburb of Lower Houghton. Houses resembling miniature palaces abound. Swimming pools are mandatory, set, more often than not, inside beautifully landscaped gardens. Depending on the owner's personal interests, everything from tennis courts to full size bowling greens can also be found. The entire area oozes contented wealth.

Situated in the heart of all this opulence lay the home of the Kirkpatrick family, South Africans of British, not Dutch, descent.

Charles Kirkpatrick, the head of the family, had for many years been an eminently successful broker on the Johannesburg exchange. It was thanks entirely to his business acumen that his wife Margaret and their only child, a twenty-four-year-old son called James, were able to enjoy such a splendid lifestyle.

Margaret, a quiet, home-loving woman, was eternally grateful for her lot in life. Not so her son. Unlike his mother, James had never known what it was like to go without. To him 'social status' was a birthright, not something that should be earned.

After completing his time at one of South Africa's finest public schools, James had left under a certain cloud. Allegations that he was a leading member of a kaffir-bashing society were made but never proved. He departed the school with a smudged rather than totally dirty slate.

Since then the young Kirkpatrick had shown little inclination to do anything constructive with his life. At first this was tolerated by his father, although his forbearance was thanks mainly to maternal influence. At Margaret's behest, and much against his own better judgement, Charles even managed to pull a few strings to arrange James' exemption from what should have been a compulsory spell of military service.

'It must not be allowed to interfere with his career,' Margaret had said at the time.

But as time passed it became increasingly obvious that a career was the last thing taxing James' mind. On numerous occasions Charles had attempted to raise the subject, at first making no more than a few gentle enquiries as to his son's plans. It was only after these efforts had met with failure that Kirkpatrick Senior became rather more insistent. Even so, he had so far stopped short of reducing any of James' many privileges. After all, the boy was still his only child, and the future of the Kirkpatrick line. Surely he would come right in time.

Margaret had undergone a hysterectomy shortly after James' birth, ruling out the possibility of further children. Too late now, Charles realised that, partly because of this, he had been influenced into creating something of a

IN THE LONG RUN

Frankenstein's monster. His only child was clearly incapable of facing up to the realities of life.

He brooded for many nights over the problem. Had the boy ever possessed any guts at all, he agonised? And if James had, then was he, as the father, responsible for eroding this quality by supplying such an indulgent and easy upbringing? Whatever the case, wherever the blame may lie, something had to be done — and soon.

It was while relaxing with a brandy in his study after another lucrative day at the exchange that an idea began to form. He sat there contemplating it for some while. Yes, it was harsh, but it would undoubtedly prove many things.

He pressed a small, white button on his desk. Within a minute there was a timid knock on the study door.

'Come in Patience,' Kirkpatrick boomed.

The door opened gently to reveal the senior of the two housemaids. 'Yes sir,' she said.

'Is Mister James in?'

The maid, a short, plump African woman with enormous breasts, shook her head. 'No sir. I've not seen him since mid-day.'

'Well, when he does return, tell him that I want to see him in here immediately.'

'Yes sir, I tell him.' The maid paused uncertainly. 'Is there anything else?'

'No, that's all thank you Patience. You can go now.'

The door closed as gently as it had opened.

Half an hour later a gleaming, white Porsche Carrera roared down the Kirkpatrick's long gravel driveway. It pulled up sharply in front of the house scattering a profusion of small stones.

James Kirkpatrick stepped a little unsteadily from the car. Just over six feet tall, he was lean and good looking. This pleasing appearance was spoilt only by his mouth, which somehow contrived to form a faint, seemingly congenital sneer.

He was slightly drunk after another long afternoon session at one of the many bars he frequented. He now looked around for the family chauffeur.

'Thomas,' he bellowed. 'Come here.'

Moments later the driver appeared from the side of the house. The African regarded James with an incompatible mixture of dislike and humble servility.

'I want you to wash this car — right now.' James clapped his hands in an impatient gesture and then nodded towards the virtually spotless vehicle.

GEORGE STRATFORD

Thomas began to protest. 'Sir, I've got other work to be—'

He was cut short. 'Just do it,' James snapped as he mounted the white marble steps leading to the front door.

Inside the spacious hallway he was timidly approach by Patience.

'Please sir,' she faltered. 'Mister Kirkpatrick wants to see you in his study right away.' James frightened her badly. Any dealings with him filled her with dread.

The message brought an immediate frown to James' face. What the hell did the old man want now, he wondered? Surely not another of his lectures. The prospect grated.

He rounded on the hapless Patience. 'Why are you waiting? Get on with your work.'

The maid hurried away as fast as her ample figure would permit.

James hesitated by the study door to take a deep breath. He then entered without knocking. His father eyed him sternly and then wrinkled his nose. 'Don't you ever stop drinking?'

James' eyes shifted to the brandy glass on the desk, but for once he restrained himself. He could see immediately that the old man was in one of his moods. The least said the better at times like this.

'Sit down James. I think you might need to when you've heard what I've got to say.'

Still silent, James did as instructed. This sounded ominous, he considered. Still, he would follow his usual policy. Listen with apparent interest, agree with what his father said, then continue as normal. A disturbing instinct however warned him that this time things might not prove to be so easy.

Kirkpatrick Senior surveyed him intently for several seconds, causing James to shift uncomfortably in his seat.

'Why are you looking at me like that?' he eventually asked. His rising apprehension was reflected in his voice.

Charles took his time before answering. 'I was just wondering exactly what you are made of,' he said at last.

James looked at him blankly. 'I don't understand.'

'Whether or not you have any real guts about you? Whether you are a genuine Kirkpatrick?'

'Of course I am.'

The claim was met with a grim little smile. 'In that case the time has finally come for you to prove it.'

IN THE LONG RUN

All James' worst fears were being confirmed. Never during their past talks had the old man sounded so determined. What the hell did he mean by 'prove it'? Whatever was coming, James resigned himself to feigning interest and playing along. It would all be forgotten in a day or so anyway, he told himself without conviction.

'What do you want me to do?' he asked, trying hard to inject a small note of enthusiasm.

'I want you to prove to me that you've got character. That you can see something through, no matter how tough it gets. I want you to learn self-discipline and the value of personal achievement.'

'And how exactly am I going to do all that?' James was unable to keep a small edge of sarcasm from his voice.

His father's grim little smile returned. 'You are going to compete in next year's Comrades Marathon.'

James blinked. Surely he was not hearing correctly. 'Say that again,' he said a little stupidly.

Charles Kirkpatrick's expression did not change. 'You heard me correctly,' he stated. 'You are to enter the Comrades. Not only that, you will complete the course. You are young and you are strong, so there is no reason why you cannot do it.' He then added with a touch of his own sarcasm: 'That is providing you put in sufficient training for the event. It will be something to occupy your time.'

James found it impossible to fake even the slightest amount of enthusiasm for this crazy idea. 'You can't be serious,' he murmured.

'I've never been more serious in my life.'

'I won't do it. It's absurd.'

'Before we go any further James, let's get one thing perfectly clear. You have little choice in the matter. Not unless you wish to leave your comfortable home here and fend for yourself in the real world outside.'

James studied his father's face. The jaw was set, the mouth was firm, the eyes resolute. With chilling certainty he knew for certain that this was not to be taken lightly. Never had the old man confronted him with such fierce determination.

Despite this, surely he wouldn't be thrown out if he did not cooperate? Not when it came to the crunch. There might be a certain restriction of privileges, but no more than that. He was, after all, flesh and blood. All this was merely a clever act designed to throw a scare into him.

Even as he tried to console himself with this thought, James knew that he was fooling himself. The stupid old sod was deadly serious, at least for the time being.

GEORGE STRATFORD

His only option was to play along for a while. Something would turn up. The Comrades was nine months ahead. Plenty of time to make a plan.

As if reading his thoughts, his father said: 'There are nine months before the event so you will have plenty of time to prepare yourself.'

James nodded. 'All right. If that's what you want, I'll do it.'

Charles was not fooled by his son's sudden change of attitude. 'Do not imagine that you can get out of this by faking some kind of injury. You will see it through no matter what. And just to ensure that there are not too many distractions to your training, your allowance will be reduced by seventy-five per cent until after the event.'

A looked of stunned disbelief came over James' face. 'That will hardly pay my petrol bill,' he stated.

The grim little smile that was becoming a precursor for bad news returned again. 'I shouldn't worry about that James. You won't be using the Porsche again, not without my specific permission. Nor any of the other cars.'

Charles held out his hand. 'The keys please.'

Silently, as if in a trance, James handed them over. This was not happening to him. It was all a bad dream.

His father looked pleased with matters. 'You can see now of course that it would be very much in your interests to get this thing over and done with at the first attempt. If however it should take longer, then so be it.'

Still James did not utter a word. His expression was of a person in profound shock.

Charles spoke again. 'I realise that this must come as a bit of a surprise to you James. But believe me, you will benefit from it in the long run.'

For the life of him, James could not see how. His temper, never far from the surface, now began to rise. He struggled to regain control. A violent row at this stage would get him nowhere. Even he could see that. Instead, he rose to his feet. 'If that's all?' he said stiffly. 'I've things to do.'

Kirkpatrick Senior waved a dismissive hand. 'As you wish.' Then, as James opened the study door, he added: 'Feel free to begin training whenever you like.'

The door, in marked contrast to Patience's earlier exit, closed very firmly indeed.

IN THE LONG RUN

CHAPTER TWO

Steve Ryan stepped from the near deserted tube at Tooting Bec station. Still as lean and athletic as he had been when winning the East Hampshire Marathon, he ran effortlessly up the long flight of stone steps leading to the street.

Now nearly twenty-five years old, his reputation had grown considerably after excellent recent performances in the London and Boston Marathons. Given that there were still two years to further improve before the next Olympics, his hopes of selection were becoming a real possibility.

Ryan's academic career at Sussex had been less successful. Thanks to his time-consuming involvement with the anti-apartheid movement, plus the long hours of commitment his training schedule required, it was hardly a surprise that his studies suffered. Almost as a matter of course he failed his degree. He returned home to Bournemouth with nothing on paper, but a host of experiences.

For the last few years his natural intelligence had been wasted in a series of dead end jobs. Washing up in hotels, casual labouring, it didn't seem to matter much. All he needed was enough money to get by on and the freedom to follow his strict training plan. He was still fervent in his beliefs over South Africa, but life away from university did not seem to offer the same opportunities for active involvement. This side of his life, if no less important in principle, had become less dominant in practice. And then, from out of the blue, he received a telephone call from Ronnie Tyler.

Before their parting Ryan had given Tyler a contact number in Bournemouth. Even so, after several years without contact, he was more than surprised to hear from the guy again. Surprised, but still pleased.

GEORGE STRATFORD

Tyler had given little away. 'I've got something for you Steve,' he said. 'Something you won't want to miss out on.' He gave an address in south London. 'Come up as soon as you can.'

Ryan did not hesitate for long. What did he have to lose? Two days later he was on the train.

Just recently he had heard on the grapevine that Tyler, unlike himself, was still deeply involved with the movement. There was little doubt that this summons was somehow connected. But why? After so long out of the action, what could he offer Ronnie that others couldn't? Whatever it was, it would be good to meet up again.

It took about ten minutes to locate Tyler's address, a large house overlooking Tooting Common. His friend had a flat on the first floor. With a mixture of curiosity and anticipation Ryan pressed the appropriate bell. A full minute passed. Ryan was on the point of ringing again when he heard the sound of feet running down stairs. Moments later the door was thrown open.

'Steve! Great to see you.' Tyler held out his hand. 'Sorry about the delay. I was on the throne when you rang.'

Ryan laughed as they shook hands. 'Another curry last night?' he joked, remembering his friend's passion for Indian food.

Together they mounted the stairs. Ryan was ushered into a small flat. He noted without surprise how scrupulously clean and tidy it was. Ronnie had always had a big thing about neatness. Always organised where others failed to cope. Even his degree had been gained with a minimum of fuss.

The same clinical approach had been applied to all of Tyler's activities with the movement. Every detail was meticulously planned. Spontaneous and risky gestures were OK for some, but not Ronnie.

Ryan felt reassured. Whatever his friend wanted of him, it would already have been well planned. This was no fool's errand that he was on.

True to his nature, Tyler would not be rushed. No reasons for his call were offered until both were comfortably seated. On the small table between their two armchairs stood a freshly made pot of coffee.

'Black for me,' Ryan reminded his friend as he poured.

'As if I could forget,' Tyler grinned. 'Quite appropriate under the circumstances don't you think?'

Ryan returned the grin. 'I suppose it is.' He leaned back in his chair, expression serious. 'So what's up? It's all very mysterious.'

IN THE LONG RUN

His friend continued to look amused. 'Yes, I did play on your curiosity a bit Steve. Sorry about that. But I know what makes you tick and I thought that this was the quickest way to get you up here.'

'You and your psychology,' Ryan observed lightly.

A trace of smugness crossed Tyler's face.

'So, are you prepared to satisfy my curiosity now?' Ryan continued.

Tyler hesitated then gave a sharp nod. 'Sure.' He paused again and then said: 'How do you fancy going to South Africa?' He threw the question at Ryan. There was no hint of humour now.

Ryan's jaw sagged in amazement. 'Say that again.'

'I'm serious,' Tyler assured him.

'I don't doubt it.' Ryan's voice was hushed.

'You know me. I don't joke about things like this.'

'Why for God's sake? When? How long for? The questions tumbled out.

Tyler held up a hand. 'Hold on,' he said. 'Look Steve, obviously I knew that this would come as a major shock to you. That's another reason I didn't let on too much over the phone.' He stood up and moved across the room. 'Before we go any further, there's something I want you to look at.'

From a drawer he produced an old newspaper, which he dropped onto Ryan's lap. 'Read that. It's South African.'

Ryan regarded the journal much like he would a pile of excrement.

'Just look at the front page,' Tyler urged.

His curiosity overcoming finer feelings, Ryan did as instructed. His gaze was immediately drawn to the main headline: TWELVE THOUSAND SET OFF ON RUN OF PAIN.

In spite of himself, it was with a glimmer of interest that his eyes then scanned the opening paragraph. The text described the kind of mass start common to nearly all major marathons. In this case though, the runners were facing an unbelievable slog of over twice the distance. Fifty-five miles.

A sudden thought rushed into Ryan's head. 'Hang on! You're not expecting *me* to run in this race are you?'

The answer was simple and direct. 'As a matter of fact — yes.'

Ryan threw the newspaper violently on to the floor. 'Stuff you Ronnie,' he exploded. 'You've dragged me all the way up here just to tell me that. What the bloody hell's up with you? Have you lost your marbles?' Bright patches of red coloured Ryan's cheeks. 'You *do* realise what you're asking, don't you?

GEORGE STRATFORD

Apart from any personal feelings I have about going there, I'd almost certainly get an international ban slapped on me if I competed. Do you honestly think I'm prepared to chuck it all down the toilet now there's a possible Olympic place up for grabs? After all the hard work I've put in. You've got to be joking.'

Calmly Tyler picked up the paper and then re-seated himself. When he spoke, his voice was soft.

'Have I ever put you wrong Steve?'

'Not until now you bloody well haven't.'

'If you'll just listen for a few minutes.'

But Ryan was in no mood to listen. 'What about all the shit we gave the cricketers when they went over there? And the rugby players. You're asking me to become like one of them.'

Tyler shrugged. 'Have it your way. If you won't at least hear what else I've got to say then you might as well go back to Bournemouth now.' His voice dropped as he added: 'It seems like I was wrong. I thought you'd be glad to strike a real blow for the cause.'

'How the hell will any of this achieve anything?' Ryan demanded. 'Apart from screwing things up for me that is.'

'I'll tell you if you're prepared to listen. Everything, and I mean everything, can be sorted out so there's not a problem. Just trust me.'

Tyler's continuing calm drew some of Ryan's anger. There was a long silence while he fought to come to terms with the situation. One side of him remained appalled at his friend's suggestion; the other reasoned that if the cause could actually benefit in a big way, then he was morally bound to hear Tyler out before making a judgement.

He sighed. 'OK, let's have it Ronnie. I'm not promising a damn thing, but let's have it anyway.'

Tyler smiled briefly. 'Thanks Steve.'

He began. 'This race — the Comrades — is a major event over there. It's reckoned to be one of the world's toughest challenges. One of the runners in it, Bruce Fordyce, is a national hero.'

Ryan was cynical. 'To the whites perhaps. What's so special about this Fordyce anyway?'

'Because he's won the race eight times in the last nine years. The other year he didn't enter. The guy is rated by many as the greatest ultra-distance runner ever.'

This talk of Fordyce was quite deliberate. Tyler knew that, like it or not,

IN THE LONG RUN

Ryan was certain to be intrigued by the South African's reputation. His friend's huge competitive nature would then demand that he gauge his own potential alongside.

Tyler continued. 'Fordyce usually does the fifty-five miles in around five-and-a-half-hours. And from what I know most of the way is covered with bloody great hills.'

This information drew a reluctant whistle from Ryan. He hated to admit it, but he *was* impressed.

A slight look of doubt then crossed Tyler's face. 'Fifty-five miles is a hell of a distance Steve. Much further than you've ever been before. Do you reckon you could manage it OK?'

'Of course I could.' Ryan felt slightly insulted as he rose to the bait. 'If you're fit enough it's only a question of pacing yourself.' He hesitated before asking: 'When does this Comrades take place?'

'The end of the month.'

'That soon eh?'

'So you're interested then?'

'Hey, hold on pal.' Ryan shook his head. 'I didn't say that. Let's face it Ronnie, you haven't given me one good reason yet why I should even think about it.'

Despite this protest, the nerve ends of his competitive spirit were already tingling. He fought against the feeling. Surely nothing Ronnie could say would justify his taking part. It went against every moral principle he held — and this was before he even considered the possibility of a career-destroying ban. But was it somehow possible for Ronnie to convince him? What exactly did his friend mean when he mentioned striking a real blow for the movement? Although confused, Ryan was now all ears.

Tyler smiled at him. 'My involvement with the movement has increased a lot since we were together,' he began.

'So I've heard.'

'I've now got a direct link with a group actually within South Africa. A very militant group.'

The light of understanding dawned. 'And you want me to work with these people.'

'Yes. They need assistance with a very special task. Something far bigger than you can imagine.'

'So tell me about it,' Ryan urged.

Tyler took a deep breath. 'You do realise that anything more I say has got to remain strictly between the two of us. Not even my closest helpers know anything about this.'

Once again Ryan felt insulted. After all they had done together. Surely Ronnie knew him better than that. A biting riposte rose up.

Tyler saw it coming. 'All right,' he cut in. 'I'm sorry. I should have known better. It's just that this really is the biggest thing I've ever been involved with.'

Placated, Ryan swallowed the remark. 'Yea, OK,' he said. His curiosity was now unbearable. 'So tell me.'

His friend took another deep breath. 'I take it you've heard of the American singer Tony Manelli?'

'Of course I have. Who hasn't? He's one of the biggest things around right now. What's he got to do with it?'

'He's due to give a series of concerts in South Africa this month.'

'The self-centred bastard,' Ryan muttered. 'They must be paying him a fortune. You'd think he had enough cash stashed away without risking his whole career like that.'

Tyler's eyes narrowed. 'Manelli doesn't know it yet, but he's risking a whole lot more than his career.'

'What do you mean?'

There was a long silence before Tyler said: 'Our friends in South Africa are planning to bump him off. You know, as a deterrent to any other performer thinking of grabbing a quick fortune there.' He then added as if by way of simple explanation: 'Well I did say they were rather militant.' He studied Ryan's face closely for a reaction.

For a long while Ryan thought that he had misunderstood. 'They actually mean to kill him?' he finally said. His voice was barely audible.

'That's about the size of it.'

'And you want *me* to help them do it?'

'Not directly of course. You're not expected to be around when the killing takes place. But they desperately need someone like you to help set it up. Do you want me to explain further?'

Ryan jumped to his feet and began to pace the room. 'No! Stop right there Ronnie. I can't be a party to murder. A punch up now and then is one thing. But murder...? No way. I can't be responsible for that no matter how much I despise what Manelli's doing.'

The outburst drew a sigh from his friend. 'Think about it Steve. You can't be

IN THE LONG RUN

naive enough to imagine that Manelli's concerts won't provoke a lot of reaction over there. Of course they will. The backlash from that could easily mean a lot of deaths amongst those brave enough to protest. Come on pal, you know the score.' Tyler's voice became more persuasive. 'Steve, listen to me. People like Manelli must be stopped. In the long run you'll be helping to save lives. Surely you can see that?'

Ryan ceased pacing to round on Tyler. 'Even if I do accept what you're saying, you're overlooking one very important fact. They hang people in South Africa. You know, a rope around the neck and all that jazz.'

His friend's voice dropped even lower. 'I've told you before Steve, you won't be involved in the actual killing. There'll be nothing to connect you, I promise.'

Ryan remained unconvinced. 'I just don't know what to think,' he said, resuming his pacing. 'I've got to think about things.' He paused by the door. 'I'm going out for a walk.' He shook his head. 'It's a hell of a thing you're asking.'

Ryan opened the door and stepped on to the landing. 'A hell of a thing,' he repeated softly before descending the stairs.

Alone in his flat, Tyler moved to the window. He eased back the net curtain just a couple of inches and stood there waiting. As Ryan came into view in the street below his eyes narrowed. They remained rigidly fixed on the runner as he crossed the road and stepped on to the common opposite. 'You'll do it Steve, you've got to,' Tyler muttered. In sharp contrast to his reassuring manner of just a few moments earlier, his voice was now full of tension.

He backed away from the window and like Ryan before him, began pacing the room. He continued like this for several minutes before abruptly ceasing. From the same drawer that he had produced the South African newspaper he now fished out a publicity photograph of Tony Manelli. Tyler held it up only inches from his own face.

'You're dead Manelli,' he snarled at the star's smiling image. 'One way or another, you've got it coming.' With precise deliberation Tyler then tore the photo into tiny pieces.

*

Ryan spent the next half-hour walking aimlessly around the common. Arguments for and against raged inside his head. It wasn't that Ronnie intimidated him in any way, but the guy had somehow always talked him around whenever they'd suffered a difference of opinion in the past. And the hard truth was that his friend had invariably been proved to be right. Even so, all that meant nothing — nothing at all — compared to what he was now being asked to do.

Every man, regardless of background, had the right to live his life with equal opportunities. That was precisely the ideal they had struggled for all along. To take another another's life, no matter who's it was, just had to be wrong.

But as Tyler had pointed out so significantly, the loss of one life may well help to save many others — innocent people. In any war casualties were to be expected. It was largely a matter of minimising them. If his involvement could really help to achieve this end, who was he to say it was wrong? The balance shifted constantly from side to side as Ryan struggled to come to some kind of conclusion.

Two teams of young boys, mostly around ten years old, were playing football way over to his left. Both sides were a mixture of races. For some unaccountable reason he approached the game and joined the thinly scattered group of spectators.

'Over here ... on me head!' pleaded the onrushing striker to the winger. Seconds later a perfect pass fell on to his forehead. The ball flew into the top left-hand corner of the goal.

The two boys ran to each other in mutual acknowledgement of a job well done. One black — one white.

Ryan watched this little scene and found himself joining the other spectators in their applause. That's the way it should always be, he told himself several times.

Suddenly his decision was made.

*

The two men were seated as before. Tyler, visibly delighted with Ryan's decision, was now keen to expand. 'The race is the perfect cover,' he explained. 'Any foreigner with an athletic record like yours will be made welcome. International competition is what the South Africans are desperate for.'

'I know that,' Ryan pointed out, remembering once more the ban he was risking. 'Just tell me how the hell we cover up my taking part in it?'

'That's the beauty, we don't have to,' Tyler told him. 'Like I said, they're desperate for international competition. So desperate that overseas runners like you are offered special licence to run under an assumed name. Lots have done it in the past.'

Ryan let out a short, hollow laugh. The world was full of hypocrites. For all

IN THE LONG RUN

that, he had to admit that the arrangement *was* very convenient. If others had got away with it easily enough, why shouldn't he? At least his motives, in a singular kind of way, were honourable.

'OK,' he finally said. 'Let's get down to the bottom line. What exactly do these friends of yours expect from me?'

Tyler's voice took on a business-like tone. 'Manelli is doing three concerts in Durban. While he's there he'll be staying at the New Holiday Inn. That's where you'll be booked in too. You'll be met at the airport and there's another contact who actually works at the hotel. He'll make himself known when the time is right.'

'That's fine, but you still haven't told me what I'm expected to do,' Ryan persisted.

'I'm coming to that. Apparently Manelli is a fitness freak and a major athletic fan. He's heard about the Comrades and he's dead keen on seeing it first hand. His Durban concerts have been deliberately arranged to coincide with the race.'

'And you want me to...' Ryan began.

'We want you to get to know him. That shouldn't prove difficult. Not once he realises that you're a top class British runner who's come to run in the race.'

'How the hell is he supposed to know who I am? What am I to do? Just walk up to this international superstar and say, "Hi Tony old pal. I'm a top class British runner over here for the Comrades. I just thought that you'd like to meet me".'

A look of anger quickly formed on Tyler's face. 'You're not taking this seriously enough Steve. It's not a bloody joke you know.'

With a rush Ryan realised the truth. His flippancy was merely a cover for the deep sense of apprehension he was experiencing. Since making his decision in a moment of conscience-inspired impetuosity, the realities were now sinking in. What the hell had he let himself in for? 'Sorry,' he said, wilting slightly under the intensity of Ronnie's gaze.

Tyler nodded. His anger faded and almost immediately he was his old self. 'As I was saying, getting to know Manelli won't be too difficult for you. Not once he realises who you are. You'll be given some help with this by your hotel contact.'

'All right. Always assuming that I do get to know Manelli, what then?'

'You'll have to play it by ear a bit. The basic idea is to win his confidence and then set him up for the others to deal with. You'll be told a lot more when you're over there. Everything else, your flight, your hotel, and your spending money, will be taken care of. Oh, and it might sound stupid, but don't forget your passport.'

'How do you know I've got one?'

Tyler came very close to smirking. 'You took out a ten-year passport during our last year at university for that trip to New York, remember? That means it's still got five years left to run.'

The guy did not forget a thing, Ryan considered. But what happened when he got to Durban all sounded a bit vague. 'Playing it by ear' was not Ronnie's usual style at all. His apprehension persisted. To cover this Ryan said: 'You make it sound easy enough. I just hope that it works out that way.'

Tyler placed a hand on Ryan's shoulder. The grip was firm. 'We've worked together a lot in the past Steve. I know you well. You're an intelligent bloke. For you it'll be easy. And just think of all the good you'll be achieving in the long run.'

There was that expression again. Ryan tried to smile. 'In the long run,' he repeated. 'A good choice of words don't you reckon?'

Tyler acknowledged this with a tightening of his grip. 'Keep your sense of humour Steve. But also keep your mind on what you're there for. You can leave in a week. Time enough before the race to get your entry in and establish your identity.' He grinned encouragingly. 'Once you get over there all you have to do is be yourself ... a runner.'

And help to arrange a man's death, Ryan told himself.

*

Under normal circumstances Stick Pearson relished his work as Tony Manelli's agent. A man of barely average height, his nickname was derived from his near skeletal frame. Despite this lack of muscle, Stick was a human dynamo and was regarded as one of the very best in the business. For once though, he was not his enthusiastic self. He gazed with exasperation at his star client.

'Goddam it Tony, won't anything change your mind?'

Seated opposite Pearson in the agent's plush New York office, Manelli smiled tightly and shook his head. 'Not a thing.'

Pearson sighed, dropping the crumpled piece of paper he was holding on to the desk in front of him. 'That's over fifty now,' he stated.

The singer reached forward and gave the paper a cursory glance. 'The same old rubbish,' he remarked indifferently as his eyes flicked over the handwriting.

Contemptuously he tossed the paper back on to the desk. 'This one didn't even have the guts to sign it.'

It had been the same ever since Manelli's impending trip to South Africa

IN THE LONG RUN

had been announced. Almost daily, threatening messages had been arriving at Pearson's office. Some were no more than a simple vow never to buy any more of the singer's records. Others were far stronger, hinting that Manelli had better watch his back if the trip went ahead. He had treated them all with equal indifference.

Pearson, who had been against the idea from the start, saw things differently. Even so, all his appeals for Manelli to change his mind had so far proved futile. This was the first major disagreement between the two men during their lucrative five years together. Not only were they a good professional team, they had also grown to like each other considerably. This did not make Pearson's problem any easier. With any other client he would have made a pious statement and then publicly washed his hands of the whole affair. In this case, loyalty prevented him from doing so. And there was always the other consideration that, should things not turn out as badly as he anticipated, he would have needlessly thrown away his main meal ticket.

Stick decided to try one final appeal. 'OK, let's forget the threats ... to hell with what some of your fans may think. But what about you Tony? With your background you should know better than most what it's like to be crapped on.'

Manelli ran his hand through his thick, dark hair and grinned broadly. It was a look guaranteed to set a million female hearts pounding with desire.

'Nice try Stick,' he said. 'I wondered when you'd get around to the social conscience angle.' His smile faded. 'Sure I know what it's like to be crapped on. When I was a kid we had nothing. We lived in a lousy goddam tenement which even the rats were busting their asses to get out of. The whole neighbourhood was crawling with junkies, muggers and hookers. There were times when I used to get beat up in the streets around there just for being Italian. That's my experience of racism. It's being scared shitless just to look outside the apartment door.' He jabbed a finger in his agent's direction. 'Can't you see Stick, my background is the very reason why I don't let anyone shove me around any more.'

Pearson sighed. This wasn't going to work either.

Manelli continued. 'You know as well as I do that the South African audiences will be multi-racial. It's in the contract. These shows ain't for a few rich whites. Hell, I can't remember the last time I did a tour that made a loss.' He leaned forward. 'And why? To make sure that tickets are so damn cheap that anyone can come. How the hell can you call that selling out?'

The agent threw his hands up in exasperation. 'I know you're not a racist Tony.

But try convincing the folks out there of that. For Pete's sake, you're risking everything and not earning a single buck out of it.'

Manelli now had the air of a man who had proved his case. 'That's the whole point. How can anyone criticise for that?' He flicked the crumpled letter with his finger. 'These guys who write this...they ain't my real fans. They don't want to know the truth, even when we try to tell them. They shut their eyes to what I'm trying to achieve, and the fact that South Africa is changing. I'm just trying to help that change come about a bit quicker. If these sons of bitches who threaten me can't see that then they can kiss my ass.'

This brief tirade caused Manelli's muscular body to tense; muscles that had been developed with a vigorous daily routine of running, swimming and weight training. Now in his mid-thirties, he looked ten years younger and had the physical capability to match.

Stick Pearson sighed again. For once his speech was slow and resigned. 'OK Tony, I know when I'm beat. Just remember what I said if things turn sour.'

Manelli, now relaxed once more, smiled and reached into a leather briefcase by his feet. He produced a video cassette which he placed on Pearson's desk. 'Take a look at that when you get time. It's a recording of last year's Comrades.'

The agent groaned. He was well aware of Manelli's fascination. 'I reckon that's why you're so damn eager to get over there. Just to see this race. You'll be telling me next that you want to run in it yourself.'

'Oh no,' the singer responded. 'Sure I'm fit, but this race is real tough. I ain't got time to train for that kind of thing.' He pushed the cassette closer to Pearson. 'Take a look anyhow. It might open your eyes a bit.'

'How's that?'

'Well it's not called the Comrades for nothing Stick. You want to see how these guys help each other out sometimes. And it doesn't matter what colour you are, everyone competes equally.'

Pearson raised an eyebrow. 'They let the blacks run?'

'Sure, that's what I've been trying to tell you. Anyone who's run a standard marathon in under four-and-a-half hours can enter. That's the only condition.'

'That's all huh.' The agent's voice was heavy with irony. Although hyperactive in business, the mere thought of running any great distance was something to be avoided at all costs. Why people did such things for pleasure was completely beyond his understanding.

Manelli ignored the irony. 'The Comrades has been open to all races for over

ND RUN

ten years.' He sighed. 'You're like so many people Stick, you criticise without knowing the facts.'

Pearson raised a defensive hand. 'OK, enough huh.' He then had a sudden thought. 'Say, if you're really so interested in this thing, why not cancel the concerts and just go over to watch the race? That way we'll avoid most of the hassle.'

Manelli's face hardened. 'No deal Stick. I'm doing them and that's final.'

'Sure, whatever you want.' Pearson was deflated.

'Let's get one thing straight Stick,' Manelli continued, his expression still severe. 'Either you're with me or you're not. We go back a long way and we've always got on well. But if I haven't got you behind me on this then we may as well call it quits. I need to know, whatever you may think privately, that publicly you're backing me all the way. Have I got that commitment?'

Pearson gave one long final sigh before holding out his hand. 'You've got it,' he confirmed.

CHAPTER THREE

The Jumbo Jet carrying Ryan touched down smoothly at Durban's Louis Botha airport. It was exactly eleven a.m. The runner gazed rigidly out of the aircraft window as they taxied slowly towards the main terminal building. It was almost impossible for his to believe that he was about to set foot on South African soil.

In preparation for this moment Ryan had constantly reminded himself throughout the journey that it was not the land itself that had caused his feelings of abhorrence. It was the administrators and their inhuman policies. Even so, as he descended the aircraft steps, he could not completely free himself of the sensation that he was about to be indelibly tainted in some way.

He paused one step from the bottom. No matter what he might think, there was no going back now. With a deep breath he took the final pace that meant his first physical contact with the land of apartheid. No massive bolt of lightning appeared in the clear, blue sky to strike him down for this act of betrayal to his conscience. No booming voice from above heaped a tirade of condemnation upon his head. In fact the whole experience was a considerable anti-climax. In a perverse way Ryan felt almost cheated. After a brief pause at the foot of the steps, he then simply moved forward in the same routine manner as all the other disembarking passengers.

Perhaps as a reaction to this strange sense of deflation, Ryan's mind switched to other matters. Seated close to him during the flight he had spotted a young black couple. They were well dressed and appeared to be fully at ease. Certainly he was forced to admit that they had been treated with the same courteous

IN THE LONG RUN

service as any other passenger by the South African Airways cabin staff. All the same, it puzzled him that they had not displayed any signs of apprehension. They were, after all, bound for a country notorious for its treatment of their race.

Intrigued, Ryan followed them as they headed towards the terminal building. On impulse he considered approaching the pair in order to discover their reasons for coming here. He then slapped his thigh in annoyance. Was he mad? It would be the height of stupidity to risk attracting any personal attention.

The long straggle of passengers began to enter the building. Once inside Ryan's attention was drawn to a glass-fronted balcony overhead. A large cluster of people looked eagerly down, smiling and waving a welcome to friends and family below. He was amazed to see that, not only were there whites and Africans mixing freely together up there, but also a large group of Asians. Several of the women wore colourful saris. Ryan frowned. This was not at all what he had expected. Where was the enforced segregation he had heard so much about? Was that now a thing of the past? From first impressions, this could be just another airport in any part of Africa.

He joined the queue designated for non-South African passport holders. Just one lone traveller — where the hell had he sprung from? Ryan puzzled — separated him from the black couple ahead. Both were now clutching the distinctive black and gold British passport. Yet again Ryan wondered as to the purpose of their visit. The white immigration officer greeted the pair in routine fashion. He even smiled twice at remarks Ryan could not quite catch. Then, with a thump of the official stamp, the couple were on their way.

There followed a long delay while sod's law in the guise of the queue-jumper caused confusion at the desk. This irritant — a gangling youth juggling with over twice the permitted hand baggage and seemingly incapable of finding his passport — appeared determined to test everyone's patience.

No one was being tested more than Ryan. Keen to see who was meeting the black couple, he did not need this idiot holding things up. Only after a ten-minute delay did the youth, barely visible under his backpack and shoulder bags, eventually continue on his calamitous path.

The immigration officer blew out his cheeks in a gesture of relief before accepting Ryan's documents. Rapidly his eyes scanned the details written on the visitor's questionnaire. The man then gave a huge smile.

'So you've come to run the Comrades,' he said. 'I wish you luck.'

Ryan forced a grin. 'It's tough eh?'

'You could say that. You wouldn't catch me doing it. Not for a million rand.'

The officer's nicotine stained fingers and ample stomach made Ryan consider that, even with the motivation of a million rand, the man would still struggle to make more than a couple of miles.

Keeping this thought to himself, he said: 'I'll give it a go all the same.'

Still grinning, the official checked his passport. The stamp then landed with an almost ominous thump on the page. 'Welcome to South Africa,' he said.

As Ryan feared, the black couple had by now already collected their baggage and departed. The cause of his delay however, was still very much in evidence. The youth appeared to have a natural gift for creating chaos. He was currently apologising profusely for having mistakenly taken someone else's case from the conveyor belt.

'Well it does look a bit like mine,' he was explaining, while at the same time bumping into almost everyone nearby with his cumbersome backpack. Ryan shot him a pitying glance before claiming his own suitcase and heading for customs. With nothing to declare he headed for the green channel.

A huge customs officer moved to bar his path. 'Are you a visitor to this country?' he asked. His voice bristled with officialdom.

Although carrying nothing incriminating, Ryan still flinched under the man's scrutiny. 'Yes, I'm British,' he responded.

The officer digested this information. 'Do you have any kind of firearms or explosives on you?' he then demanded.

This question really shook Ryan. Of all those passing through, why had he been the one selected for such interrogation? Surely he was not already under some kind of suspicion? They couldn't possibly know why he was here — could they? Nervous cramps gripped his stomach.

He forced a laugh. 'You must be joking. What would I want with that sort of stuff?'

The penetrating gaze persisted for just a few seconds longer before suddenly relaxing. The man then almost succeeded in producing a smile.

'OK. You can go,' he said.

With a struggle Ryan controlled his expression as his stomach cramps gave way to small tremors of relief. He moved on, all the time wondering if the officer was still watching him. He ached to look back. Just be natural, he instructed himself. If there were any real cause for alarm they wouldn't have let him through. But he was shaken badly, all the same. Was he really cut out for this sort of thing? At the moment it seemed unlikely. He paused in an effort to compose himself. Tyler

IN THE LONG RUN

had assured him that he would be met at the airport. At the very least he must try to look the part. Who knows who could be waiting just ahead? In a moment or two he felt steadier. Satisfied he moved into the reception area. He was now as ready as he would ever be. From here on it was down to fate.

Ryan stared into the mass of unfamiliar faces. It was true Tyler had always been reliable in the past. But say there had been a cock-up? What would he do if no one were here to meet him? He felt a pang of uneasiness as his eyes searched in vain for a friendly face to come to his rescue. To his utter relief he then spotted a hand-written card raised up. In bold lettering it simply read RYAN.

His attention then shifted to the man holding the card. Ryan had not formed any clear mental picture of who to expect, but even so, he was more than a little surprised.

The man was perhaps sixty-five years of age. His steel grey hair was closely cropped, and the thin, neatly clipped moustache gave him a military air. A retired colonel immediately suggested itself. This impression was further enhanced by his erect posture and lean, apparently well cared for body. In general build he was quite similar to Ryan himself.

Ryan approached and placed himself in front of the soldier-like figure. 'Hi, I'm Steve Ryan,' he said, at the same time extending a steadyish hand.

His contact's small, penetrating eyes assessed him. This uncomfortable appraisal lasted only a few seconds, but to Ryan it felt far longer. The stern mouth then formed into a thin line that might just have been a smile. Whether this signalled approval, Ryan could not tell.

'Welcome to South Africa,' the man responded in carefully measured tones. He took Ryan's outstretched hand in a surprisingly powerful grip. 'I'm Parker.' He did not bother to give a Christian name. There followed an awkward silence during which Ryan felt under continuing analysis.

'So what now?' he asked in an effort to end this scrutiny.

His new acquaintance suddenly became brisk. 'We'll go to the car.' It was an order, not a suggestion. Without another word Parker strode off, leaving the suitcase encumbered runner in his wake.

Parker's car turned out to be nothing less than a top of the range Mercedes saloon. After placing his suitcase in the boot, Ryan sank gratefully into the front passenger seat. Tired after the long journey, he tried to relax. Sleep had proved to be virtually impossible during the flight.

At first it was overpoweringly hot inside the Mercedes, but the car's air-conditioning soon made the temperature more comfortable. Parker made no early attempt at conversation, and in a way this suited Ryan. Although anxious to discover what lay in store for him, he first wanted a short time to gather his thoughts. So far, South Africa had proved to be far from what he had expected.

They had driven for nearly ten minutes before Parker spoke. His voice was of an educated man, his accent rather British.

'I suppose that I should fill in a few details for you Ryan.'

'As you wish,' the runner responded, trying hard to sound at ease. He hesitated. 'Are you English?'

Parker shot him a quick glance. 'South African, born and bred.'

'I just thought that—'

Ryan was interrupted by a short laugh. 'One thing you will learn very quickly, Natal is rather different from the rest of South Africa. In many ways it could be considered the country's last British outpost. You will come across a great number of various British accents in Durban.'

'I see.' Ryan paused before adding: 'You were going to fill me in on a few details.'

Parker took his time in replying. 'As you probably know, you will be staying at the Holiday Inn on Durban beachfront. Manelli booked in there yesterday.'

The mention of the singer's name brought back sharply to Ryan the whole purpose of his being here.

'Just go about your business and prepare for the race in your normal manner,' Parker continued. 'Naturally it is up to you how seriously you wish to compete. A word of advice though. If you wish to remain low profile, then do not allow yourself at any stage to be up with the leaders. I would suggest that you finish somewhere in the main pack.'

He paused before adding: 'Unless of course you have no desire to continue with your reasonably successful athletic career back home. If it were to become generally known that you had competed here, then things may become distinctly awkward for you.'

'I'll be running under an assumed name,' Ryan pointed out. 'Tyler assured me that overseas runners are permitted to do so.'

'Absolutely correct,' Parker confirmed. 'But I'm afraid that TV captures faces as well as names. If the wrong person from your point of view should happen to spot you ....'

He tailed off and shrugged. 'Do whatever you see fit.'

IN THE LONG RUN

'I'm here to do a job, not win the race.'

This statement brought about a complete change in Parker. For a moment he appeared to be genuinely amused.

'Win the race,' he echoed. 'You have no more chance of beating Fordyce than I have.'

Although having already decided not to push himself too hard, to hear his chances so casually dismissed stung Ryan. There was that name Fordyce again. Who the hell was this guy anyway? Superman?

If Parker noticed his reaction he gave no sign. His amusement faded as he continued. 'As I said just now, just carry on with your normal business. There is a week before the race. During this time make sure that as many people as possible within the hotel know that you are competing.'

He indicated a package lying on the rear seat of the car. 'In there are a variety of training vests and tee shirts, all clearly marked Comrades Marathon 1990. Wear them at every opportunity until you make contact with Manelli.'

'And how am I going to do that? I'd imagine that someone in his position is going to be pretty hard to get to.'

'You will be told at the appropriate time. The less you know for now the better. Just take things as they come.'

This lack of communication irritated Ryan. He was stung into remarking: 'It sounds as if you don't trust me. I've come six thousand miles to help you, and you won't even give me a proper idea of what's going on. I don't think I like that very much.'

If he had expected to intimidate Parker in any way with this mild fit of temper then he was disappointed. The older man merely shrugged.

'You would like it a lot less inside a South African jail, I can assure you. Security is vital in a matter of this nature. If you do not like the way in which matters have been arranged, then my earnest advice to you is to take the next available flight back to London. The choice is yours.' His expression then hardened. 'On the assumption that you do stay, let me make it quite clear that your role here is simply to obey orders. Any deviation from this could have dire consequences for you. As I have already stated, the choice is yours.' The rigid countenance remained as Parker waited for Ryan's response.

This is crazy the runner told himself. He had been in this country less than an hour and already he was being threatened by the very people he had come all this way to assist. Tyler's words came back with force. 'They are very active and very militant.' Christ, what an understatement that was. He hadn't exactly expected a hero's welcome, but at the same time he had anticipated some kind of gratitude. Instead he was being confronted with ultimatums and threats. His first instinct was to say sod it and go home. To counter this, all the deep-rooted convictions formed at Sussex came rushing to the surface. Right now his personal feelings were not that important. He was here, and he'd promised to do a job. Whether or not he liked Parker in the process was largely irrelevant. What was of consequence was the man's apparent efficiency. Despite his reticence there seemed little reason to doubt that matters would be well organised. Ryan drew some comfort from that. Also, he acknowledged, he had given his word to Tyler. That was as good as making a solemn pledge to the movement itself.

'I'll stay,' he confirmed.

Parker gave a curt nod. 'Good. I'm pleased that we now understand each other.'

Ryan hesitated. 'There is one thing I'd still like to know.'

'You are at liberty to ask. Whether or not I choose to give you an answer is another matter.'

Ignoring the negative aspect of this response, Ryan asked: 'Why me? Why bring me all the way from England?' It was a question he had asked himself many times.

For the second time, Parker displayed mild amusement. 'I wondered when you would bring that up. Yes, it may appear a little strange at first, so I suppose that you do deserve an answer.' He pulled over on to the inside lane of the freeway before expanding on this. 'For a start, you will be known to Manelli. He avidly watches all the big races, including the London Marathon. Even if he does not immediately recognise you, your name will mean something to him thanks to your performances in that event. He will be keen to talk to you.'

'All right. But why not a South African runner? Surely there was someone already here who could have helped you in the same way.'

'Perhaps, but why take the risk? You were available to us from a trustworthy source. Besides, in one rather important aspect you are far better suited for the task than any African could be.'

'How's that?'

'As an athlete coming here from overseas and competing against convention, you will hold a particular attraction for Manelli. He will quite probably admire you for this.' Ironic amusement entered Parker's voice. 'He will almost certainly see you as being in rather a similar situation to himself. Both of you coming here, as you have, to perform in your respective manners. This, in spite of popular

IN THE LONG RUN

opinion and the fact that each of you may suffer considerably as a consequence. You will, if you like, be kindred spirits.'

Ryan nodded. 'I see. The perfect basis to build a friendship on.'

'Precisely.'

The matter explained, there followed another lengthy silence. During this lull Ryan began to take a closer look at his surroundings. They were now passing through some residential suburbs. Every so often they passed small groups of runners pounding along the pavements. With a certain amount of grim satisfaction he noted that black and white did not appear to be training together. So much for earlier false impressions, he told himself.

This reflection was then shattered as the car turned a corner. Into view came by far the biggest group of runners yet. Well over a dozen headed towards them at a vigorous pace. As they neared Ryan could clearly see that there were indeed several blacks amongst their number. Many wore what appeared to be a club vest: dark blue with one red and one white horizontal band across the middle.

As the Mercedes drew alongside he stared in their direction. In response several runners of both races gave him a cheerful wave. One indicated with a cheeky grin that perhaps he should be following their example rather than cruising around in a luxury car.

Such was Ryan's interest and curiosity that, for an impulsive moment, he considered asking Parker to stop the car. The idea was quickly rejected. This was not the time to be displaying any behaviour that could be construed as weak.

Parker passed him a brief, pointed look. 'Don't be fooled by that,' he remarked. 'At the end of the day those blacks will still go back to their under-privileged areas, and the whites to their comfortable, middle-class homes.'

He gave a hollow laugh. 'Many of those white runners will then sit there at home congratulating themselves on being non-racists, whilst at the same time the only Africans they will allow through their front doors are the hired servants.' His voice rose a shade. 'Tell me Ryan, how many people do you know who would be prepared to work for the equivalent of twenty pounds a month?'

'They actually work for that?' Ryan was incredulous.

'It's better than starving.'

Ryan slowly nodded. This was more like the South Africa he had always envisaged. The pampered whites dominating the downtrodden Africans and exploiting them with wages barely fit to survive. His earlier confusion was set aside. Once again his resolve to see this thing through became strong. OK, so there had been a little window dressing at the airport. The fact remained that massive problems still existed. Until that was put right the struggle would have to continue.

Yet another silence developed as Ryan continued with these thoughts and Parker, faced with increasing density of traffic, concentrated on his driving. Soon they were in the city centre where traffic lights seemed to be located on virtually every block. Their progress became a very stop-go affair.

Finally the Holiday Inn came into view. Rising thirty stories, the building's white façade was neatly bisected by its exterior lift shaft. This rose to a domed peak that sat astride the flat roof like some huge bowler hat.

The Mercedes slid gracefully to a halt opposite the hotel entrance. Parker turned, his eyes boring into Ryan's as if attempting to read his mind. 'We are placing a lot of trust in you,' he finally said.

If there were any doubts about his commitment, Ryan felt that they should be dispelled at once. 'You can rely on me,' he responded. 'I won't let you down.'

'I'm very pleased to hear that.' Parker's words were softly spoken. 'It would be extremely unfortunate if you were to disappoint me now.'

The older man's eyes held their gaze for several more seconds. He then gave a curt nod. 'Come,' he ordered. 'You can take your suitcase out now.'

*

Ryan awoke with a start. He glanced at his watch and groaned. It was five p.m. He'd slept for over three hours. Jumping off the bed, he made for the en-suite bathroom. After splashing some cold water over his face he felt slightly better.

There could be no denying the comfort of his hotel room: it was almost embarrassing. He had come to help the poor and oppressed, yet here he was in surroundings that those impoverished people could only dream of. Although telling himself that his stay here was necessary for the job in hand, a certain guilt still persisted.

From his bedroom window Ryan was able to look down on to Durban beachfront. All races mingled freely together on the parade, signifying that at least the old days of an African stepping aside for a white appeared to be gone. Runners of various ages passed regularly along the beach road. Some were plainly serious athletes; others jogged by in a far more leisurely manner. Here, it seemed, would be as good a place as any for him to begin his own training

IN THE LONG RUN

tomorrow. For the time being, he would explore a little of Durban before dinner.

Once on the street, Ryan found himself retracing the route used earlier by the Mercedes. Parker sprang back to mind. With his colonial British air, he was the very last person Ryan would have envisaged being involved in the struggle against apartheid. The man's image suggested that of a rich land owner, one who would not hesitate to make profitable use of the cheap African labour. An exploiter rather than a crusader.

At their point of parting Ryan had, with some trepidation, suggested a diluted version of this thought. Parker had given him a withering look.

'Then I suggest that you learn rather more about your South African history,' was his terse response. 'Find out in particular about the Torch Commandos. Not all whites here supported the introduction of apartheid you know.'

The name Torch Commandos fascinated Ryan, but frustratingly Parker would not say anything further. He ended their conversation by the simple measure of just driving away. An intrigued Ryan resolved to do as he suggested.

His strolling brought him to a bar. Looking up he noted the name on the sign overhead: Thatcher's.

An immediate reaction was to think of 'that woman', the British Prime Minister. But it couldn't be, he told himself. Not here of all places. He then recalled Parker's comments about Natal. The last British outpost he had called it. Ryan gave out a short, ironic laugh. Even so, surely they wouldn't name a pub here after her. Almost mechanically he passed through the revolving doors. He had to know.

The main bar was on his left. His eyes scanned the area. At first glance there appeared nothing to suggest any kind of deference to the name. It was only when he reached the corner of the bar that it came into view. Hanging directly over the far end of the counter was a large portrait of a benignly smiling Margaret Thatcher. As he glared with disgust, Ryan had the distinct impression that the image was mocking him.

His anger rose. He had to contain a mad urge to tear the portrait from the wall. Smash it to pieces and then demand of everyone present, 'Why are you making a heroine of this woman?'

At the same time he knew the answer only too well. He was now in a country where Thatcher's policies were bound to be popular. Hadn't the woman, time and again, refused to back trade sanctions others imposed on South Africa?

'What can I get you sir?'

His thoughts were sharply interrupted by the sound of the barmaid's voice. Suppressing his rage, Ryan turned to face her. His hastily manufactured smile felt more like some strange grimace. 'What did you say?' he asked. Even to his own ears his voice sounded aggressive.

If the barmaid detected this she gave no sign. 'What can I get you sir?' she repeated. 'Something to drink?'

He began to take more notice of the girl. She was certainly attractive. Her shoulder length blonde hair framed a face that was maybe just a shade too plump. Even so, this did little to disguise her excellent bone structure. Her neat figure was shown off to its best advantage by a contour hugging white cotton top and an equally tight fitting black skirt. The outfit might have looked tarty on some girls, but not this one Ryan decided. Although she was never likely to be mistaken for an innocent, an indefinable aura of niceness still surrounded her.

All this Ryan took in at a glance. The effect was like a fast acting tranquilliser. His anger simply disappeared.

'I'll have a beer please,' he replied.

'A Castle do you?'

Although oblivious to what a Castle may be, he nodded. 'Sure. Why not?'

As she moved away, the girl's hips rolled just sufficiently enough to suggest that it was a natural rather than manufactured movement. In a few moment she returned with the open bottle and a glass. Ryan, who had not enjoyed any real relationship with a woman for more than six months, found his eyes following her every movement.

'There you go,' she smiled, placing the drink on the counter.

The smile lit up her whole face. It was infectious too. Ryan responded with one of his own. In an almost automatic reaction he asked: 'What's your name?'

She brushed an imaginary strand of hair from her face. 'Gayle.'

'I'm Steve.'

'Hi Steve.'

Their eyes met and then she was gone. A thirsty voice from further down the bar was already demanding service.

Ryan continued to watch her. Confidently she dealt with a small flurry of incoming customers. With equal expertise she neatly avoided the outstretched hand of an ageing Romeo who somehow imagined that the purchase of a drink also entitled him to a free grope. The movement was executed in such a manner that even the customer himself was forced to laugh.

IN THE LONG RUN

It was a good fifteen minutes before she returned to Ryan's corner of the bar. 'Can I get you another?' she asked.

He held up a hand. 'No thanks. I'm in training.'

Gayle made to move off and then paused, her curiosity getting the better of her. 'In training for what?'

'The Comrades Marathon.'

She gave a light laugh. 'Most guys I know who run the Comrades train on beer.'

'I'm not a fun runner,' Ryan stated, inexplicably peeved by her flippant attitude. 'I've come over from the UK just to compete.'

'To try and beat Fordyce I suppose.' Her humorous expression persisted. 'You've got no chance.'

Ryan sighed. It felt like every time the race was mentioned, so was that name Fordyce. Without knowing exactly why, he suddenly wanted to know more about the runner. Was it his competitive nature being stirred, he wondered? Or was he actually experiencing a jealousy of the South African's reputation? Whatever, he was now eager for more information.

'Is he really as good as people say?' he probed.

The girl shrugged. 'To be honest, I'm not that much of an expert on running. I suppose he must be though. He keeps on winning.'

The disappointment at her response showed on Ryan's face.

Gayle was quick to notice this. 'There's a friend of mine,' she began. 'He's run the Comrades a few times. He could probably tell you what you want to know.'

'A boyfriend?' Ryan could not resist asking.

Her smile returned. 'No, just a friend. We used to be engaged, but not any more. We're still good pals though.'

To Ryan it was an odd sounding arrangement. In his experience he had never heard of a broken engagement leading to anything but bitterness. At least on one side. Keeping this opinion to himself, he asked: 'Where could I meet this friend?'

'He's a member at Mandene Park. The club is over by the university. Do you know where that is?'

As Ryan shook his head, Gayle was called away again. 'We'll talk some more in a minute,' she promised.

His eyes continued to follow her around. She had a sexuality that, although not being deliberately flaunted, still reached out and grabbed him in a disturbingly significant way. What was even more unsettling was the fact that he was just allowing this to happen. With so much else to occupy his mind, plus his deep-rooted distaste for most white South Africans, what the hell was he thinking of?

This time it was less than five minutes before Gayle returned. Clearly she had used this short break to do some thinking of her own. Her approach was now far more direct.

'If you like I could take you up to Mandene myself and introduce you. I'm off duty all day tomorrow.'

Quickly Ryan pondered the invitation. He had very little desire to be drawn into any aspect of South African social life. The main reason for his being here was to help break up institutes like these cosy, whites only clubs. On the other hand, a small voice in his head told him, just one visit might be a good thing. It would probably add a touch of authenticity to this façade of his. It would also give him the chance he wanted to discover more about the seemingly invincible Bruce Fordyce. But what swung the balance, even if he did not readily acknowledge it, was the prospect of a few hours in Gayle's company. But that would be a bonus, not a reason, he convinced himself.

She was looking at him, waiting for his reaction to her offer. His delay in answering caused her face to cloud over. 'If you don't want to ... ' she began, at the same time turning a little red.

Quickly Ryan cut in. 'No, that's fine,' he told her. 'I'd love to go.'

IN THE LONG RUN

CHAPTER FOUR

With just a short distance of his training run remaining, Armstrong felt almost cheated. There was now only one week remaining before the big race, but during the last few days Mister Douglas has insisted that both the speed and length of his workouts be reduced. It was hard to accept. He'd never felt so fit and strong. Were it not for the vigilant eye of his coach running alongside him he might well have been tempted to make a large detour.

'We can't have you overtrained Armstrong,' the Scot had stressed repeatedly. 'It's time to ease off now.'

Well Mister Douglas must know what he was talking about. Even so, feeling the way he did, it was hard to ease off so much. The more he ran, the better he felt.

His ungainly, arm waving style was now long gone, replaced with an erect and economical technique. Not that the change had been easy or rapid. Many times during the early days he'd slipped back into bad old habits, only to receive yet another stern lecture from his coach. Breaking a natural habit was no easier for Armstrong than anyone else.

Apart from his own impressive performances, Armstrong was now drawing inspiration from another quarter. Twelve months ago Sam Tshabalala had become the first ever African to win the Comrades. Even though Bruce Fordyce had not made his customary appearance in the 1989 race, it was still a huge breakthrough for black Africans. It had taken them many years to produce a winner, and Tshabalala was already gaining the rewards of his achievement. Originally from poor beginnings, he had now been elevated to star status.

Along with this came all the inevitable sponsorship deals and comforts of life.

Armstrong began to picture himself in a similar position. Although running would always be fun for him, he could now see much further than the finishing line. The road between Durban and Pietermaritzburg represented a path to the kind of life that he and his family could only previously dream about. When a rare bad day did occur, this incentive had been more than enough to keep him going.

The pair were now approaching Armstrong's township. Relatives and neighbours began to wave and call out encouragement to him. He had already become something of a minor celebrity to the residents of Shakaville. In one week's time he would be representing them and carrying their united support.

They pulled up alongside Douglas' car, which was still being closely guarded by three of Armstrong's young cousins.

'That will do for today,' Douglas said. He then looked straight into the youth's eyes. 'I mean it Armstrong. I know what you're like. As soon as I'm gone you'll be wanting to go off again.'

Armstrong gave a guilty grin. 'No more today Mister Douglas, I promise.'

As he drove back to Blythdale for his arranged meeting with Piet, Neil Douglas reflected on the last few months. He'd been hard, almost brutal with Armstrong at times. Despite this, nothing seemed to dampen the boy's enthusiasm. He was popular too. Certainly most fellow members of the club he'd introduced him to, Dolphin Coast Striders, had a liking for the lad. And this popularity certainly wasn't based just on his ability. Armstrong was under strict orders not to reveal his full potential to anyone there. The only time his charge was put through his full paces was in private training sessions with just the two of them present.

In Armstrong's only competitive race to date he had easily qualified for Comrades entry, covering the forty-two-kilometre Hillcrest Marathon in a shade under three hours. Deliberately finishing so far behind the winner had been hard for Armstrong to bear, but somehow he had managed to restrain himself.

This lack of competitive running had been a major bone of contention between Douglas and Piet. Although he'd always got his way, Douglas was wearying of these discussions. He sighed. Doubtless this would once again be a topic of conversation this evening.

*

In the Long Run

Piet took a sip from his can of cold beer. Seated opposite him on the du Toit's back porch, Douglas did the same. The conversation had been going much as the Scot had anticipated.

'Look,' he said. 'We both want the lad to make as big an impression as possible in the Comrades, don't we.'

'Sure,' Piet agreed. 'But I don't see how—'

Douglas interrupted him. 'Do you realise how hard it was for me to make him hold back in the Hillcrest run? I don't think I could have restrained him a second time.'

Piet shrugged. 'So?'

'So think about it. If an unknown suddenly comes from nowhere and starts to win important races he immediately becomes a marked man. All kinds of people would be expecting Armstrong to do well in the Comrades. Why place him under that pressure?'

The doubt on Piet's face lifted slightly. 'I suppose so.'

'Believe me, I know what I'm doing,' Douglas pressed on. 'The programme I've worked on is more than sufficient. And before you ask again, no, I haven't overtrained him. Armstrong's worked bloody hard, but we're easing off now. He'll do well.'

The Scot's confidence began to rub off. 'You're the trainer,' Piet conceded.

'There's also something else to bear in mind. If Armstrong finishes in the top five as an unknown novice, the impact he makes will be much greater. And being so young will make it even better.'

A sparkle came into Douglas' eyes. 'Just watch the contracts come rolling in then.'

Piet noted the look. 'We're not doing this to make money out of the boy,' he stated emphatically.

'Of course not. But the lad himself will benefit far more this way. And it won't do my reputation as a coach much harm either.'

Piet decided to change the subject. 'So what's the plan for this week?' he asked.

'I'd like to keep a close eye on Armstrong for the next few days. Closer than normal.' The Scot took a long swig from his can before continuing. 'Tell me Piet, how would you feel about the lad moving in here with you until after the race? I'd put him up myself, but you know I've absolutely no spare room.'

Coming so unexpectedly, the question momentarily took Piet aback. 'Why?'

'A number of reasons. I need to be able to control his diet, get him in the right frame of mind, make sure he gets sufficient sleep. All that sort of thing.'

'How would Armstrong's parents feel about this arrangement?'

'I've already spoken to them. They've no objections.'

Piet smiled. 'You've got it all worked out, haven't you Neil?'

'That's what you're paying me for Piet. Seriously though, if you could let him stay here it would help a lot.'

Although considering himself a complete non-racist, Piet suddenly realised that he had never had an African stay at his home as a guest. Not even for one night. 'I'll have to speak to Cecile about it,' he said. 'There shouldn't be a problem though.'

Douglas looked pleased. 'I'll leave it with you then.'

He then got to his feet. 'It's time I was off. Give me a call when you've decided.'

Piet did not bother to get up himself. Full of thought, he merely waved a hand as Douglas departed.

Inside the house Michelle, who had listened to every word through a partly open window, also moved away. She was smiling to herself.

*

Ignoring the nearby dirty linen basket, James Kirkpatrick peeled off his sweat soaked training vest and tossed it carelessly onto the bedroom floor. His shorts followed. Why should he do the maid's job for her? Let her pick them up when she came to clean the room. In the months since his father's ultimatum his fitness had shown a marked improvement. His temper had not.

The farce was continuing. A condition of entry into the Comrades was that all runners must belong to a registered running association. Because of this he had been forced to join Rand Athletic Club, without question one of Johannesburg's finest. Bruce Fordyce himself was a member there. Not that this held any interest for James. Initially he had joined merely to humour the old man. It was nothing more than a token gesture towards his crazy demands. As the weeks passed however, it became clear that token gestures were not going to be sufficient this time. Every Saturday morning, like some bloody school kid, he was forced to report to his father's study and relate his progress. At first the times and distances he quoted were pure fiction. Why not, he considered? It wasn't as if this thing would be seen through to a conclusion. But then matters became more difficult.

'It's not that I doubt what you tell me James,' his father had said, his expression belying his words. 'All the same, I do think it is time you ran some official time trials with your club. Just to keep the record straight, you understand.'

IN THE LONG RUN

From then on James' problems really began. A clumsy and ill-disguised attempt at bribing a club official could well have resulted in disgrace and expulsion.

'If you are suggesting what I think you are, then I would not say another word,' the man told him. 'If you do I shall be forced to report this conversation to the committee.'

Mercifully the official let the matter rest there. Expulsion from Rand for a reason of this nature would have placed him in a near hopeless position. Even if he had managed to cover up the disgrace from his father — which would have been most unlikely — finding another club to accept him would have been damn near impossible. That of course would have meant no Comrades, which in turn meant... James did not need it spelling out.

It was at this low point that his work genuinely began. Hating every minute and cursing his father a hundred times a day, he started to train with at least a small degree of intent. His, until now, largely inactive muscles at first protested in the most painful way. Slowly though, his body adjusted to these new stresses. His times and distances, although still very ordinary in standard, were at least improving.

Even so, his first attempt at a qualifying marathon was a disaster. He hit the wall at thirty kilometres and collapsed dramatically on the roadside. Barely conscious, he was carried to a first aid tent and placed on a drip to replace lost body fluids.

This experience, James convinced himself, would surely be sufficient to make the old man call things off. Not even his stubborn bloody father could expect him to push himself any further than this. But far from showing concern, Charles Kirkpatrick actually congratulated his son. 'Well done,' he said. 'You are finally beginning to extend yourself. You must now move on to greater efforts. It's all in the mind you know.'

James could not believe what he was hearing. All in the mind! How could the stupid old bastard say that? It was OK for him. He wasn't the one putting his life on the line. His father was never going to be satisfied until he'd completed this thing or killed himself in the process.

By now James had nine weeks remaining in which to qualify. With a venomous hatred burning inside, he set about his training with a new and desperate determination. Appalled at the prospect of a repetition of his previous failure, he at last took the trouble to learn more about fluid replacement and diet. He consumed large amounts of carbohydrates to supply the extra energy required.

GEORGE STRATFORD

For the very first time in his life he found himself applying his body and mind to a specific task.

By mid-April he was as ready as he could hope to be. He started his next attempt at a qualifying marathon in the best condition of his life to date. It was all or nothing now. If he failed in this final chance he was finished. There was no way he could put himself through all this again next year.

Much to his surprise, this time he passed through the dreaded thirty-kilometre mark with relative ease. Suddenly confident of a good finish, he began to reflect on his father's words. What did the stupid old fool know? It was nothing to do with the mind. It was all down to his improved training methods. Then, with five kilometres to go, fatigue and cramp spasms set in. Blanking out all thoughts of the pain, James forced himself to dig deeper than he ever imagined possible. The old man's words returned to haunt him, this time bearing a harsh ring of truth. Gritting his teeth, he pushed on. Sheer bloody-mindedness carried him over the line. His time of four hours, eighteen minutes was sufficient. He had qualified. Briefly he gloried in his achievement.

All too soon the euphoria faded as James put things into perspective. The Comrades course was twice as long. And it would be uphill for most of the way. What he'd just achieved was nothing by comparison. Surely by now he had taken his body to the very limit of its endurance? Any lingering sense of achievement was soon swamped by these negative thoughts. With only six weeks left to recover and then raise his fitness level yet again, James' temper became even worse than before. He *had* to make the effort, no matter how forlorn the outcome may appear. The physical and mental pressures brought on by this obsession made him a nightmare to be anywhere near.

As usual, no one suffered more than the servants. Especially the timid Patience who was reduced to tears by his behaviour on numerous occasions. James was convinced that they were all laughing at him behind his back. That his reduced status in the household gave them all cause for pleasure. Twice he chanced upon the gardener and the chauffeur laughing loudly together. Their merriment ceased abruptly as they spotted his approach. Even Margaret Kirkpatrick was not safe from the sporadic verbal attack. Much to James' disgust, his normally pliable mother had backed her husband all the way over the Comrades issue. His accusations that she did not care hurt her deeply and gave her many sleepless nights.

Charles Kirkpatrick also found himself thinking long and hard. He had no intentions of abandoning his plan, but at the same time he could not help but

IN THE LONG RUN

wonder if he was maybe asking too much. Perhaps not everyone, even a young healthy man in strict training, was capable of completing the torturous Comrades course? A good, gutsy attempt — that was the most important thing, he finally decided. Providing James gave it all he had, that would be sufficient. Obviously though he could not provide an easy escape route for his son by telling him this. No, James must continue to believe that everything depended on his completing the course successfully. Apart from the enormous physical challenge, Charles had long been aware of the Comrades' reputation for bringing together people of vastly different backgrounds. The most unlikely friendships had been formed in the melting pot of mutual suffering and sacrifice. It was these sort of experiences that James needed to encounter.

And so James trained desperately on, convinced of the necessity, if not his ability, to complete the race inside the allocated time of eleven hours.

After dumping his running kit on the bedroom floor, James showered and dressed. It was now nine thirty a.m. Time to once again make his Saturday report to dear Father.

Charles greeted him in his usual stern manner. Any softening of his attitude was undetectable. James felt like a racehorse under an owner's inspection as the old man critically appraised him.

'You look fit enough,' he was told.

'I suppose so.' His response was stiff.'

'There are now only a few days remaining.'

James glared at his father, the pent-up frustration clear to see. 'Thanks for stating the bloody obvious.'

'Don't you start your nonsense with me James. I won't have it. Do you hear me?'

'How the hell do you expect me to react?'

Although striving not to, James was once again losing his temper as all the suppressed anger and hate for his father sought an outlet.

'You make my life hell,' he continued, 'and then you demand respect. Well you can forget that. I could have died in that first marathon. And what do you do? You tell me to try harder. Well screw you. I've done all this for your benefit and you're still not satisfied.'

His outburst was met with an ironic laugh. 'You did it for yourself James, not me. Remember, you could always have accepted the alternative.'

'What sort of alternative was that? I'm your son remember. Not some bloody kaffir from the townships. What do you want from me you crazy bastard?'

'I want you to *act* like my son,' Charles boomed out in response. 'I want you to act like a Kirkpatrick, not the gutless, weak-minded, self-centred brat that you appear to have become.'

A sneer spread over James' face. 'So that's what you really think of me is it?'

'At present — yes. Prove me wrong if you can.'

'By running the Comrades? What will that prove? I should tell you right now to stick the idea.'

'And are you going to do that? Are you genuinely prepared to throw away all that you have here?' A calculating look then appeared in the old man's eyes. 'That would take guts of a sort I suppose. Something that I could perhaps respect and admire. How about it James?'

For once, instead of allowing his temper full reign, James actually paused to think. His father had not said those words for nothing. What exactly was being offered here? Was the old sod implying that, if he now made a stand and refused to continue with this farce, then he had passed some kind of test? That if he proved strong enough to walk away from the comforts of home, they would in fact be restored to him? What an easy way out. But could he be certain? He agonised over this dilemma. If he was wrong, then he would lose everything.

Charles studied his son's every expression, well aware of his mental turmoil. He had quite deliberately held out this tantalising prospect to James. Would he be weak enough to accept the easy option? It had not been a planned strategy, but in the heat of their conversation the words had simply come out. Nevertheless, his mind was now like a steel trap poised to snap shut. Whether or not James was ensnared was entirely up to him.

If the boy did choose to take the bait then he wanted no more to do with him. Much as this judgement brought heartache, any son of his must have the courage and fight to turn away from the soft alternative. He prayed that James would make the right decision.

By now the temptation to quit was gaining the upper hand in James' mind. What was the point of doing otherwise, he reasoned? His chances of successfully completing the Comrades were almost non-existent anyway. So why put himself through it? Surely he had not mistaken the challenge in his father's voice. It was all there for the taking.

In that very moment of decision, with the wrong words sitting precariously on the tip of his tongue, James looked once more into the old man's face. With a life-saving flash of insight he suddenly saw everything. Not as he imagined it to

IN THE LONG RUN

be, but as it really was. How this insight was gained, he couldn't say. Perhaps it was some kind of fortuitous telepathy coming to his rescue? Whatever it was, he instantly recognised that to succumb to temptation would be the end for him. He ground his teeth. The cunning old sod. He'd so nearly fallen into his trap. Well two can play at that game. Pushing the horror of how close to disaster he had come from his mind, James struck a determined pose.

'No!' he stated with deliberate firmness in his tone. 'Why should I give in now? I've come this far, so I'll see it through. If only to prove something to you.' Immediately he knew that he had made the correct decision. For a fleeting moment he felt certain that there was even a suspicion of pride in the old fool's face. In a blink it was gone.

'If that is what you wish my boy,' Charles said without a trace of emotion.

The realisation that he had come so close to losing everything pushed James into playing his role of the righteously indignant son to the full. Briefly he even managed to believe his own words.

'You say that you want me to act like a Kirkpatrick. OK, if this is what it takes to make me one in your eyes, then that's fine. But when it's all over, will you then act like a father? No more tests of character. No more ultimatums. Trust is what I want from you. Your love and your trust.'

It was only with the utmost self-control that Charles prevented himself from reaching out to his son. Was this the beginning of the change he so yearned for? Was his plan working out for the best after all? His face remained expressionless. 'We'll see what happens,' he stated.

CHAPTER FIVE

The hotel dinner had been good. Ryan leaned back in his chair with a contented sigh. Although now feeling well nourished, his gesture of satisfaction was not entirely in appreciation of the food. Throughout the meal he had thought frequently of Gayle. For a short while all other considerations faded as he remembered her smile. She had made a far bigger impression than he at first realised. Realistically though, it was unlikely that the feeling was mutual. Barmaids, by their very vocation, were generally a cynical breed not easily taken in by the compliments and patter from customers often much the worse for drink.

Whatever she may feel, Ryan warned himself, it wouldn't pay to become too involved. Not that it was a proper date or anything they had fixed up. It was her ex-fiancé that he was going to see; Gayle was merely providing the introduction. She probably saw the whole thing as nothing more than a friendly gesture. Which given his own far from normal situation, should suit him fine. Even so, he could not deny his eagerness to see her again. Or the hope that she would be pleased to see him.

With these thought still very much on his mind, Ryan left the dining room and wandered towards the nearest elevator. The doors slid open for him to step inside. As he did so, another figure followed. A short but solidly built African. The newcomer smiled broadly but said nothing. Gayle was pushed from Ryan's mind as he surveyed the man. It had been disconcerting the way the guy just seemed to materialise from nowhere. Could this be his hotel contact? They were alone in the lift. If the man did have something to say, then now would be the perfect opportunity.

IN THE LONG RUN

'What floor are you going to?' Ryan asked, aware of a slight croak in his voice.
'The fourteenth will be fine.'

Ryan's room was on the ninth. He punched both buttons. His fellow passenger's appearance gave little away. Dressed in smart casual attire, he could be anybody. A visitor, an out of uniform staff member, or even a paying guest. There was apparently no colour bar at this hotel. In fact there had been several, very affluent looking Africans enjoying dinner at the same time as himself.

Not a word was exchanged during their smooth ascent to the ninth floor. As the lift came to rest Ryan relaxed a little. His imagination was getting the better of him. Then, as he stepped out into the passageway, the African spoke.

'Manelli will be at the swimming pool on the top floor at seven thirty tomorrow morning. Be there.'

So casually were the words spoken, it took a short while for their full significance to strike Ryan. Swiftly he then turned back to look at the speaker, but by now the sliding doors were already almost closed. He just managed to catch a glimpse of the man's still smiling face before they shut completely. The elevator then continued its ascent.

*

Ryan rose at seven a.m. It had been a restless night. The real action was now about to begin. It was one thing to merely talk about arranging a man's death — it was something completely different to look that man in the eye and pretend to be his friend. Did he really have the stomach for that kind of deception? Well he had to find it from somewhere. He was in too deep to back out now.

Ryan's convictions needed a boost. He filled his head with all the injustices and atrocities he knew had been perpetrated in South Africa. These images helped steel his resolve. By coming here, Manelli was openly condoning these acts. For that, Ryan kept telling himself, the man deserved to suffer whatever fate threw at him. His determination now bolstered, he opened the package Parker had supplied him with. He selected an eye-catching white tee shirt from amongst several inside. Printed in large lettering across both back and front were the words COMRADES MARATHON 1990. Ryan slipped the shirt on. It was now seven thirty a.m., time to make a move; although how exactly he would handle things once at the pool he had no idea. Presumably on their first meeting he was expected to do no more than attempt to befriend the guy. Assuming that

Manelli's athletic interests were as strong as claimed, maybe that wouldn't prove as difficult as he feared.

As the mysterious African had said, the swimming pool was at the very top of the building. It was deserted apart from Manelli, who was already in the water, and a tough looking character sat lounging in one of the white plastic chairs at the far end. Ryan immediately assumed him to be a minder. Getting to his feet, the man's mean eyes ran professionally over him as he entered. Evidently the bodyguard saw no danger there. With a small grunt of satisfaction, he eventually sat down once more. As he did so, his lightweight jacket parted slightly to reveal a shoulder holster and handgun. Having never been confronted with anything more lethal than a starting pistol before, Ryan was shaken. The dangers of what he was becoming involved in were brought sharply into focus.

There was no mistaking Manelli. He looked exactly as he did in a thousand publicity shots: strong, bronzed and handsome. With undoubted talent and vast wealth to back this up, it was easy to see how most men could leave his presence suffering from a huge inferiority complex.

Ryan walked slowly along the side of the pool to the near end, as far away as possible from the menacing figure with the gun. He paused by the panoramic window, apparently fascinated by the view. In this position Manelli could not fail to spot the Comrades name on his shirt. Sure enough, it did not take long for the singer to respond.

'Hi,' he greeted Ryan after completing a fast couple of lengths. Leaning against the side of the pool, waist deep in water, he was the epitome of a superstar.

Ryan turned fully towards him and stared for a moment or two. 'Aren't you Tony Manelli?' he then asked, hoping that he had injected just the right amount of surprise into his voice.

Manelli grinned as he hauled himself from the water. 'That's what they call me,' he said. He held out his hand. 'And you?'

'Steve Ryan.'

As they shook hands, Ryan was uncomfortably aware that the minder was watching him closely. Was it his imagination, or had the man's hand moved slighter closer to the concealed weapon?

'You're English aren't you?' Manelli asked.

He nodded. 'I'm just here on a visit. I came over for this.' His finger pointed towards the words on his chest.

IN THE LONG RUN

'Yea, I saw that just now. You're not running are you?'

'That's what I came here for.'

Manelli paused for a moment, his brow furrowed with concentration. He then snapped his fingers.

'The London Marathon!' he exclaimed.

Ryan nodded but said nothing.

'I've got a video of the race back home,' Manelli continued, now displaying real signs of enthusiasm. 'I never forget a face for long. Let me think. I reckon you finished in around two hours twelve. Right?'

'Two thirteen,' he was corrected.

'Yea, I knew it was somewhere around there. I watch all the top marathons you know, it's a big interest of mine. I'm sorry Steve, I should have recognised you straight away.'

Coming from one of the world's most famous entertainers, this was indeed an incongruous statement. Manelli then clapped his hands together sharply. The sudden noise seemed to bounce off the still water and reverberate.

'So you're Steve Ryan huh!' he exclaimed.

'That's what they call me,' Ryan replied with just the hint of a smile.

Manelli saw the joke immediately. He laughed out loud. 'Shit, is that what I sounded like just now?' It was a warm, genuine laugh, clearly indicating that Manelli did not take himself, or his star status, too seriously.

The American sat down in one of the poolside chairs and gave Ryan a quizzical look. 'What the heck made you come here Steve?' he asked. 'It sounds to me as if you could be risking a possible place in the next Olympics. Is it worth that much to you?'

'It's a challenge. Something I felt I had to do.'

At least that wasn't a lie, Ryan considered as he tried to meet the singer's gaze. He failed to hold the look for long. To compensate for this he made a show of dropping into the seat alongside.

'I'll be running under an assumed name of course,' he added when settled.

Manelli nodded, as if understanding. 'It still takes guts. Hell, it takes guts just to run the goddam race, let alone put your career at risk too.'

Ryan reacted spontaneously. 'But isn't that exactly what you're doing — risking your career for the sake of coming here? Even if you ignore all the other angles, didn't you think of that?' The words tumbled out before he had a chance to think of the possible consequences.

For a fearful moment he reflected that he had indeed said the wrong thing. Manelli gave him a hard, searching look before responding.

'Sure I thought about it Steve. I thought about it a lot. Not so much about my career, but about the rights and wrongs of coming to South Africa.' His expression then softened a shade. 'But you must have done the same.'

Ryan gave a silent sigh of relief as he saw that no real damage had been done. 'Yes, I did,' he replied. That again was pretty close to the truth. He certainly had agonised over the rights and wrongs, but on issues far removed from anything this man could ever imagine. His inherent curiosity then exerted itself. Suddenly it was important for him to hear the American's opinions. By luring Manelli into openly stating his racist beliefs, his own part in this matter would be fully vindicated.

'So after you'd thought it all out, what was it that justified your visit then?' Ryan probed. 'I take it there's more to it than the money?' Even as he spoke these final words, he wondered why he'd bothered. Of course it was the money. What other reason could there be?

The singer's laugh rang out again, this time even louder. 'The money,' he repeated in between spasms of mirth. 'That's a goddam joke.'

Irritated by Manelli's strangely humorous attitude, Ryan demanded: 'What's so funny about that?'

The American regained his composure. 'For a start, I'm worth well over two hundred million dollars Steve, so I sure as hell don't do anything I don't want to. Secondly, I'm losing money on this trip, not making it.'

'You're joking,' was all an incredulous Ryan could say. If it wasn't the money, then what the heck *was* motivating the man?

'Seeing as how you're so interested, I'll give you two good reasons why I came,' Manelli continued. 'There's been a lot of changes in this country recently. The people here need to be encouraged, not penalised. That's the way to stop the progress.' He shrugged. 'Hell, I'm only a singer. I'm not going to change a whole lot on my own. The truth is though, there's a lot of people here keen to see me put on a show. That's why I came. But only on the understanding that the audiences I play to are multi-racial. Mix them up together, that's what I say. If everybody wants to join up for a concert, great. Let's stop messing around — let's make music instead.'

Ryan listened to this short speech with scepticism. To him it sounded far too much like well-rehearsed lines, prepared and ready for whenever awkward

IN THE LONG RUN

questions were asked. Manelli was probably lying about the money too. Not that it mattered much. At least they had struck up a relationship, and that meant that he was well on his way to achieving what was required of him.

'And the second reason you're here?' he asked, more for something to say than out of any great desire to know. He was already beginning to tire of this particular recital.

'For the race of course.' It was Manelli's turn to point towards the tee shirt. 'I've been waiting years for a chance to see the Comrades and video it for my collection.' He grinned at Ryan. 'Now we've met up I'll be keeping a special eye open for you Steve. Do you rate your chances of a gold medal?'

The runner shrugged. 'Perhaps.' It had already occurred to him that Manelli may not even be alive when the race took place, so it didn't matter much what he told him.

'Fordyce will win again this year you know.'

This remark of Manelli's sparked a fresh interest in Ryan. If this Yank was such a student of distance running, he should be able to tell him something about this so-called King of the Comrades. The man everyone kept shoving down his throat. What was he like as a person?

'What do you know about him?' he asked the singer.

Manelli smiled. 'Not too much apart from his record. I'll tell you one thing though. He'll use a standard marathon as a training run and still finish within a few minutes of your best time. Think about that Steve.'

Before Ryan could respond, Manelli rose to his feet. He made a small, almost imperceptible movement to the man at the far end of the pool, and then headed towards the exit. 'I'll see you here at the same time tomorrow if you're around,' he called over his shoulder.

His departure was sudden and unexpected. Caught unawares, Ryan merely lifted a hand in acknowledgement. 'Sure,' was all he had time to say before Manelli, clutching the towel handed to him, disappeared from view.

*

With nothing much to do before meeting Gayle at four o'clock that afternoon, the next few hours seemed to stretch interminably before Ryan. After a quick swim he decided to give breakfast a miss and set out immediately on a training run along the beachfront.

GEORGE STRATFORD

Throughout the fifteen kilometre workout he dwelled on Manelli's remarks concerning Fordyce. Using the occasional marathon for a training run was just about acceptable when preparing for a race like the Comrades. But to hear that the guy would casually complete one within minutes of his own personal best was a massive blow to his ego. The forty-two kilometre event was his speciality. Here he was dreaming of Olympic glory, and now being made to feel totally inadequate. That was bad enough, but to have this done by a white South African was really twisting the knife.

It was because of this that he returned to the hotel in a less than perfect mood. Normally he felt good after such a run. Today there was nothing. It was if the spectre of Bruce Fordyce was sitting on his shoulder and mocking his efforts. Hell, he had never even met the guy — had no idea what he looked like — and yet the man was becoming an obsession with him. In one sense he was sick to death of the name, and yet at the same time a driving force insisted that he discover more. It was a strange, indefinable fascination.

After a shower he found that it was still only mid-morning, and left the hotel in search of a diversion. The nearby Sea World with its dolphin show and marine life exhibition passed an interesting hour or so. Then, suddenly hungry, Ryan stopped off at an Italian restaurant for lunch. Like many endurance athletes before a big race, he regularly consumed large amounts of carbohydrates to provide the extra energy needed. Pasta was a prime source. As he worked his way through a large plate of spaghetti he reflected that this time he would need all the extra energy he could muster. He would be running twice as far as ever before. Although loath to admit it, he knew that the whole concept of the Comrades was slowly taking a grip on him.

The rest of the day was spent planning his training schedule and watching TV in his hotel room. The time dragged by.

Bang on four p.m. he walked out through the main hotel doors and waited on the pavement outside. Gayle had promised to pick him up in her car. She could not fail to spot him here. Five minutes passed, then ten. With a mixture of disappointment and frustration Ryan slowly began to accept that perhaps she might not be coming. Beginning to feel like a fool, he decided to give her another five minutes before giving up. These minutes had all but passed by too when an ancient Ford Escort at last pulled up in front of him. The dilapidated vehicle's front, nearside wing sported a large dent and the wheel beneath it was minus a hubcap. Gayle raised a hand in greeting through the window. Ryan opened the

IN THE LONG RUN

door and sat down next to her. The seat springs, almost as if unused to such inconsiderate treatment, groaned in protest under his comparatively light weight. As cars go, he felt, it was best placed into the 'interesting' category.

'Sorry I'm late,' Gayle told him. 'I had a bit of trouble starting Old Martha here.' She patted the steering wheel with obvious affection.

From the look of Old Martha, Ryan considered it a miracle she ever got it started at all. He kept this thought to himself. 'Don't worry,' he said. 'It's good of you to come.'

In spite of its rough appearance, the car seemed to chug along well enough. Soon they left the city centre behind. Gayle then pointed upwards to a tall, slender building on a high ridge. 'That's part of the university,' she said. 'The club's not far from here.'

They arrived a few minutes later. Gayle parked the car by some bushes where the road ended. As she switched the engine off, Martha, as if grateful for the rest, shuddered and then with a contented mechanical whirr became silent.

Together they walked towards the clubhouse. 'I don't think David is here yet,' Gayle said. 'I can't see his car anywhere.'

Ryan hardly heard her. His eyes were darting this way and that, taking in every detail. There was a football pitch to their right. To their left, tennis courts. A quick inspection around the back of the building revealed bowling greens. With a running section as well, this was clearly a busy club. For the time being however, the club was fairly quiet. Apart from a small group gathered around the pool table, they seemed to have the place pretty much to themselves. They selected a table by the window.

'Can I get you a drink?' Ryan asked.

She smiled. 'A Coke will do fine.'

He moved to the bar. The young African behind the counter looked at him enquiringly.

'A Coke and a ... ' Ryan hesitated, 'a Castle,' he then added, remembering the beer that Gayle had served him the previous day.

While the young barman saw to his order, Ryan watched him closely. The youth appeared to be happy and confident. He was far removed from the abused and downtrodden character that Ryan had imagined would be working in a place like this. As the African placed the two drinks in front of him one of the pool players called out.

'Hey November, give us some more beers over here will you?'

The speaker was a white man aged around thirty. November turned towards him and laughed. 'Slow down man, there's plenty of time.' It was clear that the pair were on excellent terms.

'How did you get a name like November?' Ryan asked while paying for the drinks.

The African grinned. 'It was the month I started work here.' He then moved off to attend the thirsty pool players.

Ryan returned to the table and handed Gayle her drink. 'How much do you know about the barman?' he asked.

She looked surprised. 'November? Not a great deal. Everybody here seems to like him though. He's very popular.' The spontaneity of her words struck Ryan. A popular black employee in a place like this did not fit in at all with his image of things.

His thoughts must have shown. 'So what do people in England think then?' Gayle asked. 'Do they imagine that we beat our African staff into submission every day?'

He coloured slightly. 'No, of course not.'

She laughed at his obvious discomfort. 'Let me tell you, this is well known for being a friendly club. Nobody gets hassle over their colour in here. If you don't believe me, just take a look at the notice board over there.' She pointed to the far wall.

Still feeling uncomfortable, Ryan did as she suggested. Pinned up amongst several pages of club announcements were three photographs. In each one multiracial groups of runners, all wearing the club colours, were captured in impromptu poses. Most were grinning broadly and clutching beer cans. There could be no doubting the conviviality of the occasion. The club colours were red, white and blue. There was no mistaking the distinctive vest that he had first seen when driving from the airport with Parker. The large group who had waved to him.

Ryan then recalled Parker's cynical words at the time. 'Don't be fooled by that. The blacks will still go back to their underprivileged areas, and the whites to their comfortable, middle-class homes.'

Probably true. But on the surface at least, this club was clearly being operated on the right lines. He returned to the table in reflective mood.

'Well,' enquired Gayle, 'what do you think now?'

'I must admit you appear to be right.' The words were hard to say and came out sounding rather stilted. He then went on to tell her about his sighting of the club members.

In the Long Run

She nodded. 'That's what I mean. Mind you, not every club is the same.'

Ryan seized on this remark. 'You mean most clubs still don't allow black members?'

'Hold on, I didn't say that. They do. That's all part of the changing scene.' Gayle frowned before continuing. 'What I'm trying to say is that there are still a few clubs — not many — that will go out of their way to discourage members they don't want. Officially there's no colour bar at all now, but who's going to hang around for long at a club where they're made to feel uncomfortable?'

Suddenly Gayle's personal opinion was very important to Ryan. He regarded her closely. 'And how do you feel about that?'

There was no hesitation on her part. 'I think it's disgusting,' she stated.

A wave of relief passed through Ryan. That was exactly what he wanted to hear, although why he should be so concerned was still a little blurred. In a few days time he would never see her again. For the moment however, he felt good.

At that moment Gayle pointed to the door. 'Here's David now,' she said, getting to her feet. 'Hang on a minute.'

Quickly she walked over to meet her ex-fiancé, giving him an affectionate kiss on the cheek. Ryan felt a small pang of jealousy. To him this was a very strange set-up for a recently separated couple. He eyed David critically. It was easy to see why she had fallen for the guy. Tall, muscular and good-looking, he had a confident air about him. The type who would never experience trouble in finding female company. Not quite a Manelli, but a similar sort of character. Together they approached the table. 'David, Steve. Steve, David.' Gayle's introductions were brief and simple.

As expected, Ryan found David's handshake firm and strong. A little too strong in fact. 'Can I get you both another drink?' the new arrival asked as Ryan flexed his fingers beneath the table. Both he and Gayle ordered the same again.

'So that's the guy you were engaged to,' Ryan said as David departed.

Gayle gave a quick grin which could have implied anything. 'That's him.'

'You can tell me to mind my own business if you like, but why...?'

'Why did we break up?' she said for him.

Ryan nodded. 'Something like that. 'He seems like the sort of guy that most women would find very attractive.'

This amused her. 'Oh he is,' she said. 'That was the problem. The only thing David lacked as far as I was concerned was the ability to say no to other women.'

All at once Ryan regretted asking the question. He felt embarrassed, although whether this was for himself or Gayle he wasn't sure.

'Don't worry,' she reassured him as she noted his expression. 'It doesn't bother me any more.'

She cast a quick glance in the direction of the bar before continuing. 'David will never change. We get on far better now than we ever did together.' She shrugged. 'He is what he is. I can always be his friend, but I'd sure as heck never become romantically involved with him again.'

Immediately Ryan's mind flashed back to a time twelve months ago. A girl then had said something very similar to him. A girl who had later come to mean a lot. In spite of her words she had still eventually dumped him and returned to her old boyfriend. It was not a pleasant memory, and because of this he now regarded Gayle's statement with a certain scepticism.

There followed a period of awkward silence, which was only broken by the return of David

'How's that for quick service?' he asked, placing the drinks on the table.

It was already clear to Ryan that David was something of an extrovert. How he'd often wished for the same kind of confidence himself, especially when meeting new people. It wasn't that he was shy exactly, but he would often find himself stuck for something intelligent to say when only small talk was required. A fact that he had just been forcibly reminded of with Gayle.

David parked himself noisily into a chair and looked at Ryan. 'So you're running the Comrades next week I understand.'

'That's right.'

'And you want to know more about Bruce Fordyce?'

For some reason Ryan suddenly felt a bit stupid. 'It seemed a good idea,' he said.

David laughed. 'Know your enemy, that's what it's all about eh. Well I can tell you now, he'll win again this year. It's the up-run, and that's his speciality. Especially Polly Shorts.'

'Polly Shorts? What's that?'

'That, my friend, is what sorts out the men from the boys. It's a hill just outside Pietermaritzburg — a real heartbreaker. Sure you'll find steeper and longer hills on the course, but when you've already run nearly eighty k's, it's a genuine killer.'

He paused for effect. 'And Fordyce — he goes up it like that.' David made a rapid upward movement with his hand.

Gayle nodded in agreement. 'He's telling you the truth. Fordyce has won the race every year between '81 and '88.'

IN THE LONG RUN

This confirmed what Tyler had told him. Ryan turned back to David. 'So who won it last year then?'

'The first ever African, Sam Tshabalala. That was on the down run from Maritzburg to Durban. It wasn't a fast time though.' David thought for a moment. 'What was it now? Just under five hours, thirty-six I think. Nearly twelve minutes slower than Fordyce's record.'

Ryan's eyes narrowed. Was David trying to belittle the African's achievement? After a moment's consideration he decided not. There was no trace of mockery in his voice. He was merely stating facts. Obviously the guy was a bit of a statistician.

'How about the up-run?' he asked. 'What's the record for that?'

'Fordyce again I'm afraid. A touch over five hours-thirty.'

Ryan did a quick mental calculation. That meant that there was only around six minutes difference. Incredible; especially if the hills were as steep and difficult as he'd been led to believe. Interesting as all this was though, it was not really the kind of information Ryan sought. It was Fordyce the man he wanted discover. Gently he tried to lead the conversation in a more personal direction.

'If Fordyce is that good then there must be a lot of runners pretty jealous of him. How does he get on with them?'

David thought for a moment. 'I suppose the other top guys must get a bit fed up being beaten every year. I don't know what they think privately. I'll tell you what though, you won't find many ordinary club runners with a bad word to say about Fordyce. You can talk to him see. He's not a bighead.'

'So he gets on well with most people?'

'That's right.' David then shrugged. 'Unless of course they're total racists.'

Instantly Ryan was gripped. This was the sort of stuff he wanted. 'What do you mean by that?' he asked, controlling the eagerness in his voice.

'Fordyce is renowned for his liberal views,' David continued. 'He's campaigned for years on behalf of equal opportunities for all. He also detests any form of political interference in sport. He even ran the Comrades wearing a black armband one year to protest at what was going on.' David laughed. 'That didn't make him very popular with certain people, I can tell you.'

Ryan joined in David's laughter. 'So he's considered a bit of a rebel then?'

'Only by those with their heads still stuck in the sand.'

David's amusement then ceased. 'I can tell you honestly, most people around here think the same as Fordyce. It's just that being so well known, it's easier for him to make his point to those that matter.'

'So you support his views then?'

'Of course, otherwise I wouldn't be talking like this.' David gave him a hard stare. 'Look, you're new here. Exactly how much do you know about South Africa?'

'Not as much as I thought.'

'That figures. For instance, do you know the difference between a white, English speaking South African and an Afrikaner?'

Ryan hesitated. 'No, not really,' he finally admitted. 'I thought all whites were pretty much the same.'

David's eyes rose to the ceiling. 'God save us from the ignorant foreigner. Try walking around the Transvaal or Free State and saying that. You'd get lynched.'

Embarrassed at his ignorance, Ryan coloured up. 'You can't expect me to know everything,' he blurted out. 'I only got here yesterday.' Even so, he was uncomfortably aware that someone with his education and political beliefs should have been aware of such divisions.

David gave him a patronising look. 'I suppose you're right.' He took a deep breath before enlarging on the matter. 'The English speaking South African, as the name implies, is of British descent. The Afrikaner is Dutch. And believe me, there is very little similarity between the two other than colour.'

He began to tick off on his fingers as he spoke. 'The language; the religion; past attitude towards government controls—'

'Hold it there,' Ryan cut in. 'Are you telling me that you English speakers had nothing to do with the introduction of apartheid? I can't believe that.'

For a few seconds it looked as if David was on the verge of losing his temper. With a supreme effort he controlled it. When he spoke his voice was hard.

'That's exactly what I'm telling you. It was the National government of 1948 that introduced apartheid. At that time it was a party exclusively for Afrikaners. Daniel Malan made sure of that.'

'Who was he?'

'My God!' David exploded. 'Don't you know anything? He was the Prime Minister who started the whole thing off. Apartheid was his idea. I get really pissed off with people like you who want to criticise without knowing the facts.'

Gayle, who had remained silent for some time, leaned quickly forward. 'All right you two, cool it. I didn't get the pair of you together just to have an argument.'

Both men looked at her and then at each other. David was the first to speak.

'Sorry,' he said. 'I get a bit wound up sometimes.'

IN THE LONG RUN

Ryan acknowledged this with a wave of the hand. 'I was a bit out of order myself,' he admitted. It felt strange to be uttering such an apology. But what he'd learned here today had been eye opening. He was now keen to continue their conversation, although he would have to be careful not to antagonise David further.

Gayle then took matters out of his hands.

'That's better,' she declared. 'I think we'd better leave politics alone from here on, don't you?'

David quickly agreed, leaving Ryan with little option but to do the same. Some other time, he promised himself. There was bound to be another opportunity.

The next hour passed surprisingly fast for Ryan. As he had judged, David could be an entertaining individual. Once the ice had been broken and his temper calmed, he came out with a string of humorous anecdotes. It was mostly lightweight stuff, but absorbing for all that. Despite himself, Ryan actually began to warm towards the South African.

It was after completing yet another of his stories that David glanced at his watch.

'Hell!' he exclaimed. 'I've got to get moving.'

Gayle gave him a teasing look. 'Got a date have you?' As she spoke she winked in Ryan's direction.

Her ex-fiancé responded with a sheepish grin. 'You know me,' he admitted. He stood up to leave.

Ryan caught David's eye. 'Will I see you around again sometime?' he asked.

'I might see you at the Comrades. Maybe we could make a plan.' David shrugged in a non-committal manner.

'Are you running this year?'

A rueful expression crossed David's face. 'I planned to. Then I tore a calf muscle in training. There's no time left now to get into shape.' He appeared genuinely sad. 'I'll be a bit like a fish out of water on the day.'

Gayle thought for a short while. 'Why don't you act as a second for Steve?' she suggested. 'At least you'll still be involved in some way then.'

She turned to Ryan. 'You'll be needing a second won't you?'

The unexpected proposal momentarily threw him. 'I don't know. I suppose I will.'

They then both turned their attention on David. 'It's a thought,' he said, half to himself. His voice then rose. 'Let me think about it. Give me a ring at home tomorrow evening. Gayle knows the number.' He then looked humorously in her direction. 'Or have you forgotten it already?'

She pulled a face at him. 'I've got your number OK.'
With a final grin, David left them alone.

Together Ryan and Gayle walked slowly back through the darkness to the car. It was now nine o'clock. After David's departure Gayle had decided to have a gin and tonic, something she assured Ryan she rarely did. This led to another, and then a third. Neither was much used to alcohol, and any lingering inhibitions soon eased. By the time they left the club both were totally relaxed and a shade drunk.

It was quiet where Old Martha waited. Inside the car, Gayle placed the key in the ignition but made no effort to start up. Instead she gazed straight ahead through the windscreen and into the night. It was if she had suddenly gone into a trance. Thinking that perhaps the gins had proved to be too much, Ryan touched her lightly on the elbow.

'Are you all right?' he asked. 'Would you like me to drive?'

When she turned towards him he could see that she was still in control.

'No, that's OK. I was just thinking.' She gave a small, embarrassed laugh. 'I go off like that sometimes.'

'Is there anything the matter?' Even to Ryan's ears his voice sounded surprisingly gentle.

She shook her head. 'No. I was just wondering what I would do if...' Her voice tailed off.

'Yes,' he prompted.

'Nothing.'

'Come on. Spill the beans.'

'Well, I was wondering what I would do if you tried to...' There was another pause and then she suddenly giggled. 'You know. Tried something on.'

Ryan couldn't see her face properly in the gloom. Was she winding him up or what?

'And what would you do?'

'Put it this way. I'd hate to ruin your future wife's wedding present.'

'I'm not a bloody rapist,' he retorted sharply.

'Shusssh.' She placed a hand briefly on the side of his face. 'I never thought you were.' She giggled again. 'I just get these silly thoughts now and then.'

Placated, Ryan began to consider this latest development. By simply touching him on the cheek she had made him even more aware of her sensuality. His indignation might now be calmed, but other, more physical parts, were definitely

IN THE LONG RUN

aroused. Was it pure lust, he reflected, or was there more to it than that? A close personal relationship based on respect was something he sorely missed. Of course there had to be sex too, but that was only a part of things. It was the companionship and knowledge that someone cared. That was what he missed most of all.

Her voice interrupted these thoughts. 'Now who's gone all quiet? You're not still upset are you?'

He smiled. 'No. Like you I was just thinking. By the way, how do you know I'm not married?'

'You're not are you?'

Ryan was not slow in picking up the touch of anxiety in her voice. 'No,' he assured her. 'Nobody has managed to snap me up yet.'

His flippant tone masked his inner conflict. One half of him desperately wanted to take hold of Gayle, if only to remind himself what it was like to embrace a woman. The cautious half restrained him. What if she reacted the wrong way? And anyhow, the last thing he needed at present was an emotional involvement. He needed a clear head with no distractions for what he had to do. Anything less would make him vulnerable.

Without warning Gayle leaned across and kissed him lightly on the lips. The contact was light and fleeting, but sufficient to unsettle Ryan even further. Before his confused mind could decide on a suitable response Gayle pulled away and started the car. The moment, whatever it might have produced, was gone.

CHAPTER SIX

With his mind crammed full of so many different thoughts, Ryan's second night in South Africa threatened to be as restless as the first. So far just about everything he had experienced had been the direct opposite of his expectations. The apparent lack of racial segregation anywhere; his introduction to the elderly yet menacing Parker; his first encounter with Manelli; the revealing visit to Mandine Park Sports Club. All of these had made a powerful impact. And then there was Gayle! In many ways she was the biggest surprise of all. As she had dropped him off at the hotel they had kissed again, this time with slightly less haste. It was hardly a passionate exchange, but the promise was definitely there.

'Don't hurry things,' she had said as he tried to prolong the embrace. 'Why don't you come and see me in the bar tomorrow. I start at four.'

With all these contrasting thoughts running through his head, Ryan had finally drifted off to sleep at around three thirty a.m.

He woke with a start. Bloody hell! It was after eight. He would miss Manelli at the pool. Throwing on a tee shirt and tracksuit bottoms he made for the top floor. The pool was deserted.

'Damn!' he exclaimed, disgusted with himself for having overslept. He turned to leave and nearly collided with Manelli's minder. Stood right up close to him for the first time, Ryan realised exactly how big the man was. At least six foot six inches he estimated, with the shoulders and chest of a mountain gorilla. The only thing small about him was his eyes, which now bored into Ryan as if in deep disapproval.

IN THE LONG RUN

'Mr Manelli reckoned you might be here.' For such a large man his voice was surprisingly quiet. 'He says would you like to join him for dinner tonight in the Sir Benjamin Room. Seven o'clock.'

Ryan breathed a sigh of relief. It seemed that, despite his outburst during their talk, he was still in favour with the singer. 'Tell him I'll be there.' He paused. 'Sorry, I don't know your name.'

The big man completely ignored this last remark. 'Seven o'clock,' he repeated before walking away with the confident stride of a man who fears nothing.

Ryan watched him depart. A man of few words and no name. He decided to christen the giant Clint. Somehow it seemed to fit him well. He wandered thoughtfully towards the window, pausing there to gaze down at the beach below. Things were going to plan, he told himself.

A voice inside his head then butted in. 'Are they?' it demanded.

*

This time the day passed far more rapidly. After repeating the previous day's fifteen kilometre run and pasta meal, Ryan then registered his Comrades entry at the association's central Durban office. As previously assured, his request to compete under an assumed name met with no opposition. His application was duly processed and his entry confirmed. The official there pointed out that on Monday there would be a courtesy bus offering overseas competitors an opportunity to inspect the course. Ryan made a note of the bus's departure time.

His next stop was the city library. Still intrigued by the 'Torch Commandos' that Parker had referred to, it seemed to be a good place to begin his research. An attractive young Asian girl behind the counter there suggested that he should visit a nearby reference library.

'They have far more literature on the history of South Africa than we do,' she told him. 'You'll be much better off going there.'

Her directions took Ryan to the tenth floor of a building just off Pine Street. An earnest young man there, after listening to his requirements, selected several bulky volumes and motioned him to sit at one of the reading tables.

Ryan began browsing. In the third book he found what he wanted. 'The Torch Commandos. An all-white group of the 1950's, formed to oppose the introduction of apartheid.' Reading on he discovered that the name derived from their many torch-lit, night-time rallies. Not, as he had earlier supposed, due to any arsonist tendencies. Its early leadership had consisted mainly of ex-servicemen who had fought in the Second World War. At its peak, membership was around a quarter of a million. Basically a peaceful organisation, The Commandos had flourished for several years before finally fading into obscurity. It was conjectured that the cause of this decline could well have been due to the leadership's strange refusal to accept non-whites into its ranks. No reason was given for this bizarre application of double standards.

Ryan leaned back in his seat to think. So that was what Parker had meant when he'd said not all whites supported the introduction of apartheid. Had he been a member perhaps? He was certainly old enough to have been. Was it possible that he had now formed an updated version of the organisation? One that now, having learned from past mistakes, consisted of all races. The idea appeared plausible. There was one other big difference of course. The old Commandos would never have resorted to the murderous measures Parker was employing. Measures that, in spite of his initial intentions, Ryan was steadily finding less and less stomach for.

He flicked back through the pages of the book. There he found confirmation of what David had said. The National Party, at the time of winning the 1948 election, was a purely Afrikaner alliance. The incoming Prime Minister, Daniel Malan, had immediately set about creating a society in which Afrikaner control could become permanent. All opponents were neutralised. English speaking civil servants in key positions were replaced by the National Party's own supporters. The Deputy Chief of Staff, Major General Evered Poole was sacked, as was the Army Intelligence Chief, Charles Powell.

Ryan now turned to a volume entitled 'The White Tribe of Africa'. After only half an hour of reading this he was forced to admit that South African history was perhaps not so one-sided as first appeared. In a damning account of the Boer war and the years immediately succeeding it, he discovered that the British had been guilty of atrocities on a grand scale. Boer prisoners had been executed out of hand. Then there was Kitchener's destructive scorched earth policy. But worst of all in his opinion, was the British introduction of concentration camps. Thousands of Boer women and children had died in these. Not through gassing as in Hitler's later case, but through sheer starvation and disease brought about by the appalling conditions. While reading these accounts, so great did his horror at the British brutality become, Ryan soon began to experience a deep sense of shame in his own origins. He was forced to acknowledge that the persecution he

IN THE LONG RUN

had learned of here went a very long way towards explaining, at least in part, later Afrikaner attitudes.

So many unknown facts were absorbed that, by the time he eventually closed the book, he was mentally drained. For the present, even Ryan's enquiring mind could take no more. For the second time that day he looked at his watch with dismay. It was now nearly five p.m. He had been in the library for nearly four hours. Eager to see Gayle again, he had planned to call into Thatcher's before meeting up with Manelli. Now, by the time he had found his way back to the hotel, then showered and changed, it would probably be too late. The best plan would be to slip away from Manelli as early as possible. Say by nine o'clock. That way he would still have time to get over to the bar before closing time. With this in mind, he hurried out.

*

Dressed smartly in his only suit, Ryan paused by the dining room reception desk. It was exactly seven p.m. The name Tony Manelli caused the girl on duty to shoot him a curious glance. There was also a touch of envy in the look. Like royalty, he was escorted to a discreet corner table where the singer rose to greet him.

'Hi Steve. Nice of you to come.' He nodded towards his companion. 'This is Kenny. Not only does he look after me, he's also one of my very best pals.' Kenny acknowledged this introduction with a grin. 'Hi,' he said.

Although not physically quite as big as the huge minder at the pool, Ryan sensed an infinitely more subtle power about this new acquaintance. Something else that he could hardly fail to miss was Kenny's black skin. In fact, now that he looked again he could see a considerable resemblance to the boxer Mohammed Ali when he was still undisputed heavyweight champion of the world.

'One of my very best pals,' Manelli had said. This from a man he had branded as the worst kind of racist. Ryan's hand rose to his temple. Nothing was making much sense any more.

Manelli looked at him curiously. 'Hey, you OK Steve?'

The voice jerked him back to awareness. 'I'm fine thanks,' he said, sitting down.

The food, when it came, was excellent. On the waiter's recommendation they all chose fillet of beef à la crème for the main course. Throughout the meal Manelli was the perfect host, directing the conversation skilfully so that neither companion need at any stage feel left out of things. By the time they had finished eating it was clear to Ryan that Manelli had not exaggerated. There was indeed a powerful bond between the singer and the unobtrusively powerful black man sat opposite him. Tentatively he remarked on this.

Kenny nodded in agreement. 'We go back a long way, that's for sure.'

He had a similar New York accent to that of Manelli. Ryan wondered if they came from the same background.

This was confirmed when Kenny continued: 'We even went to school together.'

'And even then he used to look after me,' Manelli chipped in. He became serious for a second. 'There weren't many Italians in our neighbourhood, so for a while I had some mean guys on my case.' The grin then returned. 'Then I met my buddy here. He soon put a stop to that.'

Looking closer at Kenny, Ryan was now certain that he had been right in his earlier assessment. This man would be an even tougher proposition than Clint. The mere thought of having to tangle with the pair of them produced a small spasm in his stomach.

Kenny took up the story. 'We lost touch for a few years after school.' His eyes dropped as he studied his muscular hands for a while. 'I got into a bit of trouble with the cops. It's the same old story.' He then abruptly looked up. 'Tony was starting to get famous then. He used his influence to get me out of the crap. We've been together ever since.'

Exactly what Kenny's 'bit of trouble' had been, Ryan felt it wise not to ask. What was important was that Manelli had helped him, and then continued the friendship even after becoming a major international star. How many people who reach such heights still retained close friendships made in a background they had long since left behind? This Manelli was some kind of guy.

It was at this definitive moment that Ryan knew, once and for all, that he could never willingly go through with Tyler's plan. Sub-consciously he had probably been aware of this for some time. This latest experience with Manelli had only served to prove what he should have known all along. That no matter how much he believed in the cause, he could never be cut out for murder. Maybe, just maybe, he might have been able to force himself on if Manelli had been as imagined. But he wasn't. This man was no money-grabbing racist. He was sincere in his beliefs and had as much right to live as anyone. More than many.

'Hey Steve, where are you?' Once again Manelli's voice cut into the troubled areas of his mind. He tried to look directly at the singer and failed. For an instant all he could see was a dead body.

IN THE LONG RUN

'I hope you're livelier than this on Comrades day,' Manelli told him.

With a supreme effort Ryan pulled himself together. 'I'm OK now. It's just a touch of indigestion I think. Nothing to worry about.'

The talk then shifted to the coming race. How did Ryan rate his chances? What training was he doing? Apart from Fordyce, who else did he think would do well? This last question threw him. He knew nothing of the opposition, and surely they would expect him to. He tried to talk in general terms rather than specific people. He wanted to get away now anyhow, so when pressed on the subject, he made a show of looking at the time.

'Look, I'm sorry about this, but I've got to go now,' he said. 'I'm due to meet someone soon. Thanks for the meal.'

The famous Manelli smile returned. 'I thought you were looking a bit on edge.' He winked. 'You've got a dame to meet, right?'

Ryan nodded.

'OK Steve, don't let me hold you up. See you at the pool tomorrow maybe?'

'Perhaps.'

With the utmost relief, Ryan left. He glanced back at the table just once. Kenny caught his eye and then leaned across the table to say something to Manelli.

*

Thatcher's was busy and so was Gayle. Ryan stood watching her for some while before she spotted him. She raised a hand in greeting, mouthing: 'I'll be with you in a minute.'

A short while later he heard her say to another girl: 'Look after it for me will you. I need ten minutes.'

She then waved him over to a relatively quiet corner. 'You look smart,' she remarked humorously, at the same time fingering the lapel of his suit. 'You didn't need to put that on for my benefit you know.'

'I've just had dinner with Tony Manelli,' he explained.

Her face lit up. 'Tony Manelli! How on earth did you get to meet him?'

'He's staying at my hotel.' His voice was flat.

'You don't sound very excited about it. What I wouldn't give for a dinner with that guy.' Gayle then studied his face more closely. 'Is there something on your mind?'

That, thought Ryan, was a classic understatement. How he longed to tell her all his problems. It wasn't possible of course. The very last thing he intended to do was drag her into this mess. Since having decided to pull out of this Manelli business, the possible consequences were weighing heavily on his mind. Parker loomed menacingly in his thoughts and he needed help badly, but there was no one he could turn to. All this to deal with and six thousand miles from home. Suddenly Bournemouth seemed light years away. God how he wished he was back there right now.

'I'm just tired,' he said in answer to Gayle's question.

She touched his hand. 'Don't go overdoing it Steve. You'll need all your strength for next Thursday.'

He nodded without enthusiasm.

'I phoned David for you earlier,' she continued. 'He said that he'd be happy to act as your second if you'd still like him to.' She then added: 'I think he likes you.'

David! Would he be able to help him out of this mess in any way? After a brief surge of hope, Ryan dismissed the idea. How the hell could he tell anyone that he'd come here to help kill a man? They'd probably lock him up straight away. No, any solution could only come from himself. The sense of loneliness and fright was getting stronger by the minute but, frightened or not, Gayle must be kept out of this at all costs. It would be dangerous for her to have even a hint of what was going on.

'Tell David thanks,' he said, trying hard to sound enthusiastic.

Gayle produced a folded piece of paper from her bag. 'I've written his number down for you. This one is his home, and this is his work. You can call him whenever you like.'

Ryan stored the paper away. 'I'll do that,' he promised. It was a lie, and he knew it. Even as he spoke he was wondering when the next available flight home might be. It was vital to get away as soon as possible.

Despite his efforts to appear normal, the conversation that followed was spasmodic and strained. It came as a relief when the other barmaid came running over.

'You'll have to help me Gayle. I can't manage on my own any longer.'

'OK, I'll be right there.' Gayle then turned to Ryan. 'Are you going to hang around for a while?'

He shook his head. 'I think I'll have an early night.'

A brief look of disappointment crossed her face. 'As you like.'

Ryan wanted to take hold of her. To tell her it was not as she thought. That it was only for her own good he was acting this way. He hardened himself. 'I'll see you tomorrow perhaps,' he said with no real conviction.

IN THE LONG RUN

Her response was cool. 'You know where to find me.'

In spite of this indifferent attitude, Gayle's eyes still followed Ryan as he made for the door. There was a hurt and puzzled expression on her face. Then it was gone. She approached the nearest customer with a bright smile.

'Yes sir. What can I get for you?'

*

Ryan paused outside, hating himself. He had sensed Gayle's eyes following him as he left the bar. But what could he do? If he couldn't get a flight home quickly then there was little doubt that Parker would turn nasty. The way he had acted was in Gayle's best interests, even if she didn't know it.

Was he being watched? It seemed probable. He would have to be very careful if he were to conceal his intentions. He would also have to get some kind of warning to Manelli. He couldn't live with himself if he did not do that. Perhaps an anonymous last-minute call from the airport? Once Kenny and Clint knew the danger, he was sure that these two could protect Manelli from anything Parker could produce. And once he was on the plane, he too would be safe from any threat.

'Hello Mister Ryan.'

The voice came from behind. He spun quickly around.

Facing him was the same stocky African he had met in the hotel elevator. Even though the man appeared friendly enough, Ryan felt his stomach twist with fear. There was something about his dissembling smile and the way he kept appearing out of nowhere.

'You look worried,' the African observed. 'Is everything going as expected?'

'Of course. No problems at all.' There was a small croak in Ryan's voice.

The benign expression continued. 'Good. Mister Parker wants to talk to you.'

It took all Ryan's effort to conceal his alarm. What the hell did Parker want with him so soon? Surely he couldn't suspect his change of heart? He decided to try and bluster his way out of the situation.

'Not tonight, I'm tired. Surely tomorrow will do.'

The man's smile fell away in an instant. 'No. He wants to see you now.' He indicated an oldish car parked on the other side of the street. 'Now,' he repeated.

Ryan thought as quickly as his frightened mind would allow. To refuse would be crazy. Apart from revealing how he now felt, he had no idea what force might be used. This guy could easily have a gun on him. His smile didn't mean a damn thing.

He sighed. 'OK, let's go.'

Like a dutiful chauffeur the African opened the front passenger door and ushered him inside.

They drove through the city in silence. At last Ryan could stand it no more. 'Where are we going?' he asked.

'Not far.' The driver's tone stated very clearly that there would be no more information forthcoming.

Before long the city was behind them and they were heading along the main North Coast road. After nearly thirty minutes the car eventually slowed to make a left turn onto a rough dirt track. Bumps and potholes littered the new surface, causing their vehicle to buck wildly at times. Away from the semi-security of the main road it was dark. Suffocatingly so. Only the two small puddles of weak orange light from the car's headlights offered any relief from the claustrophobic blackness. It was like being transported to another world in a matter of seconds. A world where anything could happen and nobody would ever know. The driver's silence compounded what Ryan prayed was his irrational fear.

After another ten minutes of bumpy driving his fearful gaze began to make out a flickering glow ahead. As they drew closer he could see that the light came from a large bonfire. The flames gave fragmented illumination to several squalid looking huts. Each sullen silhouette assumed an air of grave potential menace. As they entered the small township numerous dark figures began to appear. Each one stared into the vehicle with hostile curiosity. The car had now slowed right down to a pedestrian crawl, allowing these shadowy figures to walk intimidatingly alongside in silent close escort.

Ryan's eyes suddenly fell onto a smouldering rubber tyre lying abandoned on the ground ahead. Even with the car windows closed, the stench of burning rubber was pungent. My God! he thought, now very close to blind panic. They've had a necklacing here. Several times he had read with revulsion in the British press about this inhuman form of execution. A sadistic ritual in which a car tyre was placed around the naked victim's neck, filled with petrol, and then set ablaze. It was the ultimate punishment for those considered to be informers or collaborators.

The car pulled up just alongside the focus of Ryan's horrified attention. 'Out,' the driver instructed. His tone brooked no argument. As Ryan emerged, a silent

IN THE LONG RUN

mass of inhospitable black faces stared at him. He wanted to say something — to shout out to them: why are you staring at me like this? I'm on your side. Surely these people would then understand all the support he had given them in the past. All the protest marches and demos held on their behalf. This whole area was just like the townships he had seen featured on TV documentaries back home. But this was not TV, and he was not in the safety of his own front room. This was actually happening to him. Ryan almost cried out loud in panic. Why had he been brought to such a place? Where was Parker?

Ryan's questions were soon answered. Parker suddenly appeared in the doorway of the nearest hut. As before, the man was immaculately turned out; although framed as he was by a patchwork of rusting corrugated iron and splintered timbers, his dress now appeared ridiculously out of place. In spite of this impression it was still clear that he held a position of authority here. All eyes tuned towards him as he approached Ryan.

He spoke to the driver first. 'Any difficulties?' he asked, raising an eyebrow.

The African's smile returned. 'No Boss.'

Parker nodded before turning his attention to Ryan. 'And how are things progressing?' he demanded. There was no prelude to this brusque question. No small talk. Not even a hello.

Throughout the drive Ryan had been trying desperately to work out what he would say to Parker when asked this. Now the moment was here, could he carry it off? His eyes flickered once more towards the smouldering, partially melted tyre before answering. He prayed that his performance would be convincing.

'It's going well. I've made friends with Manelli just as you wanted. He seems to like me. I even had dinner with him tonight.'

Parker gave a curt nod. 'Yes, I'm aware of that.' His tone then became a touch friendlier, although his eyes remained hard. He moved closer to Ryan and placed a hand on the runner's shoulder. 'I see that you have noticed the necklace over there. I take it that you are familiar with its use?'

Ryan swallowed hard and nodded. He said nothing.

'It is not a pleasant way to die, I can assure you.' The old man then gave a short laugh that was totally lacking in humour. 'But of course it is only used on those who attempt to deceive or betray us. That being so, there is absolutely no need for someone like yourself to be concerned. Is there?'

For a few seconds Ryan thought he was going to be sick. Now he knew for certain that Parker was completely inhuman. The thought of that rubber obscenity being placed around his neck numbed his brain, making him unable to answer.

Parker removed his hand. 'I can see that you are impressed. And in answer to your unspoken question, no, it has not been employed for such a use tonight. It is there merely to illustrate my point.'

'Why are you telling me this?' Ryan's voice was a husky whisper.

Parker's tone became hard once more. 'Your conduct since arriving here causes me to doubt your wholehearted support for our aims. This is not a holiday. Your friendship with the girl for instance — the barmaid.'

'She knows nothing,' Ryan protested. 'She's just a friend, that's all.'

'But your instructions were to make friends with Manelli. No one else. Any diversion could be viewed as frivolous conduct. Worse than that, a security risk.'

'I won't see her again. She doesn't mean anything to me.' He had to keep Gayle out of this at all costs.

'It is too late now, she *is* involved.' There was a chilling finality to Parker's words.

'I've already told you, she doesn't know anything. She means nothing.'

Parker was unmoved. 'You protest too much,' he stated. 'It is very obvious that even in the brief time you have been here, you have already developed a certain affection for this girl. A very stupid thing for someone in your position to do.'

The horrific thought of Gayle being sucked into Parker's insane world brought home to Ryan as never before just how much he did care for the girl. It was crazy that he should feel like this after just a couple of days. Crazy — but still undeniably true.

'You're not going to harm her in any way,' he said. It came out as half question, half defiant statement.

'She will be in no danger just so long as you continue to do as instructed.'

Ryan could not suppress a sigh of relief. This feeling was quickly replaced though by the awful realisation that he would, after all, be forced to carry on with this terrible business. Although Manelli clearly did not deserve to be sacrificed, there could be no question of skipping the country and leaving Gayle at the mercy of these people. The thought of that was just too horrible to contemplate.

'I warn you,' Parker continued, if you have any naive notions that the authorities here can help or protect you and the young lady, forget them. You would undoubtedly end up in jail and she would most certainly ....' He allowed the words to hang ominously before adding: 'Nobody can be protected forever.'

IN THE LONG RUN

'All right, there's no need to spell it out. Just tell me what I need to do.' The resentment in Ryan's voice was strong.

Parker allowed himself the luxury of a brief smile. 'Having formed this unfortunate friendship with the girl, it would now be better if you were to let it continue. A sudden change of attitude on your part might well cause unwanted attention. It is important that you appear as natural as possible. I would add though, should you breathe a word of our plans to her, then you will both die. Is that clear?'

'How the hell can I appear natural with a threat like that hanging over my head?' Ryan demanded.

'That is one of several problems that you will have to work out for yourself. I am sure, given the considerable incentives involved, that you will manage somehow.' This aspect was then dismissed with an imperious wave of Parker's hand. 'Turning to more practical matters,' he continued, 'I think it would be a good idea if you were to attend Manelli's first concert this Monday. You are now on good terms, so I am sure that he will provide you with a couple of tickets should you ask. Take your young barmaid. Now that she is involved so to speak, albeit unknowingly, we may as well obtain some use out of her.' Parker gave a sardonic smile. 'The combination of a pretty face and a smattering of intelligence will nearly always make an impression with our American friend. Unless I am very much mistaken, the young lady qualifies adequately in these departments. You will quite possibly find that by having her in your company, Manelli will be keener than ever to socialise with you.'

Ryan's fear of Parker was now supplemented by a total loathing. How could the bastard drag an innocent young girl so cynically into this violent mess? To think that he had come six thousand miles to help such a man. Damn Tyler for being so persuasive. Not that his old friend could possibly have known how dangerous things would become. But damn him anyway. Damn him, damn him, damn him.

'What if she won't come?' he then asked Parker.

'I'm sure that she will. She seems rather fond of you. In any case, I can't imagine there are many women who would pass up a chance of meeting Tony Manelli.'

Remembering Gayle's response when he had told her about dining with the singer, Ryan was forced to agree. 'So what then?' he asked, bitterly conceding the point.

'You will discover Manelli's plans for the day of the race. Find out whether he intends to watch it on television from the safety of his penthouse suite, or if, as is more likely, he is contemplating an actual visit to the event. I am positive that now he is taking a personal interest in your performance you will have little trouble gaining this information.'

'And what if he does choose to actually be there?'

Parker's expression barely altered. 'Then we will arrange for it to be his final public appearance.'

A loud burst of laughter from the smiling African standing just a few feet away jolted Ryan back to awareness of his surroundings. So intense had been his exchange with Parker that temporarily only the two of them had existed. Now once again he was conscious of the oppressive atmosphere and host of hostile faces still gazing at him. In spite of this intimidation, his anger gave him courage. He would do anything to protect Gayle.

'Is there anything else or can I go now?' he asked, not even attempting to disguise the enmity in his voice.

Parker gave him one final austere look. 'You can leave,' he stated. He then made a sharp movement with his hand. The African driver moved closer. 'Take Mr Ryan back to his hotel Simon. I think he now knows where his loyalties lie.'

Simon grinned broadly. 'Yes Boss.'

IN THE LONG RUN

CHAPTER SEVEN

After two relatively sleepless nights Ryan's body cried out for sleep. So strong was this demand that not even his tormented state of mind was sufficient to keep him awake. He passed out virtually the instant he lay down on the hotel bed.

Even then the stress continued. Nightmare images of a screaming Gayle, a blazing rubber tyre draped around her neck, forced their way into his dreams. Parker watched nearby, his grotesquely distorted face shrieking with maniacal laughter. And all the time a ghostly apparition of Manelli hovered in the background. Repeatedly the spectre declared in echoing tones that he had returned to haunt the friend who had betrayed him.

Dressed in his local athletic club colours, Ryan was running towards Gayle as fast as he could. In spite of his terror he knew that he must somehow rip away the burning monstrosity from her shoulders. Try as he might though, each time he came within touching distance she would vanish, only to reappear moments later once more in the far off distance. He lost count of his attempts to reach her. Finally, utterly exhausted, he fell sobbing to his knees. He cried out her name for the thousandth time. And then, inexplicably, she was suddenly right there beside him, pleading for his help. Molten rubber ran agonisingly down his bare arms as he tore frantically with burnt and blackened fingers at the disintegrating ring of fire. It was then that the flames exploded, engulfing them both. There was searing heat, followed by the nauseating stench of roasting human flesh. The only thing he was aware of was a terrible burning agony and Parker's shrieking laughter. All at once there was a huge nothing. No pain. No fear. No nightmare. Ryan spent the rest of the night in the sleep of the exhausted.

The sheets were soaked in sweat when he awoke. Memories of the nightmare immediately returned in vivid detail, causing his heartbeat to shoot up dramatically. It took several minutes for him to calm himself. Only when fully satisfied that he was in control did Ryan rise from the bed and hurriedly dress. It was time once more to visit the swimming pool.

The scene there was a replica of their first encounter. Manelli was in the water with the same stone-faced minder sitting nearby. As before there was no one else present.

This time Manelli greeted him immediately. 'Hi Steve. Glad you could make it.'

Ryan's concern for Gayle, intensified to an even greater pitch by the nightmare, reinforced his capability for deception. It was imperative that he appeared as friendly and natural as possible. There was a brief moment of hesitation as he looked into Manelli's eyes. The American had proved himself to be a good man. A steel shutter then slammed down. Gayle's safety was the most important thing in the world to him.

'Hi Tony,' he said, his mouth forming into what he hoped was a friendly smile.

Manelli beckoned. 'Are you coming in?'

'Sure.'

Discarding his topclothes, Ryan dived cleanly into the water. His lean, sinewy frame was ideally suited to the front crawl. He knifed gracefully to the end of the pool and back again.

Manelli looked impressed. 'Hey, not only are you a good runner, you're a fair swimmer too.'

Ryan wiped the water from his face before replying. Having already seen Manelli swim, he knew that the singer also had a good turn of speed.

'Fancy a race?' he asked. Even under these abnormal circumstances his competitive urge was keen.

Manelli rarely ducked a challenge. 'You're on pal,' he responded.

It was not a large pool. 'Ten lengths?' the American suggested as they got out and stood together on the edge.

Ryan nodded his agreement. His eye then caught sight of Clint at the far end of the pool. He was watching them intently. For some crazy reason Ryan briefly visualised the minder producing his gun and holding it aloft to start the race. It was a ridiculous thought.

IN THE LONG RUN

'Go!' Manelli's voice rang out.

As one they entered the pool in shallow racing dives. For seven lengths they were virtually inseparable, matching each other stroke for stroke. As they turned for the eighth time Ryan held a one metre advantage. Manelli, with his far more robust style, managed to cut this back in the penultimate length, only to lose it again in the final turn. It was an advantage that Ryan just managed to hold on to until the finish. Both were fit men, but it was the athlete's extra training that finally told.

Ryan grinned triumphantly as he stood up in the water. 'That was close,' he said in between deep breaths. For a short while all else was forgotten as he savoured his victory.

Manelli nodded his agreement. His breathing was also heavy. 'I guess I owe you one,' he said eventually.

His words forcibly reminded Ryan why he was there. He seized his chance.

'There is one thing you could do. I'd really like to see your concert tomorrow night. Can you fix me up with a couple of tickets?'

Manelli slapped him on the back. 'No problem. I was going to ask if you wanted to come anyhow.' He paused. 'You did say two tickets huh? Am I right in guessing that the other one is for the dame you dumped me for last night?'

'That's right.'

The American laughed. 'Make the most of it. Me, I made a promise to myself before I left the States. No women on this trip. I need a break.'

From most men this would have sounded like an arrogant boast. From Manelli it came out as nothing more than a naturally humorous remark.

'Thanks—' Ryan began.

'Hey, don't thank me Steve. And by the way, I'm having a small party after the show up in the penthouse. Why don't you and your girl come along? I'd like to meet her.'

'That's great. We'll be there.'

So it actually was that easy, Ryan reflected. Exactly as Parker had said. The thought of his tormentor playing with their lives like some all-powerful puppet master brought a sudden surge of anger. To conceal any outward sign of this Ryan ducked his head into the water and swam rapidly back up the pool.

The pattern of Ryan's morning was much as before. The only slight deviation was that, with the race nearing, he reduced his training run to ten kilometres.

GEORGE STRATFORD

The staff at the Italian restaurant were now becoming used to his daily visits. Luigi, the manager, greeted him that lunchtime with a broad smile and ushered him personally to his table. As if divulging state secrets, the Italian whispered confidentially that during the next few days there would be a rush on pasta as more and more runners converged on Durban. This, he announced seriously, could even result in a grave shortage of the commodity. 'Have no fear,' he assured an astonished Ryan. 'For regulars like you there will still be plenty available.' Uncertain as to whether he was being wound up or not, Ryan thanked the man anyway.

Back in his hotel room, he lay on the bed brooding for a while. Sick of this, he then tried the TV. None of the channels captured his interest. Exasperated, he eventually headed back outside. Gayle wasn't due to start work for an hour yet, but he'd go over to Thatcher's anyway. Perhaps a beer or two would help his mood.

To his surprise Gayle was already there. The place was quiet, allowing her time to chat with an elderly male customer. Even though the man must have been pushing eighty, it was clear that he was not past appreciating her charms.

Ryan made for the corner and stood beneath the portrait of Margaret Thatcher, observing them as they talked. Gayle laughed and patted the customer's hand.

'You old devil,' he heard her say. Quite unreasonably, he felt a pang of jealousy.

'Can I have a drink please?' he called out a little sharply.

She looked in Ryan's direction as if only just noticing him. Briefly she made one more softly spoken remark to the customer before coming over.

'What can I get you sir?' It was the same professional enquiry she used on their first meeting.

'I thought you didn't start until four o'clock,' Ryan stated.

She shrugged. 'I changed shifts for the day. Does it matter?' There was still no smile of greeting.

'I'll have a Castle please,' he said, deeply troubled by her lack of warmth. He knew that his attitude last night must have seemed strange, but it was now obvious that she was far more upset about it than he at first realised. Something would have to be done quickly.

She returned with his drink. 'One Rand eighty please.'

Although having the correct coins, Ryan gave her a twenty Rand note. She would have to return with the change, which would give him a few more seconds to think.

She dropped the money into his outstretched palm. As she did so, Ryan quickly grabbed hold of her hand to prevent her moving away.

IN THE LONG RUN

'Look Gayle,' he said in a soft, intense voice. 'I'm sorry if I appeared a little strange last night.'

For an instant he felt the pressure as she tried to pull her fingers free. This then eased a bit as she fixed him with a stern look. 'You were like a different person. I don't understand.'

'I was upset. I'd just had a phone call from home. One of my best friends has been taken seriously ill in hospital. Meningitis or something.' It was a blatant lie of course, but the best he could think of on the spur of the moment. At least it sounded plausible.

She visibly relaxed. Her hand, instead of resisting him, now gently squeezed. 'Why didn't you tell me?'

He shrugged. 'I suppose I try to keep my problems to myself.'

Their eyes met and he could tell from her sympathetic look that she totally believed him. 'I'm sorry,' she said simply.

He felt terrible for deceiving her this way, but anything was better than the truth. She must never know that.

'Have you heard any more news about your friend since?' Gayle then asked.

'Yes. I had another call this morning to say that he'd had an emergency operation late last night. He should be OK now they reckon.'

Another lie, Ryan thought. Once you start telling them it's difficult to stop.

Gayle removed her hand as a customer came to the bar. 'I'll be back in a minute,' she promised.

When she returned she was like her old self. She smiled at him for the first time that day. 'I finish a four o'clock. Do you fancy going somewhere?'

'We could catch a movie if you like,' Ryan suggested.

'That would be nice.' Gayle smiled again. 'Come on, cheer up. Things aren't that bad, are they?'

The next few hours, unlike the earlier part of the day, slipped by far too quickly for Ryan. The movie had been forgettable, but in Gayle's company that didn't matter. All other problems were pushed temporarily aside. They were now sat inside Old Martha close to the hotel. When they kissed this time it was with a new passion and intensity. For ten minutes the world ceased to exist.

'It's getting late,' Gayle murmured, nibbling his ear. 'I must go soon.'

'Do you have to.'

'Yes, I do.' She giggled as he tickled her ribs. His hands, perhaps by accident, perhaps by design, rested for a moment on her beautifully rounded breasts.

The laughing ceased. She made no immediate move to push his hand away. In fact for a second it seemed as if she were about to kiss him again. Then, abruptly, Gayle drew back and faced the steering wheel.

'Shall we meet tomorrow,' she asked.

Ryan ignored the question. 'What's the matter? His mouth hung open in bemusement.

She hesitated. 'Look Steve, you're only here for a few days and then you'll be going home. I hadn't meant to get this involved. Let's not spoil things by taking it any further.'

Once again Ryan was reminded of grim reality. Abruptly he wondered if any of Parker's men were at this very moment watching them? Whatever lingering magic the moment still held was irretrievably lost. Even so, he still had to ask the question.

'Do you regret getting involved with me then?'

'No, but I don't normally go in for short-term affairs.'

'Neither do I.' There was a difficult pause. Quite suddenly Ryan asked: 'How do you fancy meeting Tony Manelli tomorrow evening?'

She looked at him with disbelief. 'Are you joking? Can you really fix it? I'll change my shift again if you can.'

He gave her a superior grin. 'I just happen to have a couple of complimentary tickets for tomorrow's concert.' He paused for effect. 'And, let me tell you, a personal invitation to his private party afterwards. You're included too.' His light-hearted tone masked a deep resentment. Here we go dancing to Parker's tune again, he reflected bitterly. It had to be done though. His act must be convincing at all times.

All of a sudden he wanted to get into the privacy of his hotel room. He opened the car door. The seat, as usual, groaned under his shifting weight.

'I'll come over and see you tomorrow some time,' he said when out of the car.

She planted a kiss on the palm of her hand and blew it in his direction. 'I'll be there,' she promised.

*

The phone rang just twice before being answered.

'Hello ... David? It's Steve Ryan here.'

IN THE LONG RUN

There was a short pause while recognition dawned. 'Oh yes, Gayle's friend. How are you?'

'Fine. Gayle said I should give you a call if I still wanted your help on Thursday.'

'So I take it you do then.'

'If you're still prepared to give it a go I'd be grateful, Ryan said.

Parker's instructions were to appear as natural as possible. In that case it would seem rather odd if he were to refuse David's offer of help. Anyway, the assistance of someone experienced in the race would prove invaluable. Whatever the circumstances, personal pride still dictated that he put up some sort of show.

'Right then,' David said. 'Let's make a plan.' His brisk tone suggested that he was not a man to drag his feet once set on something. 'I've got a client to see at eleven thirty. After that I'm pretty free for the day. Shall we meet up lunchtime for a chat?'

Ryan was about to say yes when a thought occurred. 'I'd like to, but there's a bus laid on at noon today to show all the overseas runners the route. I'd be pretty stupid to miss out on that.'

David laughed. 'Perhaps it's better you don't see it. It might put you off altogether.' He became more serious. 'I've got a better idea. Why don't I drive you along the route myself this afternoon? That way I can give you some tips at the same time.'

Ryan readily acknowledged the advantages of this. 'That would be great,' he said. 'Why don't we meet at Thatchers around one o'clock? That's close to where I am.'

'Will Gayle be there?'

'She should be.'

David gave a licentious chuckle before hanging up.

It was ten minutes past one when David arrived. True to his nature he breezed in exuding confidence.

'Sorry I'm late,' he said, giving Ryan a hearty slap on the back. 'Things took a little longer than I anticipated.'

He turned to Gayle who was serving nearby. 'A couple of drinks here young lady,' he called out.

She pulled a face at him before carrying on with what she was doing. David pulled a face back at her and then regarded Ryan once more. 'How's the training going then? Have you done any hill work yet?'

Ryan shook his head. 'Not much. I'm in good shape though.'

They talked — or rather David talked and Ryan listened — until Gayle came over.

'How are you two getting on together then?' David asked her, glancing slyly in Ryan's direction.

She coloured slightly. 'However we are, it's none of your business.'

It appeared to Ryan that the question had touched a nerve, indicating that she cared a little more than she was prepared to admit. The thought pleased him. 'We seem to be getting on OK,' was all he said when David transferred the inquiry to him.

'Are you having a drink or what?' Gayle chipped in.

David hesitated and glanced at his watch. 'Actually it might be a good idea if we moved straight on. We don't want to have to rush things.'

This suited Ryan fine. With a full evening ahead, he did not want to be late back. Readily he agreed.

'I'll see you at six then,' he told Gayle as they prepared to leave.

David made no comment this time as he heard the arrangement being confirmed. Even so, his expression was one of great personal interest.

Whatever it was that David did for a living, it must pay very well Ryan considered. His car, a luxurious BMW, purred through the city streets with an elegance equal to that of Parker's Mercedes. It was on the tip of his tongue to make an enquiry about David's employment when his companion spoke first.

'This is Pine Street, the starting point for this year's race.'

At present the road was busy with traffic. Ryan tried to visualise the spot as it would be on the morning of the race. Packed solid, not with cars, but over twelve thousand enthusiastic runners. Already he could feel an anticipation of the glorious high he got on these occasions. Massed starts such as these, coupled with the hope and expectancy of what was to come, were his life's blood. Surely not even Parker could take that away.

Soon they passed through the Indian quarter. Shop after shop displayed traditional foods, clothing, and just about anything else connected with the sub-continent. On the right they passed what appeared to be a Hindu temple, colourful and striking. It was the last kind of building he might once have expected to find here. By now though he was well past being surprised by almost anything South Africa could offer. Shortly they reached the freeway. The road began to rise. Not too steeply at first, but gradually increasing in severity.

IN THE LONG RUN

'This is nothing,' David commented. 'Wait till you see Field's Hill at around twenty-five kilometres. Up until then all you're doing is working up a good sweat.'

They turned off the freeway and started the long climb up Cowies Hill. As they drove David kept up a constant chatter, pointing out all the landmarks. The road was now lined on either side with trees and pleasant looking houses. Every so often the hill twisted until, just before the summit, it banked sharply to the right. Below them lay a sprawling town. 'That's Pinetown,' Ryan was told.

They followed the gentle downward slope that led into the town centre. With its low buildings on either side of the road, Ryan was reminded of a modern industrial estate. Strange, he considered. To him the name Pinetown suggested something quite different. Something perhaps older and more traditional. There was no telling of course what the outlying districts might be like.

The road was straight and level as they paused at traffic lights. 'This whole area will be packed with spectators on the day,' David told him. 'Take all the encouragement you can from them because Field's Hill is just up the road.'

Once out of Pinetown, they joined the freeway once more. Ryan soon found himself looking up the frighteningly steep and twisting climb.

'That's it,' he was told. 'Three kilometres to the top and rising up over two hundred metres.'

Ryan was well aware that by now, in a normal marathon, he would be approaching two thirds of the way home. To have come that far and then be faced with this monster hill — and the knowledge that there was still another sixty-five kilometres of the race remaining — was a daunting prospect indeed.

Upwards they drove, the BMW twisting left and right as it followed the hill's snaking path.

'A lot of people walk up here,' David told him, now unmistakably serious. 'There's no shame if you do. It's better to get up that way and finish the race rather than knock yourself out trying to get up too quickly.'

To Ryan's stubborn pride the mere thought of walking during a race was a sign of failure, and something he had never yet been reduced to. He was determined that he would tackle this great obstacle on his toes, not on his heels.

Soon after mounting the crest they left the freeway once more. The route settled down into a gentle upward pull in pleasant suburban surroundings. 'Now we're coming into Hillcrest,' David said. 'They usually put on quite a show here. There's a fairly large running club in the village so the locals turn out in force to support them. Some of the characters tend to get a bit carried away, especially those who set up camp outside the local pub.' He laughed. 'It all adds to the atmosphere.'

A short distance further on they came to the pub David had referred to, the Hillcrest Hotel. Ryan spoke on impulse. 'How about a drink. I'd like to see the place.'

'Sure, no problem.'

The pub interior was far from new, but there was a comfortable, used feel about the place. The two men seated themselves at the bar. Ryan ordered two Castles. As David poured his beer he looked thoughtfully at Ryan. 'You've probably been asked this before, but what made you come over here? With world opinion as it is, didn't you think about the possible consequences?'

Oh yes, thought Ryan, remembering his first meeting with Manelli. I've been asked that question before OK. He gave much the same answer as he had given the American, pointing out again that he would be running under an assumed name. David listened, for once quiet and attentive. He nodded as Ryan finished. 'I asked for two reasons. Apart from the obvious one, I'm forced to say that when I first met you I got the impression that you were rather anti-South African.'

His remarks shook Ryan. Had he really been that transparent? If so, then he would have to tread very carefully from now on. This David was no fool.

'I'm sorry if I made you think that,' he said with an embarrassed grin. 'I didn't mean anything.'

David continued to look circumspect. 'One of the main reasons I decided to help you was out of curiosity,' he admitted.

Ryan picked his words with care. 'I was just interested in what goes on, that's all. You hear things back home and you're bound to wonder a bit.'

David looked at him for several seconds. Suddenly he brightened. 'Let's forget it,' he said. 'I shouldn't have brought the subject up. That's my trouble, I say what I think too much.'

'That's fine with me,' Ryan said as lightly as possible.

There was a brief lull in the conversation.

'At least you haven't got the same problems as Bellocq,' David remarked next.

Ryan thought for a moment. That name rang a bell. 'Do you mean Jean-Marc Bellocq, the French runner?' he asked.

'You've heard of him then,' David smiled.

'Of course. He's one of the great distance runners.'

He paused. How stupid of him not to remember straight away. Bellocq had been banned from running in his own country for having competed in South

IN THE LONG RUN

Africa last year. At the time Ryan had drawn some satisfaction from this outcome.

'I can see from your face you're remembering what happened to him,' David observed. 'Yes, he ran in last year's Comrades under his own name. He finished third.'

'And then got himself banned.'

'That's right.'

Ryan swallowed hard. What with Parker's threats and everything else, he had spared little time to dwell on the risk he faced by competing here. Even if in his case the risks were small, it was still an uncomfortable reminder. He did not have long to ponder on this.

'There is one other thing I want to talk to you about,' David said abruptly. 'You might think it's none of my business now, but I happen to think it is. It's about you and Gayle.' David was nothing if not blunt.

'What about us?' There was an edge to Ryan's voice.

'She told you that we used to be engaged?'

'Yes. She also told me that you were just friends now.'

'That's right — friends. And even though we tease each other a lot, very, very good friends. That's why I look out for her.'

Ryan's voice rose. 'Why are you telling me this? What are you trying to say? Bloody hell, no one was looking out for the girl more than he was right now. He was putting his life on the line for her benefit.

'Calm down,' David told him. 'All I want is what's right for Gayle.'

'So do I,' retorted Ryan.

David's manner took on a more confidential approach. 'She's pretty keen on you I'd say.'

Ryan's irritation faded. 'You think so?'

'Come on, it's obvious.' David laughed. 'It is to me anyway. I can read her like a book.'

He took another mouthful of beer. 'The thing is, how do *you* feel about Gayle? I don't want to see her getting hurt.'

Considering that over the next few days he would be busting a gut to protect her, this was the most ridiculously inappropriate statement Ryan had ever heard.

'She's got nothing to worry about from me,' he assured David.

'The thing that concerns me most,' David pressed on, 'is that you're not going to be around for very long. What happens when you go home? Is that the end of it from your point of view? If so, I think it's only fair you tell her now. Believe me, Gayle is far more sensitive than you may imagine.'

Gayle's hesitancy the previous evening, and her words about not going in for short-term affairs, came back to Ryan. He should have realised then how emotionally vulnerable she could be. Now it was being spelled out to him by her ex-fiancé. Of course he wanted to believe that they had some kind of future together. Why the hell else would he still be here? But the risks and complications were terrifying. Only when this thing with Manelli had been resolved would he be able to judge matters with a clear mind.

'It's all happened so quickly,' he said by way of defence. 'I never imagined that either of us would become so involved in such a short space of time.'

The serious look on David's face persisted. 'Let me tell you a few things about Gayle,' he said. 'For a start, did you know that both her parents were killed in a car crash when she was still a little girl? That she lived with her grandparents in Capetown until a few years ago.'

The shock showed clearly on Ryan's face. 'I had no idea.'

'Obviously it's not something she talks about easily. The grandparents are both dead now too.' David sighed. 'What I'm saying is that she's got no close family to look out for her. She lives on her own in a small flat, and since we split up nine months ago she hasn't shown the slightest interest in forming another relationship. It worries me.'

David looked Ryan straight in the eye and held the gaze. 'That's why I look out for her still. Sometimes more than she realises.'

'But how about her work at Thatchers?' Ryan pointed out. 'Surely she must make a few friends there?'

'Most of them are acquaintances, not real friends. Gayle tends to keep the people she meets there at arm's length. That's why I'm amazed at the way things have developed between you two so rapidly.'

David took another mouthful of beer before continuing. 'You might find this hard to believe, but Gayle only started work in the pub to help overcome her chronic shyness. Before that she was a verification clerk at my office.'

There was now so much more explained. Ryan felt a fresh rush of affection for Gayle. There was also a new kind of respect for David. In spite of his sometimes brash exterior, it was clear that he could be as caring as the next man. In his own way of course.

'I'll tell you this David,' he said, choosing his words with care. 'I like Gayle a lot, and the last thing in the world I intend to do is hurt her. If she wants to continue with things when it's time for me to go home, I'll be more than happy

IN THE LONG RUN

with that. I promise you now that I'll keep in regular contact. After that, we'll see how it goes. Is that good enough for you?'

David nodded. 'I guess that's about all I could ask for at present,' he conceded. In an act that was completely out of character, he then managed to appear self-conscious. 'I feel like her big brother these days. I do still love her you know.'

'Not,' he added quickly, 'like that though.' The moment passed and he was back to his old, assured self. He drained his glass. 'I'm glad we've had this talk. Now it's time to get moving.'

Only then did Ryan notice that his own beer was largely untouched. He took a sip and pushed the rest aside.

'Let's go,' he agreed.

Hillcrest behind them, they drove on. 'You can forget about the freeway now,' David said. 'This is the old Maritzburg road. We keep on this for the rest of the way.'

Soon they were rising up another steep, twisting hill. Trees and grass lined most of the way in an abundance of green. To his right, deep in the valley below, Ryan could see a cluster of mock Tudor houses. This could almost be England, he mused. Certainly the view here was very different from the brown and arid terrain so easy to associate with Africa.

'This is Botha's Hill,' David informed him. 'Not too far to Drummond now. That's the official halfway point.' He grinned. 'If you don't make it to there within five-and-a-half hours the race marshals will disqualify you. Fordyce and the other leading runners will be through in less than three hours.' David was well into his stride again. 'They fire a gun into the air to signal half-time at Drummond, and then two more at the finishing line in Maritzburg. The first one is after seven-and-a-half hours to show that time's up for the silver medals. After that there's a final shot a five o'clock to officially end the race.' He laughed. 'There's always some poor soul who misses out on a bronze medal by a second or two. You should see the state of some at the end. It would probably be more merciful if they pointed the gun at them.'

The road narrowed as they got to the top. There was a short, level stretch lined with Jackaranda trees. Then the course began to twist sharply once more as they commenced the descent into Drummond.

'Halfway,' David declared as they swept past an unremarkable stretch of road. Apart from its significance within the race, there was little else to mark the spot.

It wasn't long before yet another formidable hill loomed in front of them. 'That's Inchanga,' David said. 'A lot of runners blow it going up here. Get up this one and there's not much else to worry about for twenty ks or so. His eyes twinkled. 'And then it's the infamous Polly Shorts.'

Inchanga, although not quite as steep as Field's Hill, would still be a considerable challenge, Ryan acknowledged. Especially as he would now be running into unexplored distances.

The large car purred to the summit and then down a sharp descent which ended in a series of bumps and troughs. Then, suddenly, level ground came into view. It stretched for as far as Ryan could see.

'You can have a rest along here,' David remarked, a mischievous gleam in his eyes. 'This is Harrison Flats. Further on is Cato Ridge, which is just as easy.'

The surrounding bare countryside, although a patchy pale green, seemed barren compared with the lush area of Botha's Hill. Just a few sparse trees offered any kind of interest to the landscape. Not that, on the day, that would be important. It was, as David had said, the opportunity to coast a little. For a change they drove in silence, the uninteresting surroundings seeming to stem even David's flow of words. Only as the flats began to rise did he speak, pointing out that they were now passing the highest point of the course, a full half-mile higher than the sea level at which they had started. Then they began the descent into greener country once more.

'Polly Shorts not too far ahead,' David announced cheerfully.

'Is this it?' Ryan asked a little further on as they began to rise for what seemed like the thousandth time.

'No, this is Little Polly,' David replied. 'Don't mistake it for the real thing.'

As if on a roller coaster they went up, only to plunge downwards and then up again shortly afterwards.

'This is it,' David said. 'The last real obstacle. Get to the top and you'll see Maritzburg.'

Ryan regarded the notorious hill. The hill regarded him back with stony impassivity.

Polly Shorts, at first glance, came as something of an anti-climax. Although obviously a considerable hurdle, it did not seem to have anything like the same formidable air about it as Field's or Inchanga. Then Ryan thought back on the distance and terrain already covered. Come the day, this strangely named hill could well then take on the proportions of Mount Everest.

IN THE LONG RUN

'How far have we come now?' he asked.

'Just about eighty kilometres or fifty miles in old money,' David told him.

As with many of the other hills, Polly Shorts followed a twisting path. Obstinately it lingered on for two around kilometres before eventually levelling out. At the summit Pietermaritzburg came gloriously into view below them. Ryan tried hard to imagine how welcome this sight would be on the day. As David had said, it was the last real obstacle.

While they drove through the suburban streets leading to the finishing point in Jan Smuts Stadium, Ryan realised that from here on it would simply be a matter of keeping the legs going. There were still some uphill slopes to contend with, but nothing too demanding. Less than ten kilometres after having climbed Polly Shorts they were outside the stadium.

Innumerable questions flashed through Ryan's head as he cast his mind forward three days. Where would he finish? And in what kind of physical condition would he be? Come to that, would he even finish at all? Anything could happen in a race like this. Cramp, dehydration, injury or even simple fatigue — any one of these could be the cause of failure. And then there was the other side of matters. The side that he was doing everything in his power to sweep under some kind of mental carpet: the grim reality of Parker and Manelli. Would the singer be dead by the end of the race? If so, where and when would the killing take place? And what, if any, further part in his mad schemes would Parker demand of him? Finally, what about Gayle and himself? Did he even have the right to dare hope for a future with her? There was so much to be resolved. Only time would provide the answers.

CHAPTER EIGHT

Manelli had been superb. The capacity crowd at Kings Park rugby stadium cheered and applauded him with a series of standing ovations. The singer held them all in the palm of his hand. Even after three lengthy encores, virtually everyone present was still on their feet demanding more. African, White, Asian and Oriental, many wearing vibrantly coloured forms of traditional dress, had stood up, danced, and sung along together with all the well-known numbers. The entire evening was a personal triumph for the American, more than justifying his personal beliefs. So compelling was Manelli's on-stage charisma that even Ryan had temporarily forgotten all his troubles and instinctively joined in with the party atmosphere.

All too quickly the show was over. As he and Gayle were carried slowly along by the crush of people heading for the exits, he glanced at her face. Judging from her animated expression there could be little doubt that she had thoroughly enjoyed herself. The same sort of look appeared to be worn by just about everyone else surrounding them.

Tyler had been so wrong in his assumptions, Ryan considered. There had been no mass protest, nor a hint of violence. The music of one man had transcended all considerations of race divides and hatred. Probably amongst some the bigotry would soon return, but for two-and-a-half hours all these differing people had been united in their pleasure. Only one person could take the credit for that: Manelli. By achieving this, how could these concerts of his possibly be considered immoral, or the singer himself corrupt?

IN THE LONG RUN

Ryan gave Gayle's hand a squeeze, perhaps unconsciously seeking some kind of assurance. She looked at him and smiled. An easy, natural smile that reflected her happiness. It told him far better than words of the pleasure she drew from his company. Ryan felt a huge rush of emotion towards her. Much as he had come to like and even respect Manelli, nothing was more important than Gayle's safety. Not even his own. Any lingering doubts over pressing on with Parker's instructions were swept away by that one look. He squeezed her hand once again as the crowd moved slowly on.

*

The pair of them stood at the entrance to Manelli's penthouse suite. In contrast to her earlier relaxed mood, Gayle now appeared nervous. 'I've never met anyone this famous before,' she whispered in Ryan's ear.

It was Kenny who opened the door and greeted them. 'Hi,' he said, looking approvingly at Gayle, 'Glad you could make it.'

They were ushered into a room packed with people, most of whom were clutching full champagne glasses. The vibrant noise of so many simultaneous conversations seemed to hit Ryan full in the face. He paused for an instant to adjust. He and Gayle were provided with champagne of their own by a passing waiter.

Kenny moved closer to make himself clearly heard. 'Tony's in the back room at present. He likes a short while to himself after a big show like tonight's. I'll tell him you're here. He'll be out soon.' With that he moved off to speak with Clint who was giving his usual display of the strong, silent type in the far corner. Behind the giant minder was a door, presumably leading to where Manelli was unwinding. A little lost, both Ryan and Gayle surveyed the mass of faces before them.

'Do you know anyone else here?' Gayle asked.

Ryan shook his head. 'I don't think so.'

In the centre of the room, James Kirkpatrick was doing his best to impress a stunning brunette. The girl wore an elegant black evening dress, its low neckline displaying a generous amount of cleavage. She was made for the dress, and the dress was unquestionably made for her. James was already drunk. The girl had an agitated expression on her face.

In preparation for the coming race James had taken a room in the nearby Edward Hotel. Regarded by many as Durban's finest, his stay there had been arranged and financed by his father. Charles, still fondly imagining a change for the better in his son, had felt a small reward was at last in order. It was the same with the party. Although no great fan of Manelli's music, James knew that to be at this gathering would carry considerable prestige. When back in his old social circle, it would give him much to impress them with. By pulling certain strings the old man had arranged an invitation for him. The head of Manelli's record label in South Africa was, after all, heavily indebted to his father for past information on share dealings.

'Just remember to behave yourself properly James,' Charles had told him. 'On absolutely no account allow yourself to get drunk. Your conduct whilst there will reflect directly upon me.' This advice, like so much before it, had been totally ignored. The combination of free drink, attractive women, and party atmosphere was a test James never stood a chance of coming through successfully. Once again he leered down the front of the brunette's dress. She drew sharply back.

'I wish you'd stop doing that,' she snapped while looking desperately around for an escape route.

'If you don't like people looking, you shouldn't walk around with your tits hanging out,' James responded, angry that his advances were being rejected.

For a moment it appeared that the girl would actually strike him. She then thought better of it. Spinning around, she walked quickly away to the edge of the room; in her haste nearly colliding with Ryan.

'I'm sorry,' she apologised, plainly flustered.

'Don't worry about it,' he replied. Then, looking at her expression he added: 'Are you all right?'

Gayle also regarded her closely. She could not fail to see the obvious attraction that this girl would hold for most men. For a second or two she wondered whether this were some clumsy attempt to muscle in on her boyfriend. She then decided that it was not. The girl was genuinely upset.

'Can we do anything to help?' she asked.

Glancing over her shoulder at James who was glaring in their direction, the brunette seized her opportunity. 'Would you mind if I talked to you for a while?' she pleaded. 'There's a guy over there who's giving me a hard time.'

Gayle recognised the situation and smiled reassuringly. 'Of course you can.'

Ryan shot a quick look at James. 'Who is he anyway?'

The girl frowned. 'I'm not sure. His name is James, that's all I know. Apart from the fact that he's a conceited and nasty piece of work.' Her voice tailed off as the

IN THE LONG RUN

nasty piece of work, determined not to be cast aside so easily, made his way toward them. A look of desperation crossed the girl's face.

'Oh no,' she murmured.

Gayle put a protective arm around her shoulders and drew her to one side, as if in deep conversation. This left Ryan as the buffer between them and the advancing menace. The two men faced each other a yard apart. James assessed the figure in front of him. He was an inch or two taller than this guy, and more solidly built. There was no problem here. Roughly he tried to push past.

'It's James isn't it? How are you?'

The words caused Kirkpatrick to pause again. He looked once more at Ryan. 'Do I know you?'

'You look familiar,' Ryan lied, anxious to avoid a scene. 'Why don't we have a drink together and talk about it?'

But James was in no mood to be put off. 'Don't mess me around,' he warned. 'I've never seen you before in my life.' Once again he pressed forward, his greater weight forcing back an off-balance Ryan. He approached the two girls.

'I suppose that you're talking about me now,' he snarled at the brunette who was studiously keeping her back to him. He spun her around. 'Who the hell do you think you are, you bloody tart?'

Gayle reached forward in an effort to offer some protection. In return James gave her a violent shove which sent her staggering back into the wall behind.

A red mist floated before Ryan's eyes. He charged forward, aiming a roundhouse punch to the side of Kirkpatrick's jaw. At the same time the brunette grabbed James around the neck from behind. His head jerked back, causing Ryan's punch to miss.

With the girl still clinging to him, James delivered a thudding blow to Ryan's stomach as the runner's impetus carried him forward. The brunette was then roughly thrown to the floor as James closed in for the kill. Ryan, on his knees and gasping for breath, was in no condition to defend himself.

Gayle bravely tried to step in once again, only to receive a brain-numbing slap across the face. His features contorted with rage, James was now completely out of control. Snarling, he drew back a foot and aimed a kick at Ryan. The kick was never delivered. James suddenly found his leg being sharply dragged back even further behind him. After hovering for a moment as if poised for an ungainly pirouette, his other leg was then knocked from underneath him. With all support gone, he nose-dived into the floor. Stunned, he lay there in a painful, untidy heap.

Humiliatingly, he was then dragged back up by his hair. He found himself staring into Kenny's grim face.

'Time you left fella,' he was told.

Despite his many faults, James was not a coward. Even so, he immediately knew better than to argue with this man. One look told him that he was dealing with a true professional. Any attempt on his part to continue matters would only end in a lot more grief. He forced the cap down on his temper. 'I was going anyway,' he blustered. 'This party's crap.'

Unceremoniously Kenny bundled him to the door and out of sight.

Ryan slowly straightened up and moved awkwardly over to Gayle. 'Are you all right,' he gasped.

She forced an uncertain smile and nodded. 'I think so.'

Both then turned their attention towards the brunette, who by now was quietly sobbing.

Suddenly Manelli was at her side. He put a powerful arm around the girl and whispered something in her ear. Within just a few seconds she was smiling weakly. Whatever the magic ingredient the man possessed, it had once again done the trick.

By now all conversation had ceased as the whole room stared at their little group. Kenny returned and Manelli drew him to one side.

'What happened?' he asked quietly.

Briefly Kenny explained. The singer then turned to the watching mass. 'Hey,' he called out, 'there's nothing to worry about folks. Just carry on and enjoy yourselves.'

Slowly people lost interest. The buzz of conversation resumed. Satisfied, the singer then returned to the trio by the corner. 'Come on,' he said. 'We'll go in the back room. It's quieter there.'

Within thirty minutes Ryan had all but recovered from the blow to his stomach. Both girls also seemed sufficiently revived to join in the relaxed and humorous atmosphere created by Manelli. The brunette, particularly, appeared spellbound by the singer. It turned out that she had won a newspaper competition to discover Manelli's biggest fan in South Africa. Two of the best tickets for the Kings Park concert, plus a chance to meet the star at the private gathering afterwards, were her prizes. The girl's mother, also a huge fan, had happily accompanied her daughter to the show but had then suffered a huge bout of nerves over attending

IN THE LONG RUN

the party. Even though left on her own, the brunette, Tracy, had been determined to meet her idol. Her major fear was that alone, without moral support amongst so many important people, she may be shunted into the background and forgotten. For that reason she had nervously worn the revealing dress, hoping that in this way she would at least catch her hero's eye. It was her misfortune that she had also caught James'.

There was a short convivial pause in the conversation. Then Manelli said: 'How are you feeling now Steve? You'll be OK for the race huh?'

It was the opening Ryan had been hoping for. 'I'll be all right,' he confirmed 'But what are you doing on the day? Will you be watching on TV or coming to cheer me on in person?'

Manelli gave a throaty chuckle. 'Hell Steve, I didn't come all this way just to watch it on TV. I'll be there bright and early at the start to see all you guys on your way. After that I've hired a helicopter for the day. It'll fly me along the route and put me down wherever I want. I should get some great aerial shots on video.'

'And later?' Ryan probed.

'I was going to talk to you about that. There's a place called Hillcrest just out of town. It's on the route.'

Ryan nodded. 'I drove through there this afternoon.'

'Well I've been told that there's a great little Italian restaurant there that I should try. I reckon it would be a nice idea to get out of town and have a quiet meal with a few friends in the evening. You know, something informal without all the usual baggage.' He waved a dismissive hand toward the closed door separating them from the continuing party. 'How about it? Bring Gayle too if she'd like to come.' He grinned. 'You can give me the lowdown on how the race was for you while we eat.'

For some ridiculous reason Ryan's first thought was 'Not more pasta'. He then glanced toward Gayle sat next to him. She looked keen on the idea. He hesitated, unsure what to say. What if this was where Parker decided the killing should take place? He couldn't allow Gayle anywhere near that. On the other hand, Manelli may well be dead before then anyway, so it didn't matter a damn what he agreed to now. As Ryan continued to debate he abruptly realised that the other three were all staring at him, puzzled by his silence and indecision.

Gayle put her hand on Ryan's arm. 'It would be nice if we could go.'

Knowing that he must say something, Ryan sighed. 'It's just that this race will take a lot out of me. I don't know if I'll be up to a night out afterwards.'

'Sure you will.' Manelli sounded confident. 'You'll be fine. If that's all that's stopping you I'll get the reservations made first thing tomorrow.'

Manelli could be a hard man to refuse.

He then turned to Tracy. 'And as for you young lady — after your little upset tonight, it'd be nice if you came along too. How about it? Consider it my way of making things up to you. I don't know who the heck that guy was, but I still feel kind of responsible. Someone out there should have been looking after you better than that.' A huge smile lit Tracy's face as she accepted the invitation. Her hero was surpassing even her high expectations.

The young girl's eagerness was in direct contrast to Ryan's dread. 'I'll let you know,' he insisted.

Manelli looked at him and grinned. He, and Gayle for that matter, both seemed to consider the matter settled. As if to finalise things, the singer got to his feet. 'Come on,' he said. 'Let's go join the party.'

*

It was ten a.m. when the persistent ringing of the bedside telephone finally broke through into James' deep sleep. God his head hurt.

He snatched up the receiver. 'Yes.'

'There's a call from Johannesburg for you Mr Kirkpatrick,' the hotel telephonist told him. 'One minute please.'

As the connection was being made, events of the previous evening started to come back to James. He cringed at what his father would say should he find out. Having got the old man fooled, how could he have been so bloody stupid?

His worst fears were confirmed when Charles' angry voice boomed down the line at him. 'James. Are you there?'

'Yes, I'm here,' he replied, full of trepidation.

'What the hell do you think you were playing at last night?' His father was struggling to contain his rage. 'I've just had Paul Eastwood on the line. He tells me that you made a complete idiot of yourself at the party. Is that true?'

Paul Eastwood was the record chief who had supplied the invitation. So he couldn't wait to drop me in it, James thought viciously. The bastard.

'It was nothing much,' he said defensively. 'I don't know what he's told you, but it's probably been blown up out of all proportion.'

'Nothing much!' his father exploded. 'You call brawling in public and attacking

IN THE LONG RUN

young women nothing much. What did I say to you? Mind how you behave as it will reflect on me. And this is what you do. Well that's it James. I've finally had enough of you.'

James found himself temporarily tongue-tied.

'James, are you still there?' the angry voice demanded.

'Yes.' His tone was contrite.

'It's the last straw James. You've let me down once too often. As far as I'm concerned you're finished. At least until you prove yourself a responsible person. You can come home to collect your belongings, and from then on you are on your own. I won't be responsible for you any longer.'

The words punched their way into James' brain. 'You can't mean that,' he said in hushed tones. 'What about the race? We had an agreement.'

'Not any longer. Your actions of last night destroyed all that.'

His father's voice then became less irate. There was even a touch of sarcasm. 'Look on the bright side James. At least you will not now have to face the Comrades. That should please you considerably. You are now free to do whatever you wish, although financing your worthless lifestyle might prove to be a problem from now on. I know that you have a little money of your own, but I can assure you that it will not last for long unless you use it wisely. Try to bear that in mind. Goodbye.'

Before James could respond to any of this his father hung up. As if in a trance, he still clutched the receiver to his ear. The one thing that he had always dreaded — but never truly believed would happen — had happened. He stared vacantly into space, his mind refusing to accept the situation.

'Was there anything else you wanted sir?' It was the telephonist's voice.

Without replying, James savagely slammed down the receiver.

*

Michelle du Toit walked quickly across the schoolyard and approached the sports master.

'Please Sir, could I have a word with you?'

The master turned, surprised to see her. Normally he had little to do with the girl pupils, his duties, in their co-educational school, being mostly with the boys. Rugby, cricket, and athletics were his main sports.

'What can I do for you?' He thought for a moment. 'It's Michelle isn't it?'

She nodded.

'So what is it Michelle?'

'It's the Comrades on Thursday isn't it Sir?'

'Yes. It's always run on the thirty-first of May.' Then, ever the teacher, he added: 'Which I am sure you also realise is a national holiday to commemorate Republic Day.'

Michelle had to stop herself from raising her eyes to the heavens. 'Of course Sir.'

'So what do you want to know about the Comrades?'

'You used to run in it didn't you Sir? That's what I've heard some of the boys say.'

'That's right Michelle, I did. Five times in fact. I might even run in it again next year if I can find the time to train properly.'

His collection of two silver and three bronze medals was a source of great pride to the teacher. Because of this he was always ready to talk about his experiences if asked. Michelle was well saware of this. Even so, she was clever enough to draw him slowly. Listening to several minutes of boring rubbish was a small price to pay. Just so long as she eventually got the information she needed.

'I'm a little surprised at your interest Michelle,' the master continued.

'I know somebody who is running,' she explained quickly.

The man smiled. 'Is it their first time?'

She gave him her little girl look. There were times when it was better to be a young adult, and there were times when it was far more advantageous to still be a child.

'Yes, it's their first run,' she confirmed.

'And you want to know what it will be like for them. Is that it?'

She continued with the innocent child routine. 'Something like that,' she said in a small voice.

The teacher looked at his watch. He was not too pressed for time. He was also pleased at Michelle's apparent interest and concern. He talked for another ten minutes, all of which still held no trace of importance for Michelle.

'How about training Sir?' she asked as he paused.

Her question drew a surprised look. 'I would hope that your friend has finished most of that by now. At this late stage a runner should be easing off and saving themselves for the big day. It would be very tough luck indeed if something were to put them out of the race after all the hard work of preparation.'

This was more the stuff, Michelle considered. 'What could do that then Sir?' Her eyes were large and innocent.

IN THE LONG RUN

The master shrugged. 'Any number of things. An injury such as a pulled muscle is the most obvious reason of course. Then an illness of some kind perhaps. It's also important that you watch what you eat. Any sort of stomach upset can be disastrous on long distance runs like the Comrades.'

Michelle giggled. 'A laxative just before the race wouldn't do you much good then,' she said.

Her amusement brought a stern look. 'A laxative would be just about the worst thing possible.' The man glanced at his watch again. 'I'd better be going now, especially as you do not seem to be taking our conversation seriously any longer.'

How wrong can you be, thought Michelle.

To the teacher she said: 'Oh I am taking it seriously Sir. Thank you for your time. You've been a big help.'

Gratified, the man smiled. 'That's all right Michelle. I'm glad that you appear happier about things now.'

'Yes, I'm much happier,' she smiled. 'Like I said Sir, you've really been a terrific help.'

*

James had spent the last hour prowling around his hotel room, feverishly trying to work out his best course of action. Sick of this endless pacing, he then sat down heavily on the edge of the bed. Should he check out and return home immediately? Once his father had calmed down he might perhaps be in a more reasonable mood to reconsider. An impassioned plea and a solemn promise to change for the better — that might do the trick.

James swore softly. Who was he kidding? His father had sounded utterly resolute. This time he was not going to be swayed by words, however convincing. So what was the alternative? He tried hard to remember exactly what the old man had said. 'As far as I'm concerned you're finished. At least until you prove yourself a responsible person.' Was there a glimmer of hope in that final part? Perhaps the door was only temporarily closed? But what could he do to force it open again? His brain darted this way and that as it sought a solution.

James continued to dwell on his father's words. With rancour he remembered the sarcasm in his voice when mentioning the Comrades. He jumped to his feet. The Comrades — that might still be the answer. What if he was to still run the bloody thing? The old bastard expected him to quit now. To once again take the easy option. By competing anyway, apparently with nothing to gain, he was certain to surprise him. And capture some kind of grudging respect. After the race was over he could appear humbled and promise to alter his ways. Even actually do so for a while if necessary. He would also work on his mother. With enough emotional blackmail she could be swayed into taking his side. The old man would crack in the end. He was bound to.

Although dreading the long hard slog to Pietermaritzburg, James realised that this could be his only chance. All the training he had done should get him through. He had to try anyway. But first there was one little extra touch needed. He picked up the phone and asked to be connected to his home number.

His mother answered. It was obvious from her tone that she knew nothing yet of the latest developments.

'I've got a message for Dad,' James told her.

She sounded puzzled. 'He's at work. You should know that. Why didn't you call him there?'

'I'd rather do it this way,' he said, adding a touch of mystery to his voice. 'Just tell him that I'm very sorry and—'

'Sorry for what?' There was definite anxiety now. James smiled to himself. He'd got her going already.

'Never mind what for. I'm sure he'll explain when he gets home. Just tell him that I'm sorry and that I'm staying on here in Durban to run the Comrades anyway.'

He then added with a touch of pathos: 'I want to do at least one thing in my life that he approves of.'

'What are you talking about James? I don't understand. You must tell me if something is wrong.'

'Please don't ask any more questions. It's really nothing for you to worry about. Goodbye Mother.'

James hung up as she began to speak once more. He then summoned the switchboard. 'If there are any more calls from Johannesburg for me today, I am not in. Do you understand?' He let out a satisfied sigh. That should start something between them.

IN THE LONG RUN

CHAPTER NINE

Ryan paused by his hotel room door as he searched through his pockets for the key. He would take a shower and relax for an hour or so before going out again. He had risen that morning in less than good shape — hardly surprising after the previous night's party. The deserted swimming pool he had came across suggested that Manelli was feeling in a similar condition. Ryan did a few lengths anyway and felt marginally better as a result. For the first time since arriving he then elected to eat breakfast at the hotel. It was as he left the dining room that once again the smiling African Simon materialised from seemingly out of nowhere.

In a quiet corner of the foyer Ryan told him of Manelli's plans for the coming race, and of the small dinner party in Hillcrest afterwards. Simon listened carefully but offered no comment. As the runner finished his companion let out a loud laugh, as if having been told an incredibly funny joke. Nervously Ryan took a long look around to see if they were attracting any unwanted attention. When he glanced back again the African had vanished.

Much of the day after that was spent with David, who seemed pretty much his own boss when it came to taking time off. The two of them had driven along the race route once more, this time discussing tactics and meeting points. Polly Shorts was quiet and relatively traffic free, allowing Ryan the opportunity for a closer inspection. Three times he ran up and down the two kilometre stretch to familiarise himself with the terrain. For now it was an almost effortless exercise. How he would cope on the day however, remained to be seen. Now back at the hotel, he finally located his room key and pushed open the door.

GEORGE **STRATFORD**

For the second time that day Ryan was suddenly confronted by Smiling Simon, who this time was lounging comfortably in an easy chair by the window. Even with his flair for unexpected appearances, this one was something special.

The African's smile grew wider. 'At last,' he said, as if greeting a long lost friend.

So stunning was the effect on Ryan, he was at first speechless. 'What the hell are you doing here? How did you get in?' he eventually managed to say. Despite his fear of the man, there was an edge of anger to his voice.

The only reaction this drew was an expansive spread of the hands. 'There are ways.'

Ryan bit back a heated response. Things were dangerous enough without exacerbating them further. 'So what do you want this time?' he asked instead.

'Mister Parker would like to see you again.'

The thought of returning to that appalling township made Ryan feel physically sick. 'I told you everything I know this morning,' he said.

Simon shrugged. 'If Mister Parker wants you, you better come.' There was no overt threat in these words. There did not need to be.

Rapidly Ryan weighed matters up. He'd done nothing wrong. He had acted exactly as instructed. In that case, no harm was liable to come to him? Parker probably just wanted to deliver his final instructions in person. At least he would then know exactly what was in store for himself — and Manelli. He sighed. 'OK, let's get on with it.'

To Ryan's surprise, they headed off on a completely different route this time. Did that mean that they were not going back to the township again? Daring to hope so, he asked Simon this as he swung the car into a right hand turn.

'No, not this time. Things have changed.'

Considering the African's reticence on their previous journey, it was a remarkably informative statement. At the same time it brought a flood of new questions into Ryan's head. What had now changed? Were they about to make new demands of him — ones that might incriminate him far more than before? And if so, how would he cope? Would he still be able to protect Gayle? He was on the point of trying to extract more information when the car pulled up.

'This is it,' the African stated. 'Get out.'

They were still in the city centre. More than that, they were parked directly outside an elegant restaurant. Simon led the way inside, pausing briefly to speak to the receptionist. With a regal wave of her bejewelled hand the woman then summoned a man in full evening dress. He was allocated the duty of escorting

IN THE LONG RUN

them through to the dining area. After his previous encounter with Parker, Ryan could scarcely believe where he had been brought. This was a high-class place — an incredible contrast to that dark, foreboding township that would haunt him for the rest of his days.

They wove their way past several tables to the far wall. Here, several private booths had been installed for customers requiring a more intimate atmosphere. They entered one of these to find Parker sat alone at the table. From his satisfied expression he had just completed an excellent meal. The old man actually smiled as they made their way in. He waved a gracious hand, indicating that both should be seated.

'Ah, Ryan my boy. Nice to see you again,' he said. The runner drew up a seat, totally perplexed by this affable greeting. 'Have a glass of wine,' Parker continued. 'The South African variety can be really quite excellent.' Without waiting for Ryan's response he poured out another glass. Even in this expansive mood it seemed he still expected to be obeyed.

Ryan took a small sip before speaking. In these surroundings, although still distinctly apprehensive, he was far less intimidated than before. 'So what do you want now?' he asked.

Parker smiled again. It was almost as if he had been taking lessons from Simon sat alongside. 'I have some news for you my boy. Something that should please you considerably. Especially as we both realise that your heart is no longer fully behind this little plan of ours.'

Little plan! The phrase grated badly with Ryan. How the hell could anyone refer to the murder of a man like Manelli as nothing more than 'a little plan'? 'I'm still following your instructions aren't I?' he said warily.

Parker's next words were staggering. They hit Ryan full in the face. 'Well there is no need for you to continue doing so any longer. As of today, the whole project has been cancelled.'

Stupified, Ryan stared at Parker with his mouth hanging slightly open. Could this possibly be true? Or was it some kind of test that he did not understand?

'You're joking,' he managed to say at last. 'You telling me that it's really all off?'

The old man's face was impassive. 'I never joke about such matters. It is indeed, as you so eloquently put it, all off.'

Try as he might, Ryan could not mask his expression of relief. Could this thing which had begun as an earnest mission of conscience, and had since developed into a terrifying ordeal, truly be over? It all seemed so sudden and too good to be true. A look of bewilderment replaced the one of relief. 'Why?' he asked incredulously.

Parker now regarded him with some amusement. 'Certain facts have come to light. We are now convinced that Mr Manelli is not the racist, money-grabbing exploiter that we first imagined him to be.' He went on to explain about the singer's insistence on providing many free seats to be distributed amongst the townships. How he had incited everyone to join together at the previous day's concert, telling them that race or colour made no difference. There was also the mitigating factor that one of his best friends — Kenny, Ryan presumed — was black.

'While we still do not agree with his coming here, we now feel that his motives were misguided rather than mercenary,' Parker concluded. 'That being the case, he has now been reprieved.'

Ryan considered these words carefully. After getting to know Manelli, his opinion had been changed by these very same facts. It was feasible that such overwhelming evidence could sway even a man like Parker. Whatever the case, it looked as if both he and the singer were off the hook. His relief at this change of situation was now very nearly as much for Manelli as it was for Gayle and himself.

'Does this mean that I'm free to do what I want now?' he asked.

Parker's benign expression faded. He became far more like his old self.

'I think it would be better,' he said, 'if you were still to continue with your participation in the Comrades and also your dinner party arrangement with Manelli afterwards. An insurance policy for us if you like, just to ensure your continued silence over this matter. While intent without action is no crime in itself, it could endanger our future plans if you were to talk to the wrong people. I am sure that you understand.'

Ryan understood very well indeed. If he competed in the Comrades it would have to be kept very quiet, particularly from the press and athletic governing bodies. One word in the wrong ear and he could kiss goodbye to any dreams of Olympic glory. Parker's silence on this matter would ensure his own over the Manelli affair.

'And if I don't choose to?' he queried, already knowing the answer.

'The young lady is still extremely vulnerable. So for that matter are you.'

It was exactly as he'd anticipated. Parker might have called off Manelli's murder, but he and his group were still highly dangerous people. It was all too clear to Ryan that, as he was very nearly free of them anyway, it would be crazy to provoke trouble at this late stage. Besides, more than ever since his link up with David, the urge to test himself against the daunting Comrades course was becoming stronger.

IN THE LONG RUN

He shrugged in a gesture of submission. 'If that's what you want, I'm hardly in a position to argue, am I?' He the added: 'I wouldn't have talked anyway. I don't want the attention any more than you do.'

Parker smiled again. 'Precisely. However it is as well to increase the safeguard.'

'You swear that the girl will be safe after I'm gone?' Ryan demanded next.

'You have my word on that,' Parker assured him. 'What would we gain from harming her? As you keep telling us, she knows nothing.' He continued: 'Take my advice. Obtain whatever pleasure you people derive from these long distance tortures. Enjoy your dinner with Manelli afterwards, and then go home and forget all that has happened here.'

All except meeting Gayle, Ryan told himself. His sense of oppression was rapidly easing. Running the race under an assumed name should present little threat to his career. After viewing the route he knew realistically that, under his present training schedule, he had little chance of finishing up with the top runners even if he wanted to. Just to complete the course in a creditable time — perhaps a silver medal position — was all he now aspired to. That in itself would be an achievement. After that both he and Gayle would be safe, thank God. Something else then occurred to him. 'Does Tyler know about this change of plan?' he asked. With all that had happened since his arrival he had spared few thoughts for his friend back in London. Perhaps he should give him a call to explain matters.

Parker stroked his chin for several seconds, his piercing eyes boring into Ryan's. 'No, he has not been informed yet. You however should make no contact. I will attend to that side of things.' Then, as if once more reading Ryan's mind, he added: 'Such matters should not be discussed over an open telephone line. You will see your friend shortly and then you can talk all you wish in private. Until then, leave it with me. I am in a much better position than you to communicate with Mr Tyler on a confidential level.'

Ryan shrugged. What Parker said made sense. In any case, perhaps it would be better if his next conversation with Tyler was on a face to face basis. There was an intense bitterness burning inside. He had been misinformed, used, and placed in great danger. There would be some harsh words passed when he and his so-called friend met again.

Parker raised his wine glass. 'I doubt that you will see me again Ryan. At least not if you do as instructed. That being so, I offer you a toast. To a free South Africa.'

'To a free South Africa,' Ryan responded automatically.

'And now I will have to ask you to leave,' Parker concluded. 'As I have some personal business to attend to with Simon here, I hope that you will not consider it an imposition if I request that you make your own way back to the hotel. Or wherever else you may anticipate going to.'

Ryan did not need a second bidding. He rose to his feet. 'You are right in your judgement,' he found himself compelled to say. 'Manelli is a good man and doesn't deserve to die. I discovered that too.'

Parker gave a thin smile. 'It was not particularly difficult to see that you had come to that conclusion.' He then turned towards the African, clearly signifying that their conversation was terminated. Ryan left without another word.

Alone with Parker, Simon's smile grew even broader. 'Do you think he suspects the truth?' he asked.

There was a grim look of satisfaction on the old man's face. 'Not at all Simon. He believed every word that I told him simply because it was what he wanted to believe. It is not often one meets an educated man who is quite so gullible as Mr Ryan.'

'Are you certain that he'll go with Manelli to the restaurant?' Simon persisted.

'Oh there's no doubt about that, especially now he considers there is no longer any threat to his friends. We can, as they say, now kill two birds with one stone.'

Simon gave a deep, throaty chuckle. 'Very nicely put Boss,' he said. His eyes were full of anticipation.

*

Ryan lay in bed, halfway between consciousness and sleep. For the first time in days he felt at peace. Even Gayle had remarked that evening how much more relaxed he appeared. Manelli was now safe, and provided he went through with the formality of the Comrades, the threat to Gayle and himself would also be removed. In his present frame of mind he was now actually looking forward to the race with enthusiasm. It would be by far his greatest challenge yet. He would also be able to gauge whether or not Bruce Fordyce was as good as his reputation. The man still intrigued him.

Inevitably his thoughts then returned to Gayle. He was now fairly certain that David was correct. Everything indicated that she did care considerably for him. Gayle's smiling face was the last thing he saw before drifting off into his first truly peaceful sleep since arriving in South Africa.

IN THE LONG RUN

CHAPTER TEN

Gritting his teeth, James attempted to walk straight past his hotel bar. It was Wednesday evening: a time when under normal circumstances he would be out enjoying himself. A resentful sigh slipped out. Durban's Golden Mile of beachfront offered an array of temptations, all of which must be resisted if he were to have any chance of success the next day. A six a.m. start was bad enough without having to compete with the extra handicap of a hangover. Unappealing as it was, an early night was the sensible option.

Unable to prevent himself, he paused for an instant just to glance briefly into the bar. The long line of optic bottles tantalised him. He looked sharply away, only for his gaze to fall on a passably attractive female sat alone. It was too much. There followed a brief inner battle that James never even expected to win. He did not surprise himself. His feet, as if on automatic pilot, led him inside. He ordered a large whisky.

Leaning against the bar, he contemplated the coming day's challenge. Could he realistically hope to make it? And even if he did, would it all turn out to be a wasted effort? All day he had been expecting some kind of response from his father. It was now early evening and he had still heard nothing. Why hadn't the old bastard phoned? Surely his mother had got to work on him by now? It was unthinkable that she would remain in the background over this matter. Not now he had actually been thrown out.

Draining his glass, he ordered another drink. As he waited for it to come he glanced once more in the girl's direction. She smiled at him.

GEORGE STRATFORD

*

Charles Kirkpatrick regarded his wife with a look of exasperation that was tinged with sadness.

He sighed. 'How many more times do I have to explain?' he asked. 'Can't you see what the boy is trying to do? He is deliberately playing on your soft nature, hoping that you will then talk me around. And you've fallen for it.' He continued to pace up and down the huge, sumptuously furnished lounge. Margaret, almost lost in the massive armchair that she was seated in, eased herself up and approached her husband. She took hold of both his hands, interlocking her slender fingers with his powerful ones.

'I've supported you all the way over this Comrades issue Charles,' she told him in a gentle voice. 'You were right. James needed something to wake him up. But I never dreamed it would come to this. That you would actually throw him out.'

'He's an adult for God's sake Margaret, not a little boy. He's twenty-four years old and should be perfectly capable of supporting himself.'

'But he's had no experience in anything.'

Charles regarded her sternly. 'And whose fault is that? I never should have allowed you to talk me into arranging his exemption from military service. A spell in the army might have been the making of him.'

Margaret disengaged her fingers and backed off a couple of paces. She faced her husband, hands on hips. 'I wondered when you would bring that up.'

For a moment it appeared that Charles would continue in the same vein. He then checked himself and let out a deep sigh. 'We shouldn't be arguing like this.' He dropped down onto the six-seater settee, patting the space alongside him. 'Come on. Sit here and let's talk sensibly,' he suggested.

Margaret hesitated only briefly before doing so. She then gazed at her husband with deep concern. 'So what do we do?' She gave a nervous little laugh. 'I know he isn't the perfect son. Far from it. But he is our only child. I know he'll come right in the end. Surely you must realise Charles that no mother worthy of the name can turn her back completely.'

'Is that what you think I'm doing — turning my back on him?'

She cast her eyes to the floor. 'I don't know. Are you?' Her voice was hushed.

Charles did not answer. Instead he spoke quietly, almost as if talking to himself. 'I've given the boy so many chances, and every time he lets me down.' His tone then grew stronger. 'Nobody wants him to succeed more than I do. But there

IN THE LONG RUN

comes a time when he must stand alone. Maybe that is the only way he will ever achieve anything.'

Margaret linked hands with her husband once more. 'He is running the race despite everything,' she pointed out. 'Don't you think that he's trying to say something to you? Something like: I can do it anyway. I don't care about your money any more.'

Charles doubted this very much. It was far more likely that his son was merely trying to manipulate them both in order to re-establish his position. He prayed that this was not the case, but cynicism born out of James' repeated letdowns told him differently.

Seeing his doubt, Margaret sought to press home her point. 'At least give him a chance,' she pleaded. 'Prove to me that you mean what you say. If you want him to become a better son, you must give him some encouragement when he deserves it.'

Slowly Charles passed a hand over his forehead. Sound reason continued to tell him that this was just another of James' tricks. This discussion that they had been drawn into was the exact outcome that James would have hoped for.

The ridiculous thing was that, even with this knowledge, the trick was still working. He knew that he must give the boy every benefit of the doubt, if only for Margaret's sake. Disillusioned as he was, if there was just a one per cent chance that James had finally been jolted into doing something purely out of pride, then it had to be given some consideration.

'I'll tell you what I *will* do,' he said at length.

His wife looked at him with some expectancy. 'Yes.'

'I will try to keep an open mind on things. If James proves to be sincere in this endeavour, then we can discuss matters again. What I refuse to do at this stage is give him any more inducements. He must go through it in the firm belief that all is lost. If he can do that, then just maybe there is hope for him.'

Margaret studied her husband's face. She knew him well enough to realise that he would go no further. Given their son's past record, it was the best that she could reasonably have hoped for. 'That sounds fair,' she conceded.

'This means,' Charles continued, 'that neither of us should make any attempt to contact him until after the race. He must be totally convinced that my decision is final. That he competes with nothing to gain but the personal satisfaction of proving a point.'

'But what if he calls here tonight?'

'If he does, then I would honestly consider that he was after something. Probably information from you. He would merely be prying; trying to find out if you had softened me up yet.' Charles shook his head. 'I'm sorry Margaret, but if he does call, then I would be forced to accept this as final proof of his insincerity and weakness. James will stand or fall purely on his actions over the next twenty-four hours.'

Margaret silently prayed that her son would not be tempted to pick up the telephone that evening.

*

The entire du Toit family was gathered on their back porch, along with both Armstrong and Neil Douglas. There was a comfortable silence as they all contemplated the spectacular sunset.

Douglas was the first to speak. 'Tomorrow's the day laddie,' he remarked, his Scottish accent sounding more pronounced than ever.

The boy's large grin reflected his confidence. 'I'm ready Mister Douglas.'

'Aye, you are that,'

'You've done a good job Neil,' Piet chipped in. 'No one could have done better.'

The Scot allowed himself the luxury of a rare smile. 'Armstrong's worked hard,' he said. The pride in his protégé was well evident.

Piet's wife, Cecile, not normally the most talkative of people, spoke next. 'As we are all here together, I think now is the time when everybody should wish Armstrong the very best of luck for tomorrow. It's all in his hands now.'

Claudine giggled. 'Don't you mean his feet Mum?'

There was general laughter at the teenager's remark. Claudine then jumped up and positioned herself in front of Armstrong. Her face was now serious. 'I hope you win tomorrow,' she told him as they exchanged a solemn handshake.

'I'll do my best not to let you down,' the youth responded, clearly touched by the girl's sincerity.

'That's all anyone can ask,' Piet cut in, anxious to steer clear of any heady talk of Armstrong winning. 'As long as you do your best we'll all be proud of you, no matter where you finish.'

Douglas gave the youth a slap on the shoulder. 'You'll do well right enough,' he assured him.

Piet turned to his eldest daughter who had remained seated and silent throughout. 'How about you Michelle? Aren't you going to wish Armstrong luck?'

IN THE LONG RUN

Slowly the girl stood up and shuffled over, all the time looking at her feet. She then raised her eyes. Her features formed into a little girl smile. 'I'm sorry if I've been nasty to you,' she said, much to everyone's surprise.

Armstrong was the most surprised of all. It was his turn to cast his eyes down to the floor. His embarrassment was self-evident. He mumbled something in Zulu, his English not capable of dealing with the situation.

Piet regarded his eldest daughter. Although taken aback, he was greatly pleased. Her attitude up until now had been a considerable worry to him.

Michelle continued. 'I hope everything goes well for you tomorrow.' Her voice was demure.

There was a general murmur of accord. Piet then said: 'OK everyone, now that's over I think we should all have a drink. What's it to be?'

'Aye, one more beer then,' Douglas agreed. 'And then we should all start thinking about an early night, especially Armstrong. We need to be in Durban by five o'clock at the latest.'

Armstrong did not touch alcohol. 'Do you think I could have my Horlicks now?' he asked. Since staying at the du Toit's the bedtime drink had become something of a favourite and a nightly habit for him.

Cecile rose to her feet. 'Of course Armstrong.'

'You stay where you are Mum, I'll make it for him,' Michelle volunteered brightly.

Cecile regarded her much as Piet had done a few minutes earlier. 'That's very nice of you love,' she said, sinking back into her seat. This was indeed a pleasant change in her daughter, brought on no doubt by the excitement of the coming day.

Michelle hurried off to the kitchen. While waiting for the saucepan of milk to heat up she added three teaspoonfuls of Horlicks to a large mug. From the back pocket of her jeans she then produced a small envelope containing three brown tablets. Each of these she ground into fine grains with the teaspoon before mixing them thoroughly with the Horlicks powder. The hot milk was then added. Stirring it all thoroughly, she smiled to herself. Not the smile of an innocent child any longer, but one full of petty spite. 'That should make you run all right boy,' she murmured to herself. 'You see if it doesn't.'

*

James lay on his back staring moodily at the hotel room ceiling. The girl beside him in the double bed had been a major disappointment in ever way. She had proved to be the easiest pick-up imaginable, virtually throwing herself at him right from the start. Even James appreciated a token chase.

That wouldn't have mattered too much if she had been good between the sheets, but here he had suffered a major disillusionment. Despite all her earlier come-ons, once her clothes had been removed the girl's mood had changed completely. She became stiff and unresponsive. Nothing James tried could arouse any passion in her. She just lay there like a zombie, looking for all the world as if she might burst into tears at any moment. Eventually she did.

'What a bloody waste of time,' James muttered to himself. He listened with mounting irritation to her soft whimpering. Finally, in a burst of temper, he threw back the sheet and began pacing naked around the room. The one consolation he could draw from the evening was that she had at least kept him off the booze. After only three drinks together they had been in bed.

He snatched up his watch from the dressing table. It was now eleven p.m. He had planned to ring home much earlier than this. Instead he had got himself sidetracked with this silly bitch. Was it too late now? He knew that his mother usually went to bed quite early, but he had to speak to her. He had to know what his father had said. Before he did anything though, he would have to get rid of this snivelling cow. The last thing he wanted was her listening in to the conversation.

He glanced toward the miserable figure on the bed. She lay there virtually motionless, her body partly exposed by the drawn back sheet. As he moved to shake the girl his eyes rested on her left arm which was flung listlessly to one side. He stared stupidly at the limb for several moments. A look of horror then formed as he made a closer inspection. Scattered all around the lower part of the arm were a mass of tiny red sores. Marks that looked horribly like the legacy of a dirty needle.

'You fucking bitch,' he screamed. 'You're a bloody junkie.'

Even he had never been stupid enough to play with drugs. Because of this he was far from expert on the tell-tale signs. Nevertheless, it did not take a genius to spot the potential danger. Why hadn't he noticed these marks before, he furiously demanded of himself? Surely he should have suspected something after her inexplicable change of mood. Christ almighty — she might even have given him Aids. With this appalling thought running through his head, he tugged savagely at the inert figure. Dragging the still naked and whimpering girl from the bed, he bundled her roughly towards the door and out into the corridor.

'You fucking bitch,' he repeated, throwing the girl's clothes out after her and slamming the door closed. Momentarily unable to think any further, James then

IN THE LONG RUN

buried his face in his hands. After only a few seconds like this he suddenly jerked his hands away again. What the hell was he thinking of? He remembered all the places his fingers had explored while vainly attempting to induce some sort of passion into the girl. For all he knew they could now be infected and covered in the virus. Come to that, his whole body could be contaminated. His ignorance of such matters did nothing to calm him. If anything it made matters worse.

He ran straight to the shower and began to scrub himself with desperation bordering on blind panic. Bit by bit he turned up the heat to a point where it was almost insufferable, as if in hope that the scalding water would magically burn away any infection. At last he could stand it no more. Bright red from the violent scrubbing and heat, he gingerly dabbed his tender body dry with the softest towel available.

Still not satisfied, James set about cleaning his teeth. With sweat pouring from his face he worked the brush into every corner of his mouth and as far down his throat as he could without actually choking himself. After fifteen minutes of this feverish activity his gums were very nearly as sore as his body. Only then did he leave the bathroom. His temper flared briefly once again as he tore the soiled linen from the bed and hurled it to the floor. Anger spent, he then flopped wearily onto the bare mattress.

A shade calmer now, James sought to reassure himself. Even if she was a junkie, that didn't necessarily mean that the girl was carrying Aids. Now he thought about it more logically, the chances were probably very slight. After all, most people who caught the disease in this country were black weren't they? Gradually he talked himself into a slightly better frame of mind. Didn't he have enough real problems to deal with without agonising over something that might never happen? He would get a test as soon as possible. Until then there was nothing he could do.

The combination of stress and the earlier whisky slowly drained James. Within a short space of time he was asleep.

*

The persistent demanding ring of the bedside telephone finally broke into James' deep sleep. Barely awake, he fumbled for the receiver.

'This is your early morning call you asked for sir,' a girl's voice told him 'The time is four-thirty.'

GEORGE STRATFORD

He groaned and hung up.

Gradually his brain began to function as he lay still, making no attempt to rise from the bed. What was the point? Once again the possibility, however small, that he might have contracted Aids overshadowed all other considerations. He had to find out about getting tested. To hell with the Comrades. He had received no call from home. That told him that his father must have remained firm. If that were truly the case, he would be crazy to put himself through all the pain of the race for nothing. Even before he had doubted his ability to last the course. Now, with this new threat hanging over his head, there was no way he would ever make it. He tossed and turned, unable to get back to sleep.

It was some fifteen minutes later when the telephone rang again. After a short delay he was connected to his mother.

'Is that you James,' she asked, her voice unnaturally quiet.

'Of course it is,' he said, surprised at the timing of the call. 'Why are you whispering like that?'

'I don't want your father to hear me. He's still sleeping upstairs. You know how easily he wakes up.'

James' hopes, already stirred, rose considerably. Why the secrecy? Had his plan worked after all? 'What do you want,' he asked, his voice unaccountably dropping to match hers.

His mother related the bare bones of her talk with his father. James listed closely, his hope turning to fierce elation. The crafty old sod, he thought angrily as his mother spelled out the situation. Thank God he had never telephoned last night.

'So you see James,' she concluded, 'it is important that you do as well as possible today. I'm sure he will then reconsider your situation.'

'Why are you telling me this?' James could not resist asking. 'Especially after he particularly told you not to.'

There was a long pause during which, for some extraordinary reason, he pictured his mother's features twisted with torment. Even he could well imagine the heart-searching and anguish that this call must be costing her.

Eventually she spoke. 'I know that you've got faults James, but you're my only child. I can't help but love you. How I pray for the day when you learn the value of tolerance and achieve something of worth. Today may just be the start of that. Please, I beg of you James, try for me — try very hard.' Her voice began to break with emotion as she finished. The phone line suddenly went dead.

IN THE LONG RUN

Slowly James replaced the receiver. For the first time that he could remember he was touched with concern for someone other than himself. Never before had his mother displayed so graphically the depth of her distress over him. All thoughts of not running were now forgotten. If he only ever did one decent thing in his life, he would do this for his mother. Sod his father — and damn that junkie bitch. Both these considerations could wait a day.

Whether or not this new determination was inspired by the knowledge that he might just be terminally infected, James couldn't say. He didn't care to dwell on it. One thing he did know however was that, even though he could probably never be the type of son his mother longed for, he certainly owed her something. She wanted him to run, so run he would.

Fired by this thought, he rose from the bed. Whatever the outcome today, he sure as hell would now be giving it everything he had.

GEORGE **STRATFORD**

CHAPTER ELEVEN

The evocative theme music from *Chariots of Fire* swelled out from a multitude of strategically placed speakers, each inspiring note rising to linger imposingly overhead before finally diffusing into the black, early morning sky above Durban's Pine Street. The music, virtually an anthem to many runners, blended easily with the huge swell of energetic chatter from more than twelve thousand densely packed competitors. To every one of them there was a sense of occasion absolutely unique to the Comrades. Although not yet daybreak, the temperature was already approaching twenty degrees centigrade.

Ryan was awe-struck. Never in any of his countless races had he experienced such a feeling of nervous anticipation. Apart from the competitors themselves, it seemed that just about the entire population of Durban City had turned out to wish them luck and see them safely on their way. There were people literally everywhere, nearly all jostling, noisy and good-humoured. It was these final, nerve-jangling minutes before the start that was always one of the high points to him. It was a time when the adrenalin really began to pump in anticipation of the pain and pleasure soon to be experienced.

Specially installed ancillary lighting bathed the area immediately around the starting point in a white brilliance. Further back along the line where there was only the normal street lighting, it was much dimmer. The swell of impatiently waiting runners stretched back far beyond Ryan's vision, continuing on until appearing to merge with a blur, into the star speckled sky.

Every type of long-distance runner was represented somewhere. There were the

IN THE LONG RUN

serious athletes; some standing quietly in contemplation while others bounced eagerly on their toes. There were the exhibitionists in wacky costumes, and there were those with something to say. Hundreds of banners, some requiring as many as half a dozen competitors to support them, were held aloft to display their colourful greetings and messages. One individually held banner pleaded for all to see: CAROLINE, WILL YOU MARRY ME?

'*Shosholoza kwa zontaba stimela se gonda e Rodesia...*'

A small group of black runners began to sing. Other Africans scattered throughout the field soon picked up the words. One by one fresh voices joined in to swell the sound.

Ryan turned to David stood alongside him. 'What's all that about?' he asked.

His companion grinned. 'It's something you often hear Africans sing at sporting events. Roughly translated it means: hurry to the mountain, the train is leaving for Rhodesia.' He shrugged. 'Don't ask me any more than that.'

He then nudged Ryan and pointed. 'Look, there's Bruce Fordyce over there. The guy wearing number 2403.'

With huge interest Ryan stared at the runner indicated. So that's the man he had heard so much about, he thought. Fair-haired and slight of build, Fordyce was stood quietly a few rows from the front. Other runners constantly reached out to shake his hand, as if by touching him some of the greatness might rub off on to them. He displayed no annoyance at this almost regular infringement on his mental preparation. Frequently he gave a quiet smile and exchanged a few words.

'All those runners around him are what's known as the Fordyce bus,' David continued. 'They'll try to stick with him all the way. Whatever he does, they'll attempt to do the same.' He laughed. 'That is until Fordyce makes his drive for home. Then he'll leave most of them for dead.'

Slowly Ryan dragged his eyes away.

David pointed again. 'There's someone else who might interest you.' This time he was indicating a tall bearded figure wearing a French Foreign Legion style cap. 'Jean Marc Bellocq. Remember we were talking about him the other day?'

Ryan nodded. He regarded Bellocq, still currently banned from competition in his own country for having run this very race last year. Up until now the Frenchman had merely been a name to him. With a runner's eye he appraised the athlete. 'He seems in good nick,' he remarked. 'Strong and capable.'

'Not bad for someone who's already run in two, one hundred kilometre races during the last fortnight,' David responded. 'He finished second in one of them too.'

Ryan was astonished at such competitive intensity. Strong and capable suddenly seemed a barely adequate assessment. He shot David a wry look. 'I'm beginning to feel like a real nobody here in terms of distance.'

For once David made no comment.

A moment later Ryan spotted Gayle making her way towards them through the mass of spectators lining the street.

'I thought I'd never find you,' she said before kissing Ryan lightly on the cheek.

'She's nearly always late,' David grinned. 'You'll get used to it.'

He then glanced at the time. 'You should be getting into position soon. Have you decided which seeding area you're going in?'

Four time zones divided the start. Marshals with barrier ropes strung across the road indicated the beginning of each section. The front division was intended for top athletes anticipating a finish of less than six-and-a-half-hours. To the vast majority of the field such a time was an impossible dream. It followed that this section was appropriately small. Behind this elite body, the next, slightly larger zone, was marked out for those expecting to take no more than an hour longer. Competitors here were potential silver medallists who should be somewhere in the first thousand home. Gathered behind these was the main bulk of runners. A mass of humanity stretching back down the main road for well over a mile. These two rear sections were huge by comparison. The first was for under nine hours, and following that, one for those who were hoping to get to the finish line somewhere during the last two official hours of the race. Everyone who finished within eleven hours would be rewarded with a commemorative bronze medal.

These seedings were not enforced in any way. It was left to each competitor to make an honest assessment of their own ability. Ryan had already considered this and opted for the relative anonymity of the third section back. He informed David of this.

His second nodded in approval. 'You could be doing yourself a bit of an injustice,' he remarked. 'But you'll soon work your way through when the field strings out.' He gave Ryan a friendly nudge. 'You better get moving. I'll see you at the top of Field's Hill as arranged.'

Gayle moved forward to plant another quick kiss on Ryan's cheek. 'Good luck,' she whispered in his ear.

'You must be special,' David remarked. 'She never even used to get out of bed to see me off.' He clapped his hands. 'Get moving then, otherwise you'll be late.'

After a last minute check to ensure that his number was fixed firmly in place, Ryan gave Gayle one final smile. 'See you later,' he said.

IN THE LONG RUN

*

At the head of the field, a few rows behind Fordyce, Armstrong was eager to get started. This was his big day. So many people wanted him to succeed — he dare not let them down. There was the du Toit family, Mister Douglas, and a host of well-wishers from his colleagues at Dolphin Coast Striders. He was also running for the honour of his family and Shakaville Township. It was curious that, from amongst all these, his last minute thoughts should now centre on Miss Michelle. He had been deeply touched by her recent change of heart. It was good to know that she now liked him in the same way that the rest of her family did.

Some of the more seasoned runners regarded the Zulu youth with curiosity. He was a new face to them — an unknown quantity. Who was this determined looking youngster? Was he a threat, or was he simply in the wrong place?

Douglas' final words came back to Armstrong. 'Don't go too fast to begin with. Just follow Fordyce if you can.' It was hardly original advice for anyone hoping for a top ten finish and a gold medal. Even so, it was sound. Armstrong knew that all those in the Fordyce bus would be adopting similar tactics. The only question on everyone's mind was that, after missing last year's race, had the great man returned with the same motivation? There was absolutely nothing left for him to prove. Also, at thirty-five years old this year, he was now moving into the stage where entrants were officially classified as sub-veterans.

Armstrong felt a violent shove as James tried to force his way through to the front rank. Kirkpatrick was well aware that he had no right to be in this privileged position, but he was damned if he was going to make things even more difficult for himself by starting at the back. It was going to be tough enough as it was. Armstrong regarded James philosophically as he passed. His mind was far too occupied to worry about a bit of barging.

The tension and expectancy hanging over everyone sharply increased as the final strains of *Chariots of Fire* faded away. A semi-hush — reverent almost — descended. The brightly illuminated face of the post office clock tower showed two minutes to six. The moment they were all waiting for had nearly arrived. A cock crowed. It was in reality the recorded voice of Max Trimborn, a now deceased former stalwart of the Comrades. It had originated as a joke by him years before as he stood on the starting line. Now, captured for posterity, his wake-up call had been adopted and enshrined as part of the annual tradition.

GEORGE STRATFORD

The cock crowed a second time. Ryan, as he always did at this moment in a big event, felt his mouth turn dry. Unconsciously he began to bounce up and down on his toes.

A church bell across the street began to clang as six o'clock was struck. On a platform high above the impatiently waiting runners, the Mayor of Durban, resplendent in his chain of office, raised the starting gun. An instant later it was fired. A massive roar of jubilation erupted as the seething mass of humanity surged forward. The sixty-fifth running of the Comrades Marathon was under way.

*

Ryan was not used to starting a race from so far back. For a lengthy period after the gun sounded he remained hemmed in and virtually motionless as those around him waited for the forward momentum to filter through. For almost the first time he noticed how many women competitors there were sprinkled around. Up until now he had naturally concluded that the course would be too demanding for most females. Although no sexist, the prospect of possibly being beaten by a woman was not one that he particularly relished. He was also now noting how many in his section were far older than himself. The forty to fifty age group appeared to be particularly well represented.

Gradually they began to inch forward and get under way. Small shuffling steps at first, slowly increasing as the congestion eased a little. By the time Ryan actually crossed the start line it was more than five minutes since the gun had been fired. From here on a steady jog was now possible.

As he moved into the brightly lit section of Pine Street Ryan spared a thought for Manelli. Where was he at this moment? Had the American spotted him? As a visiting celebrity he had probably secured a privileged viewing position well away from the crush. This thought passed quickly through his mind and was then forgotten. The race itself, and what lay ahead, took over completely.

*

As the starting gun had sounded, those at the front with unimpeded progress took off in two very different fashions. as always there were a handful determined to be famous for five seconds. Runners who set off at a frantic sprint, determined that TV would capture their moment of glory. For a brief span they could claim

IN THE LONG RUN

to have led the race, before inevitably falling back to blend anonymously with the thousands behind. Fordyce, along with all the other genuine contenders, totally ignored the frenetic few. Each one set out with measured strides, wondering if this was to be their year for glory.

Apart from Fordyce himself, Armstrong had been made well aware of who else might pose the biggest threat to him. Mark Page, a team mate of Fordyce's from Rand Athletic Club, was strongly fancied. There was Shaun Meicklejohn, who fooled many people with his uncanny resemblance to Fordyce. Boysie van Staden, a stalwart representative of Natal for many years could never be disregarded. The same could be said of the powerful Frenchman Bellocq, although his two recent long races might just prove to be too great a handicap. Another to watch out for was 'Iron Man' Nic Bester whose strength matched his reputation. Of the fellow Africans, there was the tall, long-striding Hosea Tjale, and of course the defending champion, Sam Tshabalala. Although declaring himself fit, there had been rumours about the champion's health and training injuries. How true these were remained to be seen.

As instructed, Armstrong settled in a short distance behind Fordyce. He was running easily and felt good. To his right he noticed the runner who had barged past him at the start. Their eyes met for a moment before James spat onto the ground and looked away.

The seemingly endless stream of runners passed through the Indian quarter and began the slow rise out of Durban. Every bit of the way was lined with spectators from all races, each one cheering, clapping and shouting encouragement.

By the time he got to this point Ryan was into a good steady rhythm. Already the leaders were well out of sight to him as he pushed easily along the uphill slope. Further along the freeway the crowds were less, although every now and then he passed a group ready to provide vociferous support. The line of runners was now stretched out over many kilometres and lengthening all the time as he pressed on into the slowly increasing daylight.

About eight kilometres out of Durban Ryan passed the first of fifty-seven refreshment tables that David had assured him would be available. Apart from the heat, the humidity level was currently running at ninety per cent, making the possibility of dehydration an even greater risk than usual. Already sweating profusely, Ryan took full advantage of the offered drinks. He stuck to plain water, knowing that David would be waiting for him with a specially prepared drink at the top of Field's Hill.

Supplementing these tables were long watering troughs, their lengthy design allowing the competitors in front of Ryan to dip in a sponge whilst still on the run. These sponges were then squeezed out over the top of the head and discarded onto the roadside. Ryan followed suit.

Without pushing himself too hard, he gradually threaded his way through the field. His competitive nature was now on the rise. He wanted that silver medal. Briefly he wondered exactly how far Fordyce was now ahead of him. He lengthened his stride just a touch.

The Fordyce bus had in fact already left the freeway and was on its way up Cowies Hill some ten minutes behind the early leader. Still trailing them, Armstrong passed a hand over his brow. For some unaccountable reason he was starting to feel dizzy. But they had covered less than twenty kilometres — that was nothing. Why should he feel like this?

Never in his countless miles of training had he experienced anything similar. He knew for certain that he was not over-extending himself. So what was the reason? Not knowing what to do, Armstrong shook his head and carried on. Surely the feeling would soon pass.

*

James scowled as even more runners passed him and then disappeared into the far-off distance. He was not yet in real trouble, but he knew for certain that it would be suicidal for him to attempt the same sort of pace. At least he had gained himself a bit of time by starting at the front, he consoled himself. Even if he were to walk up all the major hills he could still make it inside the eleven-hour limit. An average of seven minutes a kilometre would see him home with a bit to spare.

As James fell yet further behind the leaders, Ryan, pushing on right behind him, moved out wide to overtake. As the two men became level their eyes met. Recognition dawned on both faces. Each tensed, waiting for a reaction from the other. James spoke first.

'You're a lucky bastard,' he snarled in between deep breaths. 'If this had been any other time I'd have given you a bloody good hiding for the shit you got me into.'

Ryan clenched his fists in an effort to control his own temper. He remembered the slap that Gayle had received from this guy. His desire to lash out was equally strong. It took a supreme effort to control himself.

IN THE LONG RUN

'Any time you like,' he responded, his harsh tone surprising James. Ryan looked with derision at the other's laboured pace. 'I'll see you at the finish. That is if you ever make it there.'

Having slowed down for a few moments, he then got back into his proper stride. Rapidly Kirkpatrick was left behind.

James glared viciously at his ongoing figure. 'I should have hit you harder,' he growled. 'If I get another chance you won't be able to run like that for a while. That's a promise.'

*

The gentle slope down into Pinetown came as a huge relief to Armstrong. He was still keeping going as best he could, but the ascent up Cowies Hill had left him feeling horribly weak. Fordyce and his followers were steadily drawing further and further ahead. Apart from this strange dizziness which refused to go away, he was now suffering from the occasional spasm of stomach cramp. Also his legs seemed to have nothing like their normal power. How he wished that he had arranged to meet up with Mister Douglas somewhere earlier in the race. His coach would surely know what to do.

Both of them, confident of his ability, had decided on Hillcrest as the first meeting point. Piet had commented on this at the time, suggesting that it was too far from the start. Eventually he had been talked around. 'It's only just over thirty kilometres,' Douglas had said. 'The lad will do that easily. There's plenty of refreshment points before then, so he'll not be wanting for anything. And by the time he gets to Hillcrest I'll have a good idea as to how the race will develop. I can advise him accordingly.'

And so Hillcrest it was. To Armstrong now, the next fifteen kilometres suddenly seemed a very long way indeed. But he had to get there, he told himself. And he had to do it without letting the leaders get too far ahead. Mechanically he continued. The huge crowds in Pinetown spurred him on. One large group of Africans, as if seeing the distress in him, chanted in chorus as he passed by: '*Amandla! Amandla!*'

They were calling on him to have strength. Armstrong responded with a tired wave and a pale imitation of his usual smile. Apart from his physical problems, he was now also feeling huge embarrassment at what these onlookers must think of him. Surely nobody dropped out of the race this early. It was a combination of pride, determination, and the crowd's encouragement that kept him going. He must not disgrace himself. If only he knew what was wrong? As he left Pinetown behind, the sickness started. It was violent and sudden. Armstrong spent five minutes retching onto the side of the road. He tried to draw comfort from this. Maybe that will help, he told himself hopefully. Perhaps he had now gotten rid of something bad inside. He grabbed a drink of water to help rinse the foul taste from his mouth. It made him feel slightly better.

Field's Hill then towered before him.

At the top of Field's Hill the Fordyce group continued to move smoothly along some eight minutes behind the surprise leader, a virtually unknown African, Elphas Ndlozi. The pace he was setting was murderously fast. Amongst those still with Fordyce at this stage were Bester, Tjale, and Meicklejohn. Ahead of them were Page, and Durban's ever consistent van Staden. Running alongside van Staden was the aptly named African, Jetman Msutu. Two years previously van Staden had guided Msutu to his first gold medal. It appeared that today Msutu was again adopting the same policy of sticking with and listening to the advice of the seasoned Durban shopkeeper.

Tactics would play a large part amongst the top competitors, and none was better at this game than Fordyce. In the past he had been quoted as saying that the real race did not begin until the last thirty kilometres. That it was important not to leave all your energy behind in the hills of the previous sixty. At the same time it had been consistently demonstrated in the past that it was fatal to try and take on the King of the Comrades in the closing stages. He had invariably proven to have more in reserve than anyone else. Many now thought that the only realistic way to beat him — if there was a way — was from the front. That was the theory. Whether anyone could successfully put that theory into practice today remained to be seen.

As every year, the crowds at Hillcrest were particularly large and noisy. With the leading runners due soon, the party atmosphere was growing by the minute. In common with many other small communities, Hillcrest possessed a fierce pride in all things local. Black or white, small child or pensioner, this was a day for the whole village to turn out and show the runners, plus the watching millions on South African TV, what sort of show Hillcrest could put on.

IN THE LONG RUN

A little surprisingly for such a small place, Hillcrest boasted a large and successful running club of its own. The Villagers, as they were known, had over two hundred members entered into this year's race, a figure exceeded by only four big city clubs. Current champion Sam Tshabalala had close links with the Villagers and could be certain of a big welcome as he passed through their banner festooned main street. Aside from his normal popularity he was running this year in support of the Zamdela Children's Welfare fund. This quiet and religious man stood to earn over fifty thousand Rand for the charity should he pass through twelve specified checkpoints within the required times.

The car park and forecourt of the Hillcrest Hotel were packed solid with festive spectators. Many already had their own *braais* sizzling with food. Numerous crates of beer, several already empty, testified that it was not only the competitors who got thirsty during the exhausting duration of the Comrades.

Directly opposite this gathering, on the other side of the main road, the du Toit family and Neil Douglas waited for Armstrong's arrival. Twice Douglas had crossed over to the hotel to check Armstrong's progress on the TV there. Both times he'd returned with a confident grin. 'Aye, he doing OK,' he said on each occasion.

Michelle frowned but said nothing.

Now, with the leading runners due to appear at any time, Douglas checked the contents of the cool bin resting by his feet. Six bottles of the boy's favourite glucose were inside. Armstrong would certainly need one by the time he arrived. It was turning out to be far hotter than forecast.

'He'll not be long now,' the coach predicted. There was a confident note to his voice.

Halfway up Field's Hill Armstrong finally staggered to a halt. For the last ten minutes he had been reduced to a laboured walk. Now even that was too much. His young face twisted in anguish and bemusement. Yet again he asked himself what was wrong? Every time he took a drink it just came straight back up again. The stomach cramps were now unbearable. He reeled around in a precarious full circle. Runners in their ones and two — he lost count of how many — streamed up the hill and then passed him. He gazed forlornly up to the sky. His eyes, already stinging badly from running sweat, were immediately caught in the glare of the now fully risen sun. Almost at once the dizziness increased.

One of the accompanying recovery vehicles paused. 'Do you want to get in?' the driver asked. His voice sounded a long way off. Armstrong waved him away.

'I must get to Hillcrest,' he mumbled. The vehicle moved slowly on, although he was aware that the attendant in the back was still watching him. They can't make me stop yet, Armstrong told himself. But all the same he should do something to convince them that he was fit to continue. He began to move forward again in a torturously slow and stumbling run. The effort needed was enormous — he felt as if a powerful adhesive had been placed on the sole of each running shoe. After fifty metres he was forced to pull up once more.

His own heartbeat thudded against his eardrums. Everything was now a blur. Then, from somewhere deep inside his head, a whirring noise started. The noise was getting steadily faster and louder – faster and louder – faster and louder. As the sound reached its final crescendo Armstrong pitched forward onto the grass verge, completely unconscious.

IN THE LONG RUN

CHAPTER TWELVE

The excitement in Hillcrest grew to an even greater pitch as the first runner appeared. It was the early leader Ndlozi who was continuing to set the pace — and what a pace it was. Seven minutes elapsed before the next two men, van Staden and Msutu, still side by side, followed him through. The lone figure of Mark Page, looking strong and full of running, was a couple of minutes behind these two.

A whole procession of runners, rapidly increasing in frequency and numbers then gave the Hillcrest crowds plenty to shout about. Fordyce and his followers received a special cheer from the Hillcrest Hotel army. The race legend responded with a wave and a brief smile. But was this a sign of confidence from the eight-times winner? He was already a good way behind. There was some hard work ahead if he was to make up ground.

As Fordyce disappeared into the distance, Douglas and Piet exchanged glances. Where was Armstrong? He should at least have been in sight by now. They continued to wait. After thirty minutes their puzzlement had turned to increasing concern. Only Michelle appeared unperturbed.

'I guess he's not as good as you thought he was,' she said with a slight smile.

Her father studied her closely for several seconds. He then turned to Douglas. 'What should we do?' he asked.

The coach's frown deepened. 'Something is obviously wrong. I'll head back down the road and try to find out what. The rest of you stay right here just in case I miss the lad along the way. Don't move until I get back or you get a message from me. OK?'

Piet nodded his agreement. 'We'll be here,' he promised.

*

Ryan pushed steadily on to the top of Field's Hill. Just ahead he could see that David and Gayle were standing in exactly the arranged spot. Each waved as he approached. He pulled up and accepted the bottle held out to him.

'What did you say this concoction of yours was called?' he asked David, looking at the container with mild suspicion.

'A Corpse Reviver. Glucose, salt, sugar, bicarbe and lemonade. Get it down, it'll do you good I promise.'

Ryan drank a little and then grunted in approval. 'It seems OK.'

Gayle consulted her watch. 'One hour fifty minutes so far.' She turned to David. 'That's pretty good isn't it?'

'Yes, not bad at all. Especially considering how far back he started.' He gave Ryan an encouraging slap on the shoulder. 'Keep up this pace and you'll get a silver medal no trouble.'

Ryan had never revealed to either the true level of his athletic achievements. He could see now how much he was surprising David with his performance. This knowledge gave him a mischievous kick and provided just the lift he needed to spur him on.

'A silver medal eh,' he remarked. 'That would be nice.'

'Just don't get too confident,' David warned. 'There's a hell of a way to go yet. And a lot more hills to come.'

Ryan took another swig from his drink before asking: 'How far is Fordyce ahead?'

The question brought a laugh from David. 'Listen to him? Tell him he might get a silver medal and he wants to take on Fordyce.'

He consulted a notebook. 'If you must know he's about fourteen minutes in front of you by now. So if you think you can catch him you'd better get moving. We'll see you at the halfway point at Drummond. If you keep going as you are you should get there in around an hour and a half.'

Gayle moved closer, prompting Ryan to give her a quick kiss.

'No time for that,' David chastised. He clapped his hands sharply twice.

His ex-fiancée pulled a face. 'He's only jealous because *he's* never managed to win a silver. You show him how it's done Steve.'

Ryan winked at her. 'See you both at Drummond then.'

IN THE LONG RUN

He set off once more and was soon back into an easy stride. In spite of the heat and humidity he was now feeling confident about his chances. There was a definite feel-good factor building up inside. He smiled to himself. And why not? Within a few hours all this crazy involvement with Parker would be behind him. He would then be in the clear to pursue his relationship with Gayle; a relationship that was without doubt getting better all the time. And to top this special day off, there was also an evening with the reprieved Manelli to look forward to. Tonight would be a celebration meal for many reasons, although thankfully the singer would never be aware of them all. Yes, Ryan decided, life at present was not so bad after all. He had a lot to be thankful for.

Still full of running, he put his head down and made for Drummond.

*

Neil Douglas made his way quickly back along the race course. He was totally baffled over Armstrong's non-appearance. The lad was so fit and strong. The thirty-two kilometres to Hillcrest should have been a doddle for him. It must be an injury of some kind, he decided. Never once in all the training they had done together had Armstrong ever complained of even a slight muscle strain. For something like that to happen today of all days was the worst kind of luck imaginable.

Douglas was well aware of all the medical centres set up at various points along the route. There was one about ten kilometres back, just by the top of Field's Hill. It seemed an obvious place to start. If Armstrong *was* injured, then that was the most likely place he would be receiving treatment. All the time keeping a sharp lookout for his charge, Douglas pressed on through the crowds.

The first thing that Armstrong became aware of was his horizontal position. Then he noticed the drip tube inserted into his left arm. Where was he? He groaned and tried to take in his surroundings. There was a man in a white coat nearby. His back was turned. At the sound of Armstrong's stirring the man looked over his shoulder and smiled.

'Ah!' he exclaimed. 'So you're with us at last.'

Armstrong groaned again. 'What happened?'

His eyes then widened as he touched the tube. 'What's this for?' He felt weak and at a loss to understand. Surely he should still be running, not wasting time lying here. He did not remember finishing the race. What would Mister Douglas think of him?

Seeing the alarm on the boy's face, the man moved closer to place a reassuring hand on his shoulder. 'Take it easy,' he said gently. 'You dehydrated and collapsed, but you'll be fine if you just relax now.'

'Armstrong looked at him blankly. 'Dehydrated?'

'Loss of body fluids,' the man explained. He pointed to the suspended drip bottle. 'This is putting some back for you.'

Armstrong gave a deep sigh and closed his eyes. He had heard of this happening to other people, but it had never been a problem for him. Mister Douglas had always made sure of that.

'I don't get dehydration,' he said simply, as if it were a disease he was immune to.

'Well you've got it today,' he was told.

After a few moments thought Armstrong asked: 'How long must I stay here? I have to get back running soon.'

The doctor laughed. 'I don't think that you'll be doing any more running today.' He glanced at the bottle. 'Your drip should take another half hour or so.'

Armstrong could not believe what he was hearing. What did this doctor mean? Of course he had to run some more. Another thought then struck him. He tried to look at his watch but the tube in his arm made this difficult. 'How long have I been here?' he asked. For all he knew, many hours may have passed by. The race may even already be over.

'About forty-five minutes.'

The boy's head fell back in relief. So there was still time. He did not care what this doctor said. He would get back in the race somehow. Even if his chance of winning was now gone, he must at least make it to the finish in time. If he did not manage that he would be letting everybody down even more than he had done already.

Mistaking Armstrong's sudden relaxation as acceptance of the situation, the doctor gave a sympathetic smile. 'There's always next year,' he said encouragingly. 'You just relax for now and I'll come back later. There's quite a few like you that need attention today.' He hurried off, leaving Armstrong to his thoughts.

The youngster knew without moving that he was still very weak. All his earlier distress was now coming back to him. Why, he continued to ask himself? What was causing all these problems? He looked once more at the drip. Maybe when the bottle was empty he would have more strength?

IN THE LONG RUN

Rapidly he did some mental arithmetic. If he stayed here another thirty minutes like the man said, he would still have nearly two-and-a-half hours to get to Drummond before the cut off. If he could only manage that, then he would somehow make it to the finish. He had to. With a sigh he lay back and waited.

*

A similar thought about getting to Drummond was passing through James' head at roughly the same time. Even though he had walked up for most of the way, Field's Hill had still taken its toll. His legs felt lead-heavy, his knee joints stiff and painful. He forced himself along at a slow jog, well aware that if he were to preserve energy by walking up all of the major hills, then he sure as heck needed to keep running most of the way between them.

Try as he might, he could not prevent himself from dwelling on the possibility that he may have contracted Aids. Even though the chances were probably small, the spectre of the virus hovered over his head like some malevolent vulture waiting for its victim to die. And all for what? Some tart he normally would not look at twice. He should have strangled the bitch when he had the chance.

Anger alternated with logic. There's nothing you can do for the moment, he kept telling himself. Forget about it until tomorrow. Concentrate on the race. His mind was like a lock gate, one minute wide open and flooded with doubt, the next closed to everything but the increasing pain and task in hand. He had to make it to Maritzburg for his mother's sake — and his own. If he never achieved anything else in life, this was to be his one gesture of serious intent. Should his father reconsider because of his efforts — great. If not, well fuck him. He wasn't doing it for him any longer.

With this jumble of tortured thoughts endlessly revolving around in his head, James pressed painfully on.

*

The doctor removed the drip tube, allowing Armstrong to get hesitantly to his feet. Cautiously he flexed his leg muscles before drawing several deep breaths.

'Remember, take it easy for a while,' the medic instructed. He handed Armstrong a small packet of dextrose tablets. 'Take two of these every hour or so, they'll help give you back some energy.'

GEORGE STRATFORD

The youngster popped a couple of the tablets into his mouth and stored the remainder in his shorts pocket. 'Thank you,' he said, his smile a little more like normal.

'And remember, no more running for a day or two,' the doctor stated firmly. Despite his stern expression, he was quite warming to Armstrong. The sharpness in his warning was only to ensure that the boy did nothing more to endanger himself. 'Have you got someone who can pick you up?' he asked next.

Armstrong nodded. 'My friends and Mister Douglas my coach are just down the road at Hillcrest. They'll look after me.' He knew better than to argue over his continuing the race. The people here had been kind, but they would never understand his reasons. Almost certainly they would try to prevent him. It would be far better to say nothing and just get on with things.

The doctor looked doubtful. 'Perhaps I should arrange for a vehicle to take you there.'

Armstrong's heart sank. That was the last thing he wanted. He was now feeling much better and far more confident that he could complete the course.

Fate, in the shape of a nurse, then took a hand. 'Excuse me Doctor,' she said, hurrying over to them. 'There's someone over here I think you should look at straight away.'

The man gave Armstrong one final look. 'We'll talk again in a minute,' he said before moving off with the nurse.

Armstrong's eyes followed him. The doctor was soon preoccupied with his new patient. He probably would be for some while. Now was the time to make a move.

He slipped out of the exit and back onto the road.

Apart from the crowd milling around outside, a constant stream of runners was still passing by. Several were pulling up for minor treatments before continuing. No one took any great notice as one more competitor simply rejoined the race.

Still not yet nine o'clock, and less than three hours into the race, the leading runners passed through the halfway point at Drummond, a standard marathon already behind them.

Also behind them were many of the worst hills, although still to be faced almost immediately was the formidable challenge of Inchanga. Finally, just over thirty kilometres further on, the infamous and dreaded Polly Shorts awaited them. These two aside, much of the remaining course would be gentle compared to the

IN THE LONG RUN

almost continuous climbing of the first half. Easing conditions further, the humidity level had now dropped to a less oppressive seventy per cent.

The early leader, Ndlozi, as expected had now dropped back, unable to sustain his searing pace any longer. Gradually he had been reeled in and then engulfed by the tidal wave of pursuers.

Mark Page had by now worked his way up to join the seemingly inseparable Boysie van Staden and Jetman Msutu. It was these three who were first past the halfway mark. The rest of the field was not that far behind. Figuring strongly were Shaun Meiklejohn, looking more like Bruce Fordyce than ever with his swept back fair hair and dark glasses, and the ungainly shuffling but highly effective Hoseah Tjale.

Barely a minute behind these two, and almost inevitably beginning to close, came the great champion with the remains of his bus. These included Nic Bester and the big surprise package so far, Meshack Radebe, a twenty-nine year old first time runner.

Conspicuous by their absence at this stage were the Frenchman, Bellocq, and the current champion Sam Tshabalala. The latter, though, still well on schedule for his charity fund-raising effort.

The never ending procession of runners continued to pour through Drummond, most mentally preparing themselves for yet another long, hard uphill slog. This time Inchanga.

Armstrong resumed the race at a steady twelve kilometres an hour, well below his normal pace but still sufficient to get him through Drummond before the five and a half hour cut off point. He had a bad feeling that he was not yet free of whatever had caused him his problems. For that reason he did not push himself too hard. All he could hope for now was to complete the course before the final gun. After having started with high hopes of a gold medal, a bronze one was little enough with which to repay everyone for their faith. The shame, should he fail to achieve even this, was unthinkable.

Without warning, after around thirty minutes running, he was struck by a violent stomach spasm. The sheer unexpectedness of the attack caused him to gasp out loud and pull up. The pressure from his bowels was immediately intense. He needed a toilet badly.

Temporary closets were scattered all along the route. With massive relief Armstrong spotted a line of these a short distance ahead. He made for them as fast as his condition would allow.

The first one he came to was vacant. He dived inside and disappeared from sight.

GEORGE STRATFORD

Two minutes later Neil Douglas hurried by, his eyes constantly scanning the passing runners in his search for the boy.

It was fully ten minutes before Armstrong emerged. More time had been lost, but at least his stomach pains had eased. He set off again at the same earlier pace. There was no panic yet. His thoughts turned once more to the waiting group in Hillcrest. By now they would be getting very worried about him. With not far to go he now wanted to get there as quickly as possible, just to reassure them that he was OK.

A dark cloud then developed. What could he say to them? How could he explain his failure when he did not understand it himself? Would they perhaps feel that he had already let them down too badly and lose interest in him?

With a mixture of embarrassment and trepidation, he entered the village outskirts.

Claudine was the first to spot him. 'Here he comes,' she shouted out. Piet's eyes followed her pointed finger and locked on to the approaching figure. Even from this distance he could see that Armstrong's step was slow and laboured. Whatever problem had held him up, he must still be suffering from it. Cecile put his thoughts into words as three pairs of sympathetic eyes tracked Armstrong's movements. Only Michelle seemed unmoved.

As the boy pulled up alongside them Piet could see the pain in his eyes. Not just the physical stress, but something more that went much, much deeper. An uncertainty — no, it was a dread — of what they would think of him now.

The Afrikaner put a protective arm around his shoulders. 'What's wrong?' he asked gently. 'You can tell me.'

Armstrong's large eyes dropped to the road in abject humiliation. 'I'm sorry Boss,' he mumbled. 'I got sick and slowed down.' He face began to twitch. For a moment it seemed likely that he would cry with the shame of his performance. 'I'm sorry,' he repeated.

'Don't worry Armstrong,' Michelle chipped in brightly. 'I'm sure that Dad will still let you do the garden for us.'

Piet rounded furiously on his eldest daughter. It was easy to see that she was untouched by Armstrong's plight. If anything, she seemed to be drawing a fair amount of satisfaction from it.

'Shut up,' he told her.

Michelle's bottom lip jutted out. 'I was only trying to cheer him up,' she said.

IN THE LONG RUN

Piet gave her a withering look before turning back to Armstrong. 'What do you mean, you got sick?' His tone was full of compassion. 'How bad was it? Maybe you should pack it in now?'

The youngster looked up, his eyes growing wider than ever. 'No Boss!'

There was panic in his voice. Apart from what he owed the du Toits, he was also representing his family and the township of Shakaville. Zulu's never gave up. If he did so now he would never be able to face the people at home.

And then there was his coach. What would Mister Douglas think if he quit at the first sign of trouble? 'Where is Mister Douglas?' he asked, suddenly aware that his coach was not there.

Claudine took Armstrong by the hand and looked up at him. 'He went back to look for you. He was worried — we all were.'

Her spontaneous gesture of affection touched him deeply. He swallowed hard and smiled at the young girl. 'I'm OK now,' he said.

There was no point in telling them the truth, he considered. His earlier fears of rejection had been removed. It was plain that they still cared for him. If he mentioned what the doctor had said then the Boss might well order him to stop. That was unthinkable. His eye caught Michelle's and she looked quickly away. He did not understand her. She had been nice to him last night, now it was more like before; as if she resented his presence.

This thought was interrupted as Piet handed him a drink from the cold bin. Gratefully he swallowed half the bottle in one long swig.

'Are you absolutely sure you're all right to carry on? Piet asked. He gave the youth a long, searching look.

Armstrong nodded vigorously. The action sent beads of sweat flying from his hair and face. 'I'm good now Boss,' he assured him. 'I'll finish, no trouble.'

Piet continued to study his face. There was no doubt that the boy appeared to be in a better state of mind now than when he first arrived. It was his physical condition that concerned him more. This wasn't like Armstrong at all. He was normally so full of energy.

'If you're sure then,' he said, still not entirely convinced. But he could see how important it was to the youngster that he continue. It would be cruel to deny him that chance if he was now honestly getting over his problems.

The normally quiet Cecile stepped in. 'Look at me Armstrong,' she said softly. 'I know that you always tell me the truth. Do you promise me that you feel well enough?'

A small tremor of guilt made Armstrong blink. It was true, he had never lied to her before. All the same, he could not stop the race now. It was far too important. 'I'm good,' he promised Cecile. He met her gaze for only a brief time before shifting his eyes.

It was enough however to convince Piet. He gave Armstrong a pat on the back. 'Go on then,' he told him. 'Just don't worry about where you finish. We'll all be proud of you anyway.'

These words had an instant effect on the youngster. It was exactly what he needed to hear. His slightly sagging shoulders straightened up and he flashed one of his broad smiles. He finished his drink almost with a flourish.

'See you all later,' he said, raising both arms briefly in a gesture of joy and relief.

Michelle watched as he rejoined the race. There was a heavy frown on her young features.

Neil Douglas entered the medical centre. After finding no sign of Armstrong along the route, his concern was now rapidly rising.

There were several stricken runners about – casualties suffering everything from torn muscles to mild cramp. A strong smell of liniment hung in the air. He took a long, careful look around. There was no sign of the lad. So where the devil was he, Douglas pondered? A doctor passed close by. He stepped across into the medic's path.

'Excuse me.'

The doctor paused and regarded his a shade impatiently. He was busy and could see at a glance that this man was not in need of any medical attention.

'Have you seen a young lad in here?' Douglas asked. He went on to describe Armstrong and relate his race number.

The doctor's expression changed. 'Yes, I treated him myself for dehydration. I put him on a drip and gave him some dextrose tablets. He was actually unconscious for a short while after they brought him in.'

Douglas could not believe what he was hearing. Armstrong unconscious! 'So where is he now?' he demanded.

'That's what I'd like to know too.' The doctor frowned. 'I'll tell you one thing though, he's in absolutely no condition to continue running. I thought he'd accepted that fact.'

He paused. 'Who are you anyway? Are you the Mister Douglas the boy spoke about?'

IN THE LONG RUN

The Scot became more impatient. 'Aye, that's right. But what happened when he left here? Which way did he head?'

'I told the young man that I would arrange a lift for him to Hillcrest. Unfortunately I then got called away. When I returned he had disappeared. Naturally I assumed that he had met up with you.'

'No, I've not seen the lad at all. There's no sign of him on the road, running or walking.'

A serious look crossed the doctor's face. 'I sincerely hope that he is not attempting to run again. That would be extremely foolish after his earlier collapse.'

Douglas was only too well aware of the dangers attached to dehydration. He was also very well aware of Armstrong's determination that could sometimes reach incredibly stubborn proportions.

'Exactly how bad was he?' he asked.

The medic sighed. 'Put it this way. If he were stupid enough to try and complete the course, I for one would certainly not want to be responsible for his condition when they pick him up off the road again.' He mopped his brow as if to make a point. 'Especially in these conditions.'

The Scot said nothing as his mind worked. Surely if Armstrong had resumed running then he would have spotted him on the way down here? But what if they had somehow missed each other? It would be so typical of the lad to press on regardless of the consequences.

'The thing is,' the doctor continued, 'he might feel well enough for a short while after the treatment. Enough perhaps to be lulled into a false sense of security. But after that he could be heading for serious trouble.'

'How serious exactly?'

The Scot's question was met with a non-committal shrug. 'Not everyone is the same of course. People have different levels of resistance. Looking on the worst side though, it is no exaggeration to say that further severe stress on the body could quite possibly be fatal.'

Douglas stared at the doctor for several moments. 'Where's the nearest telephone?' he demanded.

GEORGE STRATFORD

CHAPTER THIRTEEN

The three leaders, van Staden, Msutu, and Page, arrived at the bottom of Inchanga still close together. Van Staden was a strong, steady runner, not given to any great turns of speed. The long and arduous Comrades route suited his style perfectly. With seventeen race medals to his name, including four golds, he was well acquainted with what was required for success in this event. In 1988 he and Msutu had run side by side for virtually the entire race. Then, the vastly more experienced Durban athlete had coaxed and advised Msutu all the way home. It resulted in the African gaining his first ever gold medal. Today was looking as if history may repeat itself.

Quite suddenly Page decided to make a break. Increasing the pace he moved rapidly up Inchanga's steep slope. Msutu hesitated briefly and then went after him. All three runners were aware that Fordyce was now only a few minutes behind and possibly poised for his legendary drive over the latter part of the race. Van Staden let the other two go. He was not suited to fast breaks like this. It crossed his mind that Msutu had made a bad mistake in pursuing Page. That perhaps the African would have been better off staying with him as before. He gave a small shrug. Time would tell.

*

The African waiter from the Hillcrest Hotel ran across the road and then paused to survey the host of faces in front of him. He had been told that the man he wanted would be standing in the crowd just about here.

IN THE LONG RUN

'Mister du Toit,' he called out, feeling a touch embarrassed as people looked at him. 'Is Mister du Toit here?'

Piet heard the call and identified himself. Relieved that he had fulfilled his task so easily, the waiter lost some of his self-conscious air.

'There's a telephone call for you at reception,' he said, pointing to the hotel. 'The man said it's very urgent.'

Together they hurried through the packed forecourt and into the hotel. The girl behind the reception desk handed Piet the phone.

'Is that you Piet?' Douglas' voice sounded agitated.

'Yes. What's up?'

'Has Armstrong been through yet?'

'Yes, about twenty minutes ago. We're just waiting for you to get back.'

Douglas swore. As concisely as possible he then related his conversation with the doctor. Piet listened with growing alarm.

'Armstrong seemed pretty sure he was OK to continue,' he said as Douglas finished. 'We wouldn't have let him go on otherwise.'

The Scot made an impatient noise. 'Aye, but it will catch up on him shortly. If he's not stopped there's no telling what damage he could do to himself. You know as well as I do how stubborn he can be. He won't ever willingly quit.'

'I'll drive ahead and try to catch him,' Piet suggested. 'If I can make it to Drummond quickly then I'll be able to stop him before too much harm is done.'

'Aye, you do that. I'll get a lift from someone here. If I don't meet up with you before, I'll see you at the stadium in Maritzburg. Just make sure that you stop the lad as soon as possible. He'll do what you tell him Piet, even if he doesn't like it very much.'

As he hung up, Piet prayed that it would be as simple as it sounded.

'I don't bloody well believe it!'

Piet very rarely swore, especially in front of his family. On this occasion however he could not contain his anger and frustration. A field close to the main road had been set aside as a temporary car park. His Toyota, placed correctly in a designated space near the centre, was completely blocked in. There wasn't a hope of getting it out without at least two of the offending vehicles first being shifted.

Angrily he made a note of their registration numbers.

*

Ryan passed through Drummond in three hours, twenty-one minutes. It was by far his slowest ever time for a marathon, but he was pleased nonetheless. With the same distance again to go, he felt that he had conserved himself pretty well. What happened from now on of course was a trip into the unknown.

Even before arriving at the halfway point Ryan had decided not to stop this time when he saw Gayle and David. As he approached them he signalled that they should have his drink ready. Without so much as breaking stride he took it from David's outstretched hand. Now that he was on a roll he had no intention of losing the rhythm. The expression on his second's face was especially gratifying. There was a definite look of surprise. Obviously David had expected him to be weakening by now. It was almost certainly unintentional on the South African's part, but the guy did have a disturbing habit of making others feel a touch inadequate.

He carried on for several metres before looking back briefly and waving. Gayle said something to David and then burst out laughing, leaving her ex-fiancé with a rueful look on his face. This increased Ryan's pleasure. He might not possess the guy's overwhelming confidence, or his good looks come to that, but he sure as heck could show him how to run. He checked himself. 'Don't get too smug,' he murmured under his breath. There was a long way yet to go.

*

One hour, forty minutes later Armstrong laboured through the same halfway point. He had made it with just under half an hour to spare.

Several times he had been forced to stop with a recurrence of his earlier bowel problem. No matter how much he drank he seemed incapable of retaining any of these valuable fluids. All passed straight through his system. It had to be something bad he'd eaten, he told himself. There was no other explanation.

Every so often, usually after one of these delays, he would begin to feel slightly better. Each time though the cycle would soon repeat itself. Tiredness, stomach cramps, and recently now, the dizziness was returning. He pressed on, resolutely trying to shut all this from his mind.

Once again the road began to rise sharply as Armstrong encountered the early stages of Inchanga. It was now a case of just putting one foot in front of the other at little more than walking pace. Only his superb physical conditioning and the natural strength in his legs kept him going up the vicious climb. He reached the top totally exhausted — his head swimming with the latest bout of dizziness. Much as he hated

IN THE LONG RUN

to, he knew that he would have to stop here for a short while to regain some strength.

A short way ahead he could make out another competitor flopped out face downward on the side of the road. The figure looked to be in a similar or even worse condition than himself. Armstrong had heard many stories of how, in the past, distressed runners had helped and encouraged each other over the latter stages of this cruel and demanding course. Perhaps, he considered, he and this runner ahead could draw some strength from each other in the same way. He sank down onto the grass verge beside the prone figure. He waited for perhaps a minute as, hypnotised almost by the rhythmically heaving shoulders of the man's shoulders, he first tried to clear his head. Tentatively he reached out and touched the figure on the back. 'Are you alright?'

James Kirkpatrick groaned and lifted his head. A contemptuous scowl then formed on his face. A bloody kaffir — that's all he needed.

'Of course I'm not you stupid bastard,' he snarled. 'Just fuck off and leave me alone.'

Armstrong regarded him woodenly. He recognised James immediately as the one who had barged past him at the start. Of all the people to come across, why this one? His stubborn streak then came out. 'I'm just as bad as you man,' he told James. 'I need to rest too, so I'm not going anywhere for a while.'

'Suit your bloody self then.' James dropped his head back down. 'Just don't waste your breath talking to me.' He then reverted back to his own bleak thoughts. He was never going to make it. Every muscle in his body was screaming with pain. The ten-minute break had done little to revive him. How he'd got up Inchanga he'd never know.

Once again the Aids thing crawled back into his mind. How the hell could he ever tell his mother if the worst did materialise? He recalled his last conversation with her. Her final words. 'Please I beg of you, try for me. Try very hard.'

'I did Mum. I just couldn't do it,' he found himself murmuring.

Armstrong, still hurt and angry at the man's earlier response, thought he was being spoken to. His curiosity got the better of him and he leaned closer. 'I can't hear you,' he said warily. 'What did you say?'

Such was the depth of James' despair, he did not even hear this. All his mother's words were now repeating themselves painfully inside his head. 'How I pray for the day when you can learn the value of tolerance and achieve something of worth. Today might just be the start of that.'

But it was not going to be. He had let her down even in this.

GEORGE STRATFORD

This final admission of failure was the bitter end for James. Everything inside him briefly collapsed, only to well up moments later with a huge, choking rush of emotion. The loss of his inheritance, the Aids risk, and most of all, his mother's anguish. For the first time since he was a child, James cried. At first he tried to hold it back. And then suddenly it didn't matter any more. The trickle of tears turned into great sobs of despair.

Armstrong, now embarrassed, drew back. He did not know what to say or do. Perhaps he should just leave? Time was getting on anyway, and after what had been said to him, why should he concern himself? Didn't he have enough problems of his own? Then the more dominant side of his nature took over. It was distressing to see someone so upset. Perhaps it was only this man's anguish that had made him so abusive, he reasoned. Maybe he would hang around a little longer.

Slowly James' sobbing grew less. With a rush he then remembered where he was. He raised his head to look once more at the black boy.

'Are you still here?'

It was meant to be a biting comment, but somehow it did not come out like that. To Armstrong it sounded more like a cry for help.

'Are you feeling better now?' he asked.

It was on the tip of James' tongue to tell him to mind his own bloody business. He bit the remark back and thought for a moment. Briefly he saw his mother's face. Was there a chance he could still make it to Maritzburg? He would certainly need someone to lean on — it didn't matter who. If this kaffir could fit the bill, why not use him? Somehow he would force himself to be civil to the boy. He could always dump him if someone better came along.

James forced the semblance of a smile. 'I still don't feel so good,' he said.

Warmed by this response, Armstrong relaxed a little. 'Me neither,' he admitted. 'But I'm going to make it. Are you coming with me?'

James had a sudden crazy impulse to laugh out loud. Him being led by a black boy! It was crazy. Still, at the moment he sure as heck needed help from somebody. 'I'm coming,' he said. 'Just a couple more minutes.'

Armstrong looked at his watch. 'There's no time,' he said. 'Come on, it's downhill for a way now. You can do it.'

With a deep breath, James got to his feet. He could see that this kaffir would not wait much longer. What the hell are things coming to, he reflected bitterly as they set off down the slope? Now I'm taking orders from the bastards.

IN THE LONG RUN

Piet was becoming more agitated by the minute. It was hopeless trying to locate the two car owners in such a large crowd. They could be anywhere. He had already lost too much valuable time with futile enquiries. As he stood amongst the crowds thinking of what to do next, a small voice beside him piped up.

'You got trouble with cars Mister?' Two African boys, no more than ten years old, were looking at him with wary interest. Piet regarded them back with surprise. Obviously they had been listening to him.

'Do you know who owns these cars?' he asked, showing them the scribbled down registrations. It seemed unlikely, but anything was worth a try.

The boy who had spoken shook his head. 'No, but we can help you if you want.'

Piet was mystified. 'How?'

'Show us the cars, then we talk,' he was told.

He passed a hand across his brow, trying hard to work out what they were up to. 'Look, this is very important,' he said. 'I haven't got time to mess about.'

The youngsters exchanged glances. 'We not mess around,' the second one assured him. The look on his face was deadly serious.

Suddenly understanding dawned on Piet. He shouldn't, not really. But this was an emergency. He bent down so that his face was level with his new companions.

'Are you going to—?' he began quietly.

His small helpers both grinned. 'You've got it,' the first one interrupted.

Piet straightened up and hesitated only a second before cocking his head. 'Come on then.'

Cecile and the two girls were waiting for him at the car park. Michelle, fed up with hanging around, regarded the two boys with exasperation.

'Don't tell me *they* own the cars,' she remarked sarcastically.

Piet ignored her and indicated the two offending vehicles. The boys looked at them and then went into a short conference.

'Ten Rand,' the first one said.

'Each,' added the second.

Cecile looked concerned. 'Why do they want money?'

'You'll see,' Piet told her.

With a rueful grin he pulled out two, ten Rand notes. He handed one over.

'The other when you've done it.'

The boys nodded their agreement and approached a car each. In less than five minutes both had somehow got the driver's door to their respective vehicles open.

GEORGE STRATFORD

'Now we all push,' Piet was instructed as they released the handbrakes.

Cecile was appalled. 'You can't do that!' she exclaimed.

Up until now Piet had had kept the full seriousness of the situation from his family. He had seen no reason to worry them unnecessarily. Now however he had to justify his actions. He explained in more detail just how bad the consequences could be for Armstrong if they did not catch up with him.

Everyone, including Michelle, appeared shocked. It was she who responded first. 'Come on then,' she called out, a slight tremble in her young voice. 'Let's get pushing.

*

It had been a brave and positive break by Mark Page, allowing him to finally pull away from Jetman Msutu just before the seventy kilometre mark. The African was now fading, possibly reflecting that he should have once more stayed with the unspectacular but dependable Boysie van Staden.

Page, still running strongly, now had only one more major obstacle to overcome. The dreaded Polly Shorts. Fordyce was just under three minutes behind, but had the King of the Comrades left his renowned drive for home too late this time? If Page could just keep going as he was until reaching the top, he would then see Pietermaritzburg sprawled out below him. Surely this welcome sight, coupled with the knowledge that there were only seven, mostly downhill kilometres to go, would drive him on to victory.

He started the last major ascent in determined fashion, gritting his teeth as the crowds cheered him on nearly every step of the way. All his reserves of strength and courage were being called upon as his eyes searched longingly for the summit. The sun, now practically at its height, continued to bear down on his unprotected head. Any victory today would be hard won in the most demanding of conditions.

Behind him, Fordyce had been in overdrive for some time, finally shedding the remains of his bus and steadily closing the gap. During this surge he was averaging seventeen kilometres an hour. In the past when climbing Polly Shorts he had actually achieved the impossible by increasing this pace to eighteen kilometres. Never in the long history of the race had any other runner been capable of this. Polly Shorts was not known as Fordyce's killing fields for nothing. The only questions were, after a year off, did the aging master still have it in him? And if he did, how much did Page have left to counter with? Both were to be answered in a very short space of time.

IN THE LONG RUN

Halfway up the hill, after five hours and ten minutes of continuous running,, Mark Page began to walk. Spots floated before his eyes, his head began to swim alarmingly. The curse of dehydration had struck yet again, suddenly and dramatically. Had his supreme effort over the last eighty kilometres all been for nothing? Was he now on the point of collapse? He looked back over his shoulder and there, just coming around the bend and into view, was the sight he dreaded. Fordyce in full flow.

The gap between them had closed to barely a hundred metres when Page reached to the bottom of the well and came up with a response. Mechanically be began to run again in an effort to beat off this challenge. It was brave — in many ways it was heartbreaking. It was also completely futile. The greatest runner the Comrades had ever known had returned, and he wanted his crown back.

Fordyce drew alongside Page and grasped his hand in a gesture of supreme sportsmanship. For several seconds he urged his team mate to try and run with him. Page shook his head and waved him on. He was beaten now and he knew it. All that he could cling to was the hope of second place, or at the very least a gold medal. Surely if there was any justice he would not be denied that? A single thought common to all competitors, whether humble fun runner or athletic star, burned into his brain. 'I have to keep going'. Through hazy vision clouded even more by his own dripping sweat — or was it a small tear? — he watched Fordyce drive on to the crest of Polly Shorts and home.

*

Just over an hour later Ryan arrived at the foot of the same dreaded hill. For the first time in the race he was now feeling genuine strain. Since leaving Drummond he had suffered a couple of mildly bad spells, but had run through them both. This time it was different. The heat and the distance were really getting to him. Never had his legs felt so tired, nor his breathing so difficult. Only now, as he looked up, did he fully appreciate just why this hill was so feared.

The prospect of being forced to walk up at least part of Polly Shorts filled him with dismay. To be reduced to that when so close to the finish would be soul-destroying. In any case, Gayle and David would be waiting at the top. It was their final meeting place along the route. What if they should see him slacking? He knew that his time was still good for a silver medal. To drive himself on he tried to picture David's face when he got to the summit. If his second had been surprised at Drummond, then he would give him an even bigger one this time.

There was a good number of other runners tackling the hill at the same time as himself. The tremendous strain showed on nearly all of their faces. Urging them on, the spectators lining the way were noisy in their encouragement. Several patted Ryan on the back as he passed. He found himself running alongside a man much older than himself. They glanced across at each other. The man grimaced. 'Hard work eh,' he said between deep breaths.

Ryan responded with a tired grin. 'You can say that again.'

In that single short exchange a silent, mutually understood message flashed between them. 'We'll get up this bastard together' it said.

A spectator — a large balding man brandishing a beer bottle — ran a few paces alongside them before finding the effort too great.

'*Hardloop* man! *Vasbyt!*' he shouted after them in Afrikaans.

'What did he say,' Ryan asked his new companion.

'Run hard man. Hold on,' came back the translation.

There were shouts of encouragement like this all the way to the top. Smiling Zulu women, surrounded by their children, danced and clapped to their own songs. Enthusiasm and support was expressed in a hundred different ways, but with one common aim. To urge the runners on. It was a mixture of this atmosphere, the largely unspoken support of his fellow runner, and his own pride that got Ryan to the top without pausing. Admittedly the pace was slow, but he had done it and was justifiably proud of himself.

Gayle, when he saw her, was cheering as loudly as anyone. So, to his surprise, was David. 'That's brilliant man,' he shouted as Ryan once more took his drink on the move. 'You've still got nearly an hour left to get that silver. All you have to do is keep going.'

As they rose over the peak, the veteran by his side spoke. 'What do you think of that for a sight?' he asked.

Way below, Pietermaritzburg and the finish beckoned them. There were only seven kilometres to go.

'Brilliant — bloody brilliant,' Ryan responded.

The very essence of the race, which by now had been well and truly imposed on Ryan, was summed up in that moment. He offered the older man half of his drink, which was gratefully accepted.

'Come on then,' Ryan said as his companion drained the last few drops from the bottle. 'Let's cross that line together.'

IN THE LONG RUN

CHAPTER FOURTEEN

All efforts by the du Toit family to trace Armstrong at Drummond had failed. 'Nobody seems to know whether he's gone through or not,' Piet said after making yet another fruitless enquiry. There was an awkward silence, broken by Michelle.

'What are we going to do now Dad?'

Piet regarded her. She was a funny girl. One minute she gave the impression of not caring about Armstrong at all. Now she appeared to be more concerned than anybody. He put it down to the fickleness of youth. 'I don't know,' he said in answer to her question. He pondered for a moment. 'Perhaps he hasn't got here yet. If he's as bad as Neil says then he's probably still back there somewhere.' He waved a hand helplessly in the direction of Botha's Hill.

'Why don't you walk back along the course and take a look?' Cecile suggested. 'We'll stay here and watch out just in case you miss him.'

'Mr Douglas missed him last time,' Michelle chipped in. 'I'll come with you Dad. Two pairs of eyes are better than one.'

There could be no doubt about her anxiety. The look on her face said it all.

'Thank you Michelle,' Piet responded. This difficult situation was certainly bringing the best out in her, he considered. He began to feel proud of his eldest daughter. In spite of her recent tantrums she was now showing great maturity.

'We'll give it half an hour,' he told his wife. 'If there's no sign by then we'll come back and try in the other direction.'

Cecile took his hand. 'Try not to worry too much. He's a fit boy. He might well have got over his problem by now.'

Piet tried to convince himself that she may be right. He gave her hand a squeeze. 'It's possible I suppose.' Still he hesitated. 'All the same, if we don't find him soon then I think we should maybe contact the police.'

Michelle tugged hard at his free hand. 'Come on Dad. Let's get going.'

*

Bruce Fordyce crossed the finishing line in five hours, forty minutes, twenty-five seconds. It was well short of his record time, but given the abnormal early winter heat and humidity, still a superb performance. The King of the Comrades had returned to prove that he was still the best. Behind him there were some dramatic late surges, resulting in much shuffling of the pack.

Hoseah Tjale, despite his awkward looking style, powered through to claim second place five minutes behind the winner.

Meshack Radebe, in his first Comrades run and for so long Fordyce's shadow, kept going strongly to claim third spot less than half a minute behind Tjale.

The cheers a minute later for Mark Page were tinged with sympathy as he struggled bravely home in fourth place. For so long victory had looked to be his. At least he could console himself with his second gold medal.

Probably the strongest finish of all came from the Frenchman, Bellocq. After barely figuring throughout the race he stormed in, arms aloft, for fifth position. It was an even more incredible performance when one remembered what he had already put his body through during the last two weeks.

Boysie van Staden proved his point to Jetman Msutu by claiming seventh spot and his fifth gold medal. Msutu came in twenty minutes later in twenty-fifth position for a silver.

The remaining solid gold medals of the day were claimed by Ephraim Sekotlong, another clubmate of Fordyce's; the champion's look-alike Shaun Meiklejohn; Gary Turner; and 'Iron Man' Nic Bester. Defending champion Sam Tshabalala came in to a tremendous cheer. Although his thirteenth position meant that he had this year missed out on gold, his time of five hours fifty-five minutes ensured that the children's charity he was representing would receive the maximum amount of fifty thousand Rand.

These were the runners that shared most of the limelight for 1990. But there were still over five hours of the race remaining. There was much drama still to unfold for thousands of people.

IN THE LONG RUN

*

The incongruous pairing of Armstrong and James plodded wearily down the long, flat stretch of road leading away from Cato Ridge. They had now covered sixty kilometres. The race was nearly seven hours old.

Armstrong was going through one of his better periods. Only once had he been forced to stop since meeting up with James, who grateful for the respite, had waited for him. So far the conversation between them had been limited to brief exchanges, all of which had been instigated by Armstrong. James shot a quick look in the youth's direction. It was a silent plea to rest up for a few minutes. Armstrong caught the meaning and shook his head.

'Not now, later,' he said.

It was too much for James to be ordered like this. He stopped running and threw himself on to the grass verge. 'I've had it. With you — and the bloody Comrades. Sod off and leave me if that's what you want.'

Armstrong paused to look down at him. 'One minute then,' he stated quietly.

It was only after taking several deep breaths that James spoke again. 'What is it with you anyway? Why do you care whether I finish or not?'

The boy shrugged. 'Everyone wants to finish.'

'So why is it important to you?'

'Pride,' Armstrong replied simply.

James let out a hollow laugh. 'Is that all? Christ, I wish that was all I had to worry about.'

'You got something else?'

'Nothing I want to tell you about.'

Armstrong shrugged again. 'It must be very important.'

'You could say that.'

'But not so important that it keeps you running now,' Armstrong pointed out. 'Maybe my pride is better eh?'

'What the hell do you know?' James retorted. 'Why don't you just piss off and leave me alone.'

Armstrong ignored this remark. He bent down in an effort to haul James to his feet.

'Come on. We've got to get moving,' he said.

The indignity of being manhandled in such a way was too much for James. His already simmering temper boiled over completely.

'Leave me alone you black bastard,' he shouted, at the same time swinging a tired and clumsy punch.

The blow bounced harmlessly off Armstrong's shoulder. The Zulu then drew back. 'Okay, you stay on your own. I don't want you around now anyway.'

He made to move off. 'You got no guts man.'

James recoiled from this remark. Gutless — that's what his old man had called him. And now he was being called the same by a bloody kaffir. Well he'd show this bastard.

He struggled to his feet, anger momentarily blotting out self-doubts. 'I'll get to Maritzburg before you,' he retorted.

Armstrong regarded him with a blank expression. 'You can try.'

*

Ryan and the veteran he had befriended were on the final kilometre. Steadily they pushed up the slope leading to Jan Smuts Stadium. Crowds on both sides of the street urged them to make one final effort. It had been the same through most of Pietermaritzburg. This support, plus the knowledge that the finish was close at hand, inspired them both to increase their pace slightly. They were almost level with the stadium when a great cheer went up somewhere behind them. Both glanced over their shoulder.

'Looks like the first woman is coming in,' his friend remarked.

Ryan was astounded. 'Already?'

He had never considered the possibility that any woman might be capable of beating him over this course. And yet here was one just a short distance behind. After feeling well satisfied with his performance, he now felt slightly deflated. This soon passed. Instead he found himself staring back at the oncoming figure in total admiration.

'Step on it,' his companion suggested. 'That is unless you want her to beat you.'

Together they entered Jan Smuts Stadium to be greeted by even louder cheers.

From an enclosure reserved for VIP's, Manelli grinned as he saw Ryan come into view. He raised his video camera to record the scene.

The singer had been inside the stadium since just before Fordyce's arrival, enthusiastically recording whatever caught his interest. It should be a great tape, he felt. Steve would almost certainly be interested in seeing himself finish.

IN THE LONG RUN

He would get a copy made for him if it turned out OK.

*

Footsore, Piet and Michelle arrived back at Drummond.

'There's no sign of him anywhere,' Piet sighed to the other two. 'God knows where he is.'

Michelle looked more worried than ever. 'We've got to keep trying Dad,' she urged.

Cecile did her best to be positive. 'He might have recovered better than we imagine after receiving that treatment. And you know how doctors tend to exaggerate. For all we know Armstrong could be way ahead. He might even be close to finishing by now.'

She gave a small laugh to help ease the tension. 'And we won't be there to see it.'

Piet remained doubtful. 'I still think we should talk to the police,' he said. 'They might be able to help.'

'No Dad,' Michelle cut in. 'We don't need the police. We can find him without getting them involved.'

The young girl was badly frightened. Why had it turned out like this, she asked herself yet again? She had never intended for things to go so far. All she had wanted to do was prevent Armstrong from winning the gold medal everyone kept talking about. To slow him down and pay him back for taking up so much of her father's time and attention. How could she know that a simple thing like a laxative could produce such dangerous results? If anything really bad happened to Armstrong and the police found out that she had put those tablets in his drink... She trembled at the thought. The police *must* be kept out of this. They had all sorts of ways of getting to the truth.

Her mother came to her rescue. 'Michelle's right you know. I don't think we should involve the police just yet. We'd look pretty foolish if they did find him at the finish and perfectly all right.'

The fact that Armstrong must have gone through Drummond without a problem some time ago began to sway Piet. And it was true that doctors did have a habit of over-stressing things at times, always leaning heavily on the side of caution.

'There's marshals and pick-up vehicles all along the route,' Cecile continued. 'If anyone is in trouble they are always on hand to help them.'

Piet sighed. 'Okay, we'll leave the police out of it for the time being.' He got into the car. 'Let's try further ahead.'

GEORGE STRATFORD

*

There was a sustained silence as Armstrong and James continued to run side by side. No longer were they together by design. It was just that neither had sufficient energy remaining to pull away from the other. Both were taking on water at every opportunity.

For ten kilometres they had run this way, merely exchanging frequent hostile glances. This silent rivalry made each one even more determined not to be the first to crack. They were now eight hours into the race and had just passed the highest point of their long journey, over eight hundred metres above the sea level of Durban, For both of them, the start there seemed an eternity ago.

At present the going was downhill. But soon they would be arriving at the nightmare of Polly Shorts. Of the two, it was James who doubted his ability to defeat the monster. Armstrong's fierce determination, plus his supreme fitness and strength, had enabled him to partially overcome the distress of his body. Unknowingly he had begun to adopt a form of self-hypnosis, his mind closing itself off completely to anything that might prevent him from achieving his purpose. Perhaps it was a throwback to his warrior ancestors who, before a battle, would frequently convince themselves that they were invincible and could feel no pain. In this condition a man could do things way beyond his normal capabilities. Only in the aftermath of such actions might the consequences become apparent.

In contrast to this, the doubt in James' mind became ever stronger as the dreaded hill grew close. He began to panic. Was it possible to repair the damage done between him and this black boy? There was no way he was going to make it without further support. And the kid did still look reasonably strong. His anger was fading now and he knew that, despite his boast, he would never beat this kaffir. But there was an outside chance that he might still scrape home if he could only persuade the boy that he had not meant what he'd said earlier. It all depended on how gullible he was.

He glanced across at Armstrong and forced a smile. 'Don't you think it's time we called a truce?'

Armstrong looked at him without expression and said nothing.

'Look, I'm very sorry for what I said,' James persisted. 'You don't understand the problems I've got. It makes me bad tempered.'

'That's no reason.'

IN THE LONG RUN

James drew up. 'Please, hold on for a minute and let me explain.' Armstrong continued running. 'Please!' James pleaded after him at the top of his voice.

This time his note of sheer desperation found a mark in the youth. He paused and then walked slowly back. He still wanted to be angry, but he could not deny his softer side.

'Why do you call me a black bastard?' he demanded. 'Why do you hit me when I try to help you? Tell me that.'

James thought rapidly. He would have to come up with a good story, but at least the fool was now listening.

'I'm trying to finish this race for a very special reason,' he began. 'It's for my father — I promised him I would.' He then added the part that he hoped would swing matters. 'He was murdered by some blacks three weeks ago. I suppose I was blaming you for his death.' Almost immediately James could see that he had hit the mark. First shock and then deep sympathy showed on Armstrong's face.

'I'm sorry,' he murmured, his eyes casting downwards. Now he knew why this man had been crying earlier. His heart went out to him. 'We're not all like that,' he added in an attempt to defend his race.

He's hooked, thought James. 'I know that,' he said looking suitably remorseful. 'I shouldn't have taken it out on you.'

Armstrong shuffled his feet in embarrassment. 'I understand.' He then raised his hand in the direction of the road ahead. 'Come on. We'll get there together for your father's sake.'

*

Ryan was still on a high. After almost any race it took him a while to settle down, but today the sense of achievement was greater than ever before. This despite the fact that his time of just over seven hours was less than two minutes faster than Naidene Harrison, the first woman home.

Manelli had sent out an invitation via Kenny for himself, Gayle and David to join him in the VIP enclosure. Ryan turned to the veteran he had run the final stages with. The two runners shook hands warmly.

'Perhaps we may see you again next year?' the older man suggested.

Ryan gave a rueful grin. 'I don't know. Do I really want to go through all that again?'

'That's what nearly everyone says after their first time,' the veteran smiled. 'But most come back anyway. It sort of gets in your blood. Me, I've run twenty Comrades and I still can't give it up.'

Ryan shook his head in admiration as they parted. He turned to Gayle. 'Some guy.'

A thought then struck him. 'Do you know something? We ran together and talked like old friends, and I've only just realised that I didn't even find out his name.'

David overheard and grinned. 'That's the Comrades for you Steve.'

*

The pair of them pulled up at the bottom of Polly Shorts. Absolutely wrecked, James once more flopped in an exhausted heap on to the roadside. Even with this boy's help it now seemed unlikely that he would be able to get himself to the top.

Although not thinking such negative thoughts, Armstrong was also resigned to the fact that he too would have to rest up for a short while before tackling the hill. He dropped down beside James and glanced yet again at his watch. They had two-and-a-quarter hours remaining. Under normal circumstances that would have been sufficient time for him to do it three times over with ease. But these were not normal times. He could see that James was very close to final collapse. Also, now that he had stopped running, he was becoming more aware of his own problems.

For the second time within a few minutes he felt a violent spasm of pain in his right side. As before, he gritted his teeth and waited for it to pass. When the pain did ease, instead of the expected relief, he found himself fighting off wave after wave of fatigue that up until now he had closed his mind to so successfully. For just a few moments his mental defences slipped. How he longed to sleep. Soon he would do just that — he would sleep a whole day if necessary. But only after he had got them both to the finish. In spite of everything, he knew that he could still make it. It was this other man who was the problem. After learning about his father he could not possibly leave him behind. It was not only for his friends and township that he now was acting. It was for all decent black people everywhere.

He looked across at James once more and his heart sank. The man now seemed in an even worse condition than he was before they had rested. 'How do you feel? Are you ready?' he asked, knowing full well the response he would receive. It was true. Now that he had stopped, James had deteriorated to a point where

IN THE LONG RUN

he simply did not care about anything any longer. All his conflicting emotions paled into insignificance compared to how he felt at this moment. He just wanted to lay there and die.

'You go on,' he told Armstrong. 'You can't help me now. I'm going to get into the recovery truck in a minute.'

Armstrong said nothing. He merely placed his hands beneath James' armpits and hauled him slowly to his feet. It was a dead weight. How he managed it when so weak himself he had no idea. James, his body limp, did not even have the strength left to resist him. With both of them in an upright position, Armstrong struggled to steady himself. The weight now leaning against his one side was throwing him off balance. He closed his eyes and softly murmured a prayer in Zulu. A prayer for the strength he would need.

Firmly fixing James' right arm across his own shoulders, Armstrong then set off at a laboriously slow shuffle.

Thirty minutes later they were still barely halfway up the hill. Occasionally James assisted by moving his feet a little. Mostly Armstrong dragged him. Both were in a trance-like state. Every so often James mumbled incoherently.

It was a matter of move a few metres and stop — move a few more and stop again. The man in the recovery vehicle repeatedly asked them if they wanted to quit. Armstrong refused with such violence the final time that the man eventually left them alone. There were plenty of other shattered bodies around who were finding this last great obstacle just too much for them.

After another fifteen minutes of this torture, Armstrong staggered to a halt one final time. This, he knew, was the end. All the willpower in the world could not sustain him any longer. The agony in his side stabbed through him with ever increasing frequency. The pressure, even on his powerful legs, was just too much. He cried out loud with the pain and frustration of his faltering effort. Had it all been for nothing? Was this the finish for them both? What he did know beyond any doubt was that he could not bear to shoulder this man's weight a moment longer. Slowly he sank to his knees and lay James down in the road. The relief was enormous. Still crouched on all fours, Armstrong looked around for the recovery vehicle. He had done all he could. They would now have to pick up his burden after all. Perhaps himself as well.

And then the prayed-for miracle happened. James stirred and suddenly became aware of his surroundings. He looked into the pain-racked face close to his and knew immediately how he had got to this point. It was incredible. This black boy — a bloody kaffir — had actually dragged or carried him to within sight of the top. Why the hell had he done it? What could he possibly hope to gain from such self-sacrifice?

More than half-blinded by dizziness and running sweat, Armstrong sensed as much as saw the recovery in his companion. His parched lips tried to form a smile. His voice was a mere croak. 'Have you had a good rest now?' he asked.

Exactly one hour and five minutes after Armstrong had first lifted James up from the roadside, they reached the top. The final part had been nothing more than a desperately slow walk, but each had made it under his own steam. They now had less than an hour to cover the final seven kilometres.

As the road levelled out and Pietermaritzburg came blessedly into view, James took a deep breath. He knew that he would still be lying there at the bottom of Polly Shorts were it not for this Zulu beside him. Even allowing for the load of bull about his father, he could still not fully understand what had motivated the boy. If his shattered looks were anything to go by, he had now ruined his own chances. And all to help someone who meant absolutely nothing to him. It was crazy.

The situations were now reversed. With over forty-five minutes of little activity behind him, James was now recovering to a small degree. Armstrong, on the other hand, had just about reached the limit of human endurance. It was obvious to James that the boy was now a liability rather than an asset. He had served his purpose very well — far better than he could ever have hoped for. But that was now over. Common sense said that this was the time to ditch him. It was tough luck on the kid, but nobody had asked him to make such a sacrifice. That was enough, James considered, to release him from any moral responsibility.

With a virtually clear conscience he steadily began to draw away from the distressed Armstrong.

He did not look back.

With two minutes to spare, James collapsed over the finish line. He lay there, fighting for breath. The still cheering crowds were a hazy blur. Every muscle in his body screamed with pain. He could hear his own heart beating loud and furiously. The sweat in his eyes caused them to sting with a fierce intensity.

But he had made it. Admittedly he'd had a little help, but who would know that? Certainly not his mother. She could at last be proud of him. And as for his father — well now the old bastard would now be forced to reconsider.

IN THE LONG RUN

As willing hands sought to help him to his feet, James smiled to himself.

*

'There he is, look Dad!' Michelle's voice called out, urgent and compelling.

Piet saw him too. She was right, Armstrong was about fifty metres ahead. He was barely moving as he swayed drunkenly from side to side.

After several fruitless stops along the course, they had eventually driven to Jan Smuts Stadium and linked up once again with Neil Douglas.

At first the Scot had been furious that they had not yet found Armstrong. 'Did I not make myself clear to you?' he demanded. 'The lad could be in grave danger. Surely you could have got someone to stop him?'

Even as he tried to explain, Piet knew that the man was right. He should have done more. That did not help matters now though, and he suggested as much to the agitated coach.

Douglas calmed down a little and became more pragmatic. 'I'll try and check if he's been picked up somewhere. You lot just stay here until I get back.'

As soon as he was gone, Michelle tugged at her father's arm. Douglas' anger had served to stoke up her own anxieties to an even greater pitch. 'Let's go and have one more look,' she implored.

After only a brief hesitation, a guilt-filled Piet agreed. Leaving Cecile and Claudine to wait behind for Douglas, he and Michelle left the stadium to search the streets of Pietermaritzburg.

They had reached the outer limits of the town when Michelle finally spotted him. They hurried forward, father and daughter both blaming themselves for the pathetic sight wobbling around in front of them.

Armstrong was aware of nothing except overwhelming pain and dizziness. Totally disorientated, it was pure instinct that enabled him to somehow continue placing one exhausted foot in front of the other.

Without any awareness of who it was, he suddenly felt arms being thrown around him. And then he heard a voice he recognised. It was his name the voice was calling. He could barely answer for his dry and swollen tongue.

'Have I finished?' he managed to mumble.

'Yes,' the voice answered back.

With this comforting reassurance Armstrong closed his eyes. A huge nothingness engulfed him. Everything ceased to be.

CHAPTER FIFTEEN

David's BMW pulled up to a halt outside Ryan's hotel. The traffic congestion on the re-opened roads between Pietermaritzburg and Durban had been nose to tail in many parts, forcing David to take a longer but ultimately quicker route. Even so, the return journey had still taken over twice as long as normal.

Manelli, with his hired helicopter, faced no such difficulties. After apologising for not having any spare seats available in the aircraft, he suggested that Ryan and Gayle meet him in his penthouse around eight o'clock that evening. 'I'll have a small surprise for you before we go out to eat,' he promised.

David now regarded Ryan and grinned. 'All joking aside, I reckon you did bloody well today. Far better than I expected.' He allowed himself a brief look of modesty. 'And far better than I could have done myself, come to that.' He offered his hand. 'Well done. Any time you want to come and run for Mandene, just give me the word.'

There was genuine warmth in their handshake. 'Thanks for everything,' Ryan responded.

They had already dropped Gayle off at her flat to shower and change. It was during the short journey from there to the hotel that Ryan realised just how much he had now come to like David. Before he had always regarded the self-assured South African with a degree of suspicion — maybe even a touch of envy. Perhaps, he considered, it was the knowledge that he could do at least one thing better than Gayle's former fiancé that had allowed this barrier to be breached. They exchanged a quick look of mutual respect before Ryan got out of the car.

IN THE LONG RUN

'Don't forget,' David said as he slipped the BMW into drive, 'we'll have a couple of beers together before you go back to England. Give me a call.'

'I'll do that,' Ryan promised.

He stood on the pavement watching and reflecting as the big car eased its way into the traffic. Only when it had turned out of sight did he enter the hotel.

*

He met Gayle as arranged in the hotel foyer just before eight p.m. Gone were her shorts and tee shirt of earlier. She now looked stunning in a simple but eye-catching red dress. Ryan also noticed that, for the first time since they had met, she was wearing a hint of make-up. Clearly she had gone to a fair bit of trouble to look her best for the occasion.

He too had made an effort, once again getting out his one and only suit. The pair of them regarded each other with approval before taking a lift to the penthouse.

As they waited for the suite door to be opened Gayle pulled a face. 'Do you remember that awful guy from last time we were here?'

Ryan raised his eyebrows. 'How could I forget?' His brief encounter with James early that morning also sprang to mind. What an asshole, he thought.

Putting this memory aside, he took Gayle's hand and smiled reassuringly. 'Never mind, tonight will be different. I guarantee you this will be a night to remember. I can feel it in my bones.' He laughed before adding: 'Along with all the other aches and pains that is.'

Ryan was both surprised and delighted when Manelli produced his video.

'We haven't got a lot of time right now,' the singer stated. 'All the same Steve, I reckon you'd like to have a quick look at yourself finishing eh.'

Everybody in the room except Clint, as ever a remote figure, gave a cheer as they watched him cross the line. Kenny gave him a congratulatory slap on the back, while Tracy, now fully recovered from her experience with James, clapped enthusiastically.

After centring on Ryan for several minutes, the camera then began to pan around the spectators gathered inside the stadium. Ryan, still smiling quietly at his performance, continued to watch with interest. Abruptly his smile faded. He stiffened as a face from the crowd jumped out at him.

Parker! There was no mistake. It was a face he would never forget. The vigilant old bastard must have been there checking up on him; making sure that he had completed the race as promised. The shock of seeing Parker was nothing however to what followed next.

'Hey, I know that guy!' Manelli exclaimed.

Ryan stared at him in utter astonishment. 'Which one?' he asked, aware that his mouth had suddenly turned very dry.

Manelli froze the picture and then jabbed a finger at Parker. 'Him.'

No, it couldn't be, Ryan told himself. Manelli must be mistaken. He expressed this opinion out loud.

The beginnings of doubt crept into the singer's voice as he sought to remember.

'You could be right,' he admitted. 'All the same...' He shook his head as his voice tailed off.

Ryan's mind was now working frantically. It was best that he said nothing more on the subject. Parker had already confirmed that the deal was now off, so there was no danger to anyone. Why complicate things for himself unnecessarily?

Manelli turned to Kenny. 'Do you know him?' he asked.

His friend was positive. 'Never seen him before Tony.'

This seemed to convince the singer that he was wrong. 'Well I've never known you to forget a face,' he said. Quite suddenly he dismissed the topic. 'Hey, let's get moving,' he said. 'Our tables are booked for nine o'clock and I'm getting real hungry.'

His mind still confused and uncertain, Ryan followed the others out of the door.

*

Although never the most popular of people at Rand Athletic Club, James had persuaded one group of team mates to meet him after the race and drive him back to Durban. First though, the group were determined to enjoy themselves. A *braai* was set up near to the stadium. Steaks and beer were the traditional way of celebrating both individual and club performances. Thanks largely to the achievements of Bruce Fordyce, Ephraim Sekotlong and Mark Page, Rand had this year regained the team trophy. It was party time. Apart from the Rand members themselves, a steady stream of athletes from other clubs stopped by for a quick chat and a beer with old rivals before returning noisily to their own celebrations nearby.

James had surprised even himself with his rapid recovery from the race. His body would ache for days, he knew that. But aches aside, little else appeared to

IN THE LONG RUN

be physically wrong with him now he had spent an hour or so recuperating. Perhaps those weeks of serious training had been worth the effort after all.

His mood was black however. He could not put this Aids thing out of his head. For a short while the joy of having completed the race in time had blotted out all else. Now, as he sat alone on the fringe of the crowd, his euphoria was eroded as the dread returned to haunt him. For all he knew, he may only have months to live. He sat there brooding on this prospect, a solitary and out of place character amongst so much festivity.

Perhaps due to his introspective frame of mind, James now also found himself feeling less than proud over the way he had deserted the black boy. There was no way he would have made it without his help. Although he tried hard to deny it room, this knowledge still managed to plant itself too damn close to where his conscience might be.

Another group wandered over for a chat at the *braai*. The voice of one visitor reached James quite clearly.

'Did you hear about the guy from Dolphin Coast Striders?' he was asking. 'He collapsed just outside of town. He's in a bad way apparently, kidney damage or something. They reckon he might not make it.'

His words hit James like a powerful punch in the face. Surely it wasn't— it couldn't be? It mustn't be! But it almost certainly was, and in his heart James knew it. Dolphin Coast Striders had one of the most distinctive club vests of all. Even he could not mistake it. And there was no doubt that it was these colours that the boy had been wearing. Christ almighty — kidney damage! This bloke wasn't joking. He really could die.

He had to know for sure. He approached the newcomer and grabbed him roughly by the arm.

'This guy. Was he white or African?'

The visitor looked for a moment as if he were going to object to the force of James' grip. Then, seeing his desperate expression, he changed his mind.

'African. Zulu I think they said.'

'And where is he now?' James demanded, his voice rising.

The newcomer shrugged. 'Maritzburg hospital I suppose.'

Without another word, James hurried away. Several of his fellow club member, well aware of his normal attitude towards Africans, glanced at each other in total bemusement.

GEORGE STRATFORD

*

An atmosphere of gravity and misery pervaded every corner of the hospital waiting room. Piet, with his face buried in his hands, was blaming himself for all that had happened. Cecile, along with some help from Claudine, was unsuccessfully doing her best to convince him otherwise. At the same time Neil Douglas paced the room relentlessly, while Michelle, sat slightly apart from the other members of her family, sniffled quietly to herself.

For more than two hours the five of them had been waiting, praying for Armstrong to pull through. At present he was still in a coma. Possible kidney damage had also been mentioned. That was all they had been told so far. No definite prognosis could be made until further tests had been carried out. Yet again Michelle glanced across at her father. He was still deep in despair, utterly convinced that Armstrong's condition was all his fault.

'But it was me who started this whole thing off,' he said yet again in response to Cecile's words of comfort. 'Armstrong would never have been running in the first place if I hadn't pushed him into it.'

Suddenly Michelle could stand it no more. Wiping a hand over her reddened eyes, she approached her father and knelt down in front of him. 'Dad,' she said in a small voice. The fear was building up inside her.

Piet raised his head and gave her a weak smile. 'Yes love.'

Michelle swallowed hard. 'It's not your fault Dad, it's mine.'

Piet placed a hand gently on top of his eldest daughter's head. He stroked her hair for a short while before answering.

'Thank you for trying Michelle,' he almost whispered. 'But I do know where the real blame lies.'

If there was one tiny fragment of good to come out of this terrible affair, Piet considered, it was her change for the better. He always knew she was a good kid at heart.

Michelle was losing her courage by the second. Only her father's pain drove her on. But if she did not speak up now, then she doubted she would ever be able to.

It came out with a rush. 'No, you don't understand Dad,' she cried our forlornly. 'It was me. I put some laxatives in Armstrong's drink last night. That's why he's ill now.'

Douglas ceased his pacing. Everyone in the room stared at her, dumbfounded. Michelle could feel the almost physical pressure of their gaze.

IN THE LONG RUN

'It was me,' she repeated, her young face rapidly breaking up. 'But I never really meant to hurt him — I swear I didn't. I just wanted to stop him from winning so you'd pay me more attention again.' The child threw herself into her father's arms, sobbing wildly. 'It's not your fault Dad. I'm the one to blame.'

James arrived at the hospital shortly afterwards. A nurse repeated what the du Toit family already knew. Listening to her, James found himself experiencing an emotion that was totally alien to him. He did — he actually cared about this black boy. Suddenly, to his utter amazement, he cared deeply.

A vision of Armstrong's pain-filled yet still smiling face floated before him; the look he had first seen when regaining his senses halfway up Polly Shorts. It must have been the strain of that final effort that had brought all this on for the kid. And now he might die because of it. The sound of the nurse's voice jolted him back to the present. The hallucination vanished.

'There's nothing you can do here tonight,' she was telling him. 'Why don't you come back tomorrow? We might be able to tell you more by then.'

He nodded without replying. Then, as the nurse made to move off, another thought entered his head.

'Excuse me,' he called after her.

She paused. 'Yes.'

It was so difficult to say. 'How does someone get an Aids test?' James eventually blurted out.

The nurse's expression did not change. 'For yourself?'

Again he nodded without saying anything.

'When do you think you may have contracted the virus?'

'Yesterday.'

She smiled sympathetically. 'You do realise that these tests can not be done immediately? It takes approximately six months before you can be put in the clear.'

James stared at her, his mouth hanging open. 'Six months,' he repeated at last.

This can't be right, he told himself. The stupid bitch must have made a mistake. He couldn't possibly wait six months to know. Bloody hell, one day had been bad enough.

The nurse studied his reaction and saw the disbelief.

'I'm sorry,' she said, 'but I'm afraid that's how long it takes. I suggest that you see your usual doctor as soon as possible. He will be able to advise you where best to go.' With one final compassionate look she then hurried away, leaving James staring desolately into space.

*

Piet's temper rose. 'Just leave her alone,' he shouted at Douglas. 'Can't you see how upset she is?'

'And I've no right to be I suppose,' Douglas responded. 'All I did was train the lad for twelve bloody months you know.'

His voice rose. 'The girl deserves to be a lot more than just upset. Or is she entitled to poison the lad without so much as a slap on the wrist? Is that what you're telling me?'

Claudine leapt to the defence of her big sister. 'She didn't mean to poison him. Not like you're saying.'

Douglas turned to her. His voice was withering 'Aye, that's what Lucretia Borgia said as well.'

The young girl looked at him blankly. 'Who?'

'Just stop this, all of you,' Cecile cut in fiercely. Even her normally quiet composure was cracking under the strain. 'This isn't helping Armstrong at all.'

A heavy silence followed her plea. Douglas, tight faced, began pacing the room once more. Cecile and Claudine whispered softly together. Piet resumed stroking Michelle's head, which had remained buried deep in his chest throughout. He tried hard to understand why his eldest daughter had done such a malicious thing. Had he really become so wrapped up in Armstrong that he could not see the need in her? One thing he *was* certain of — it had taken enormous courage on her part to own up the way she had. It was unlikely that the truth would ever have been known had she kept quiet. Michelle had confessed purely to spare him his own guilt. No longer the spoilt and difficult young adult, she was now nothing more than a very sad and frightened little girl.

He felt a lump rise in his throat as he continued to comfort her.

*

The road back up to Hillcrest was now a lot less busy, allowing the vehicles to make good time to the restaurant. The group had travelled in two cars. Kenny drove the first with Manelli beside him. Ryan and the two girls were in the back.

IN THE LONG RUN

The silent and solitary Clint followed them in an otherwise empty vehicle. Unlike those ahead, to him the evening was just part of the job. There was no difference between a dinner party in Hillcrest and press conference in New York. Either way he could not afford to relax if he was to perform that job efficiently.

The restaurant owner, a loud and cheerful Italian, greeted them enthusiastically. Kenny had made the booking in his own name. It was only now that the man realised just who his famous customer was. He shook Manelli's hand warmly. 'You make great music Mr Manelli,' he said. 'I got nearly all of your records.'

He escorted them all to the far corner where three small tables had been pushed together to accommodate the group. Three flickering candles and soft overhead lighting created an atmosphere of intimacy. A short distance away a lone singer accompanied himself on a Spanish guitar.

Several of the diners looked up at the arriving party as they passed through. Whispers of recognition were soon buzzing.

Manelli was the perfect gentleman, ensuring that the ladies were seated comfortably before settling down opposite Tracy. Ryan and Gayle faced each other next to them, whilst both Kenny and Clint positioned themselves with their backs to the wall. Side by side they had a good view of the entire dining area.

Within minutes the owner had returned with two bottles of fine red wine. 'With the compliments of the house,' he told them.

A cute little waitress, no more than seventeen and with a winning smile, took their orders. Far from being overwhelmed by the famous singer's presence, she was soon exchanging cheeky banter with him. This amused Manelli enormously. It was a refreshing change for him not to be fawned over. After the girl had left, he raised his glass. 'Here's to you my friends,' he toasted. 'May tonight be a special one.'

Ryan drank with the others. All the same, he was still tense. The mere sight of Parker on the video had been enough in itself to unsettle him. But to then discover that Manelli felt he may know the man too... He smiled across at Gayle and tried to put it out of his head. You're being stupid, he told himself. There's no danger now. All that's in the past.

*

The car park was unlit apart from a small light over the restaurant entrance. Almost invisible in the deep shadows of a large tree some twenty metres away, a black sports car had been carefully positioned.

GEORGE STRATFORD

Parker sat erect in the driver's seat. Next to him, nursing an AK47 automatic rifle, was Smiling Simon. Except on this occasion he wasn't smiling. His mouth was set in a grim line as he listened to Parker's instructions.

'When they come out, on no account do anything until I have the car moving. Remember, Manelli and Ryan are the main targets, it is vital that they both die. If you have to take the bodyguards first, then do so. But be sure to get the other two. Are you absolutely clear on that?'

Simon's smile returned. 'No problem Boss. Not with this.' He patted the AK47 lovingly.

Parker gave a curt nod of satisfaction. 'Excellent. Oh, and Simon, do not concern yourself about the young ladies at all. If they happen to get in the way then it is just unfortunate. Do not let the thought of killing them distract you in any way from your main objective.'

The African gave a throaty chuckle. 'As if I would Boss.' You should know me better than that.'

*

Once again Manelli had been on top form. Entertaining, witty, and the perfect host. Even the normally stone-faced Clint was seen to register a tiny smile every now and then, although he continued to say little and remained very much a man on duty.

Once the party's meal had been finished, one or two diners cautiously approached their table seeking the star's autograph. Others, seeing their success, then ventured over themselves. Eventually the trickle turned into a queue. Everything from scraps of paper to menus were placed in front of Manelli to sign. Despite this lengthy intrusion, no one left disappointed.

The highspot of the evening came when, after repeated requests, Manelli finally agreed to get up on the small stage and do a few songs with the resident guitarist backing him. He sang his final number – a version of the Elvis Presley recording *It's Now or Never* – in its original Italian. Although ideal given the surroundings, it was not a song normally associated with Manelli. This did little to harm the impact.

He returned to his table amid loud cheers and applause. Before re-seating himself he leaned over and placed an affectionate kiss on Tracy's cheek. This brought the noise to a new crescendo. For several seconds it seemed that the girl did not know whether she wanted to die of embarrassment or sheer happiness.

With great reluctance the last of the customers were now leaving.

IN THE LONG RUN

'You and your friends stay for a while Mr Manelli,' insisted the beaming proprietor. 'I will get out some of my finest champagne. It is the least I can do after the wonderful entertainment you have given us tonight.'

*

'What's happening in there? Why haven't they come out yet?' Simon was getting restless. His smile had become a frown.

'Patience,' Parker told him. 'The later the better as far as we are concerned. See how quiet it is now?'

'So we just wait?'

'That's right Simon, we just wait. We may have a little more time to kill yet.'

This final remark amused the African. His frown disappeared. 'Time to kill,' he giggled 'I like it.'

*

For the first time that evening there was a lull in the conversation. At two thiry a.m. the owner had reluctantly suggested that he should be closing up for the night. He was now attending to matters in the kitchen while his guests finished off the last of the champagne.

Ryan was on the point of saying something when Manelli suddenly snapped his fingers.

'Got it!' he exclaimed.

Everyone looked at him. 'Got what?' Gayle asked with an amused expression.

'That guy on the video. I know where I've seen him before.'

Ryan's heart gave a violent lurch. The evening had become so pleasurable that Parker had eventually slipped from his mind. Now the man was back again, once more bringing with him uncertainty and fear.

Manelli turned in Kenny's direction. 'You wouldn't know him because it was just before I met you. I was barely fourteen at the time. There was this guy, some kinda middleman I guess, who was pushing hard drugs all over our neighbourhood. Anything you wanted that son-of-a-bitch could supply. They used to call him the powder man, something like that.'

Ryan listened to these words with increasing horror. 'And that was—' he began. He all but added Parker, but stopped himself just in time. 'The man you saw on the video?' he finished lamely.

'You've got it,' the singer confirmed.

Everyone was now staring at Manelli, absolutely riveted. Kenny, his face grim, spoke. 'So what happened to him?'

Anger showed clearly in Manelli's eyes as he continued. 'A young girl I liked a lot died from some of his shit. She was only a year older than me. I knew I was sticking my neck out, but after that I had to do something. I tipped off the cops. They set a trap and nailed the bastard next time he made a delivery. He got ten years and was then deported somewhere.' He paused for a second. 'Come to think of it, I reckon it was South Africa.'

The look on Kenny's face grew even grimmer. 'Did he know it was you who set him up?'

Manelli shook his head. 'I don't reckon so. I didn't give evidence or anything. They got all they needed when they picked him up off the street.'

'But he might have found out?'

'It's possible I suppose.'

Amazingly, Clint then spoke. 'Are you *sure* that it's him?' he asked. 'It was over twenty years ago.'

Manelli was quite definite. 'I'm sure. OK, obviously he's changed a bit. But not that much. Some guys seem to get to a certain age and then stay like that for years. I'll have another look at the tape when we get back, but I don't reckon I'll be changing my mind.'

Ryan was now very close to panic. He couldn't seem to think straight. Parker a drug pusher with a grudge against Manelli? It was unbelievable. So what about his supposed anti-apartheid group? Was that all a façade? Had Tyler and he both been used by this evil bastard? It was only thanks to the fact that all eyes were fixed on Manelli that nobody noticed the confusion on Ryan's face. He knew that he had to get away from everybody for a while. He couldn't think clearly with them all around.

Trying hard to control both his voice and expression, he got to his feet. 'I think I need some air,' he said. 'I'll see you all outside in a few minutes.'

Gayle shifted her attention to him. 'Do you want me to come with you?'

'No!'

His sharp reply clearly hurt her. 'All right then, go on your own,' she said in hushed tones.

Ryan made as if to say something, then stopped himself. Instead he made rapidly for the exit.

IN THE LONG RUN

CHAPTER SIXTEEN

Ryan stepped through the doorway and immediately took a huge gulp of the night air to help steady himself. He hesitated by the threshold for several seconds before moving on down the short stone path that lead to an ornate wrought iron gate. Everything seemed quiet as the grave as he passed through it and out into the deep gloom of the car park.

Away from the crowd his mind began to function a little better. Perhaps Manelli had made a mistake? After all, twenty years was a hell of a time. Certainly long enough for the memory to play tricks. It had to be that, he reasoned. Parker had been so utterly convincing, and besides, what on earth would a man like him be doing thousands of miles from home in America? No, Manelli must be wrong. It was a stupid case of mistaken identity, nothing more. He was working himself up for nothing.

Even though this logic sounded plausible, Ryan was not fully convinced. What if the singer was right, he agonised? That meant that Parker, in spite of what had been said, was still using him in some way. For what? To help him gain revenge for something that Manelli had done as a child? If that was true then all that had gone before had been nothing more than a bloody charade. There would be no links with any anti-apartheid group. No moral issues at stake. The whole thing had been a set-up from the word go — and he had been the fall guy.

His mind was sharper now, as he continued to pace around. The dark shape of a large tree loomed before him. Past conversations came back. After being told that Manelli's murder had been cancelled, Parker had insisted that he still run in the Comrades. That was understandable. But the man had also been emphatic that he attend the dinner here tonight. At the time he had been so relieved at the calling off he had not given this demand much thought. But now it became significant. Why was it so important to Parker that he came here with the American this evening?

Unless?

An awful thought dropped into Ryan's head. He pulled up sharply. His mouth suddenly developed a foul taste. The hit was planned for tonight. That had to be the answer. And he was meant to die along with Manelli.

Both these notions rapidly took root. It was a near certainty. With what he knew, Parker couldn't possibly let him live. The taste in his mouth grew worse. He had been taken for a fool all along the line. Now, because of his stupidity, both he and Manelli may end up dead. He had to get back into the restaurant to warn the others. Revealing his own part in this didn't matter any more. It was at this point that Ryan became aware of the car a few metres ahead. The door made a soft click as it opened.

He found himself staring with horror at the smiling African, his teeth reflecting in the gloom. The evil looking automatic weapon he held was pointing directly at his chest. To make the nightmare complete, Ryan then heard the cultured yet menacing voice of Parker coming from further back.

'I think you had better get in Mr Ryan. I would prefer not to kill you just yet.'

*

Inside the restaurant, the rest of the party was preparing to depart. Once again the owner thanked Manelli profusely for his performance that night. 'Come again before you leave South Africa,' he insisted. 'Everything will be on the house.'

As the group moved toward the exit Gayle said: 'You guys go ahead. Tracy and I want to use the ladies room before we go. We won't be a minute.'

'We'll get the car started and see you outside then,' Manelli smiled.

The two girls disappeared through a door to their right. While Clint and Kenny led the way out, Manelli paused to wink at the owner. 'I've never seen a woman yet that can leave a restaurant without paying a visit to the powder room first.'

The proprietor laughed as Manelli took his leave.

*

IN THE LONG RUN

Ryan was sat in the front passenger seat of the car. Parker was next to him, his austere features cadaverous in the gloom. He held a Smith and Wesson revolver pressed firmly into the runner's side. Behind them, Simon waited, the barrel tip of the AK47 resting on the ledge of the open rear window.

'Here they come now,' Parker said softly. 'Are you ready Simon?'

The African licked his lips. 'I'm ready.'

There was a soft click as Parker turned the ignition key. A light on the dashboard glowed red. The revolver in his other hand never wavered.

Ryan's eyes, like those of the other two, were fixed on the restaurant exit. Clint was the first to emerge, followed by Kenny. He could make out Manelli, still just inside the door, passing a final remark to the owner. But where was Gayle, or Tracy for that matter?

His greatest fear, far outweighing anything for Manelli or even himself, was for Gayle. Nearly every action of his during the last week had been motivated by a need to protect her. Nothing could change that now.

Clint paused. He was uneasy after listening to Manelli's story. Seeing no sign of Ryan outside compounded that feeling. Although a man of few words, his instincts were sharp.

Manelli emerged from the door and moved down the path toward the wrought iron gate. 'Where's Steve?' he asked.

As the singer spoke, Clint turned toward him. Kenny, picking up the tension in his colleague, also tensed. A second later there was the sound of a car engine starting up.

Ryan knew that it was now or never. Gayle must still be inside. She was relatively safe for the moment. He had literally seconds remaining if he was to save Manelli.

The car was already in gear with Parker holding the clutch down. Ryan could still feel the revolver digging into his side. Even so, the old man's attention was bound to waver a fraction as they moved off. At the very moment Parker flicked the headlights on and pulled away, Ryan acted.

Amazed at his own courage, he made a wild grab at the revolver. Somehow he managed to force it away from himself before the surprised Parker could respond. At the same time Ryan shouted out a desperate warning.

Parker cursed loudly as he fought to keep control of the moving vehicle with one arm and resist Ryan with the other. The runner managed to get his other hand across to assist him in the struggle. For an instant he felt that he would actually wrest the weapon from Parker's grasp.

Behind them, Simon, torn between two necessities, hesitated for a vital few moments. He crashed the butt of the AK47 across the back of Ryan's head.

At the first sound of the starting engine Clint reached for his own weapon. When Ryan's shouted warning came he already had the powerful handgun out of its holster and ready for use. At the same time Kenny bundled Manelli to their right and down behind a low brick wall.

By now Clint was flat on his stomach a short distance in front of the gate. Both arms were extended in an effort to pick up his target. The AK47 began chattering out its message of death as the black car drew level in front of him. He fired once in return before the tracer began to tear lumps out of the tarmac just ahead. Small pieces of flying tar kicked up like a swarm of spiteful hornets, attacking his eyes and then blinding him. Even as the giant minder's head began to drop, the closely pursuing tracer ran straight through the length of his prone body. His destroyed torso jumped and twitched and then lay still as bullets continued to spray indiscriminately all around the area, shattering the windscreens of both parked vehicles.

The black car steadied itself from its erratic path, revved loudly, and then swung hard left out of the car park. Kenny caught a glimpse of it as he looked up from behind the wall. He managed to get off two shots at the rear occupant clutching an assault rifle before the vehicle disappeared into the dark.

*

Parker's normal steely self-discipline was under severe strain. The whole thing had been ruined because of Ryan's interference. He glanced across at the unconscious figure beside him. My God he would regret his actions. No more the quick bullet for him now. Ryan would discover what real fear was before dying.

Ex-Lieutenant Colonel Parker (a largely self-bestowed rank during numerous mercenary campaigns throughout Africa) was a man who demanded unquestioning obedience. No one under his command had ever so much as queried an order and lived. In one particularly messy campaign, over a dozen of his own men had died from his hand. The merest hint of dissent, insubordination or cowardice was sufficient for him to justify summary execution. In his world, fear was the key to loyalty.

IN THE LONG RUN

In the late sixties Parker had tired of soldiering for a while. Aware of the rapidly growing drug culture in the USA, he saw this as an opportunity to expand his interests. If people were stupid enough to take drugs, why should he not benefit from their dependence? With his self-acknowledged ruthless streak and ability to organise, it seemed the perfect outlet for him.

Soon after arriving in America he made his first contacts; names supplied by a grateful Central African dictator he had helped to power. His plan was simple. He would learn the business from the bottom up before organising his own empire. Source of supplies, methods of distribution; these were the kind of things he needed to discover. Then he would be in a position to truly expand and profit.

The police on the beat in young Manelli's neighbourhood were nearly all on the drug cartel's payroll. Unfortunately for Parker, most members of the Narcotics Bureau were less corruptible. Aware of all this, it was to the bureau that the youngster passed on his information. Information that directly sealed Parker's fate.

Whilst held on remand, Parker managed to learn from one of the local beat cops the name of his betrayer. This though, was as far as any on the payroll were prepared to go. Justifiably nervous about an ongoing internal enquiry into corruption, they would have no part in reprisals against the kid. Not that there was much opportunity for that anyway. Shortly afterwards the Narcotic Bureau arranged for the Manelli family to be moved to another part of town. Soon all was forgotten.

Except by Parker. He was forced to serve virtually all of his ten-year sentence before being deported. To a man who could shoot another out of hand for merely disagreeing with him, Manelli's actions, child or not, deserved only one fate. Every day of those ten years was spent vowing revenge.

Parker's continuing frustration at not being able to strike back at Manelli was immense. News of the youngster's rise to fame and wealth made it even worse. When he picked up a newspaper one day and read about the singer's determination to go ahead with a series of concerts in South Africa irrespective of death threats, it was as if fate had at last given him his opportunity.

By this time the deported Parker was making a comfortable living out of his drug dealing. Apart from his many rich clients, by also supplying a large number of townships in the Natal area he had created for himself a widespread power base. His American experience, although bitter, had not been entirely wasted. For several years now Simon had been his enforcer-in-chief. There was no question that the African was as ruthless as himself. Unlike Parker though, who saw violence merely as a tool and who could kill without the slightest emotion, Simon drew an almost sexual delight from such matters.

The main problem for Parker was how to actually get to Manelli. A star of his size would not be easily accessible. He needed someone who could provide him with the singer's private movements. Someone who could help set up a safe opportunity for him to personally oversee the execution. After brooding on the problem for a couple of days he came up with what seemed like a good solution. In a televised pre-tour interview Manelli made no secret of his enormous interest in the Comrades Marathon. It was logical to Parker therefore that a competitor from overseas, especially one that Manelli might know of, would not find it too difficult to befriend him given the right opportunity.

It had been so easy from there on. Posing as the head of a large anti-apartheid group, Parker had found Tyler pathetically eager to help. It appeared that fate was on his side as the pieces fell magically together. That was, until now. Instead of helping him to enjoy his moment of triumph, the very man whom he saw as the vital link had instead destroyed everything. Well at least Ryan would not escape retribution for having crossed him, even if Manelli had done so for the time being.

Parker drove rapidly away from the restaurant along the dark and twisting country road. Simon's voice suddenly broke into his concentration.

'I've been hit Boss.'

His iron composure already under strain, Parker gave a start. He flicked the interior light on for a moment and shot a quick look over his shoulder. From what he could see the injury looked bad. A large circle of blood was spreading across the centre of Simon's chest.

'Damn everything to hell,' he muttered furiously. What else could possibly go wrong?

'Hang on Simon,' he said. 'We'll be changing cars soon.'

Ryan stirred as Parker turned down a dusty side track and pulled up a short way along. The large Mercedes was parked just ahead. Tipping his seat forward, Parker helped ease the injured African out. He then removed the AK47 before turning his attention to Ryan.

'Out you get,' he commanded, delivering a stinging slap across the runner's face.

The shock forced Ryan's eyes open. He stared at Parker with fear and horror. It took several moments for his brain to unscramble itself. Then he remembered what had gone before. How much time had elapsed? Where was he now? Had anyone been killed?

IN THE LONG RUN

Parker, his eyes gleaming with rage, gave him an even harder slap. 'Out you get,' he repeated, his voice rising.

With unsteady legs Ryan stepped from the car. He placed a hand gingerly on the back of his head and sucked air in sharply as his fingers found the sensitive spot.

'You'll live for a little while longer,' Parker remarked. He then handed Simon his revolver. 'Watch him,' he instructed.

The three of them moved towards the Mercedes, which Parker unlocked. 'You will drive,' he told Ryan, pushing him into the driver's seat. He placed a key into the ignition and then retrieved the revolver from Simon. Getting into the back, he left the rear door wide open. The AK47 lay on the seat beside him.

Simon looked ghastly as he stood by the open door. His entire chest was now covered in blood. He swayed slightly. His smile was nowhere to be seen.

'Where do you want me to sit Boss?' he asked. Even the small effort required to speak appeared to cause him severe distress.

Parker hesitated for only a brief instant. 'I'm sorry Simon — I really am,' he said. 'You've always been loyal.'

Now the African's smile did reappear. Only this time it was a smile of confusion laced with fear. A refusal to believe what his brain was telling him. 'What do you mean?' His voice was a croak.

He was still smiling when Parker placed a single shot just above the bridge of the nose. The upward trajectory of the bullet allowed it to pass straight into the brain. The African died in an instant.

The sheer suddenness of the shot made Ryan jump. The rear door slammed closed. Parker's voice barked out. 'Drive! Turn left at the road.'

Never before had Ryan witnessed anything like it. To see a murder so casually committed, and at little more than arm's length away, placed him in temporary shock. Automatically he did as he was ordered. This was just another bad dream, he kept telling himself. It wasn't really happening.

He kept repeating this mantra to himself over and over again.

*

Tracy was crying hysterically. Sat beside her in the restaurant, Gayle was trying hard to offer some comfort and at the same time cope with her own tears.

Clint's bullet-riddled body still lay exactly where he had died. A tablecloth had been placed over his corpse, but other than the formality of ascertaining death, it had not been touched. The Italian restaurant owner hovered around the body, doing his best to keep at bay a large group of onlookers alerted by the sound of gunfire.

Just inside the restaurant door, Kenny was talking to Manelli. 'I've spoken to the cops. They're on their way,' the minder stated.

Although shaken by the incident, Manelli managed to conceal it well. The death of his other bodyguard, plus Ryan's uncertain fate, troubled him far more than any personal threat.

The face from his past was now also figuring in his thoughts. Was it possible, he wondered, that the drug dealer had somehow discovered who was responsible for his arrest all that time ago? Did the guy, over twenty years later, still bear a large enough grudge to kill innocent people in his search for revenge? The possibility was becoming strong. He expressed these thoughts to Kenny. His friend agreed. The man's unexpected appearance on the video was too great a coincidence to be ignored.

Although he had said nothing yet, something else was also troubling Kenny. Just why had Ryan left the restaurant ahead of them? Was that a coincidence too? The guy looked pretty shaken when Tony had finally managed to identify the face on the video. Could it be that the limey was somehow involved with all of this?

Against this idea, Kenny conceded that Ryan *had* shouted out a warning. Without the extra few seconds that had bought them, they might all be dead by now. Even so, he was unconvinced. He would keep an open mind on this angle for now. He would also keep these thoughts to himself.

A few minutes later the police arrived.

*

A petrified Ryan followed the directions given to him by Parker. After driving around a series of dark back roads they had eventually joined the Durban North Coast highway. Apart from the curt instructions issued, neither man had spoken for well over half an hour.

During these silences Ryan had slowly emerged from his state of shock. Fighting back the fear and horror, he forced himself to think logically. There was no doubt that Parker meant to kill him. Any flicker of hope to the contrary had been snuffed out by the ruthless manner in which he had disposed of Simon. If Parker could do that so easily to one of his own, then there was not the remotest chance that he would show him any mercy.

IN THE LONG RUN

Once resigned to this, Ryan became surprisingly calm. Now that he had acknowledged the inevitable, what could he do to save himself? For a crazy moment he considered the possibility of slowing the car down sufficiently to jump out into the road and make his escape. The plan was dismissed almost at once. Parker would shoot him before he even had the door open. The overpowering tendency to cling to life for every available second was still strongest of all.

He began to wonder where they were going and what it would be like to die. A bullet in the head like Simon would at least be quick. And then Parker spoke. 'You will be turning left shortly. Do not miss the track.'

It took a moment for the full significance of the old man's words to sink in. Then, with a rush, it became all horribly clear. They were returning to that appalling township. That terrible isolated place where anything was free to happen. That was where Parker planned to finish him off. That prospect alone was terrifying enough to Ryan. His next thought however caused him to literally shake with panic. No — not the necklace! Surely to God not even Parker would do that to him? The claustrophobic nightmare of this prospect closed in, engulfing Ryan in its evil embrace. Already he was smelling the foul stench of burning rubber; vividly imagining the horrendous, searing pain.

Parker, sensing his terror, smiled wickedly. 'Yes Ryan, I think that you are now beginning to get the idea. It is not a pleasant way to meet one's Maker, but one you richly deserve after tonight's performance.'

This callous confirmation of his worst fears was the final limit for Ryan. Something went snap inside his brain. Anything — anything at all — was better than what Parker intended. Even if it did mean sacrificing some of the short time left to him.

A large lorry was approaching at speed from the other direction. Now clinically calm and deliberate, Ryan swung the steering wheel over and drove the Mercedes straight towards it.

There was a series of deafening blasts from the lorry's horn. Parker screamed something and then lunged forward from the rear seat, his strong, bony hands striving desperately to turn the wheel away from the onrushing vehicle.

Like a prematurely developed dead man's grip, Ryan's hold on the steering was vice-like. Even if he had made a mess of everything else, he was not going to be denied what would probably be his last act on earth. Only a few metres separated them from the looming mass. Ryan could quite clearly see the African driver as his whole body twitched from side to side in panic. The man's eyes were literally bulging from their sockets.

Now was the time. Ryan suddenly released his grip on the steering wheel, grabbing instead at the handbrake. Ducking beneath Parker's arm, he yanked the lever fully upwards and then threw himself flat across the front seats. Without Ryan counteracting Parker's frantic tugging, the steering wheel swung hard to the left. With the rear wheels now locked by the brake, the car swung only slightly away before slewing broadside on to the lorry in a half turn.

Ryan started to laugh. 'Goodbye Parker,' he just had time to shout before the world ended in a scream of tearing metal, sudden pain — and fierce jubilation.

IN THE LONG RUN

CHAPTER SEVENTEEN

Ryan was only vaguely aware of being lifted from what was left of the Mercedes. Pumped full of pain killing drugs, everything appeared to be flimsy and unreal. The voices he could hear had a far-away quality about them. It was almost as if the whole thing was really happening to someone else; that he was a temporary stand in for another person. Soon, very soon, things would return to normal. Until then he would just have to continue with this eerie performance.

The spectre of Parker, a haunting memory that seemed to have been with him for a lifetime, began to return. Ryan found himself speaking to the face above. 'The other guy. What happened to him?'

The medic exchanged glances with a nearby colleague. 'Was he a friend?'

Ryan let out a childlike giggle. 'Hardly,' he said. 'I hated him.' At this precise moment he did not care what he said.

There was a pause before the man answered. 'Well you don't have to worry about him any more. He's dead. You should be too. I suppose you're lucky.'

Parker dead! And he was still alive. So he had beaten the bastard in the end. Ryan felt a surge of joy run through him. He had a crazy, irrepressible urge to sing. What was that big hit by that Australian girl?

'I should be so lucky...' he began weakly.

He was still singing as they put him into the ambulance. The medic closed the doors and turned once more to his assistant. 'Poor sod,' he murmured. 'If only he knew.'

The other man nodded in agreement. 'Wait until he finds out that they had to cut his leg off. He won't feel so much like singing then.'

GEORGE STRATFORD

*

James lay on the bed in his hotel room. Although stiff and sore all over, these pains were the last thing on his mind. They, at least, would soon be gone. That morning had only confirmed what the nurse at Grays Hospital in Maritzburg had told him. He would have to endure an agonising six-month wait before he could be tested and pronounced clear of infection. All the money in the world could not hurry this process along any faster. The time now stretched before him like a life sentence. His frantic efforts to trace the girl involved had failed miserably. She was not a resident at the hotel and nobody seemed to have a clue who she was or where she came from.

Later he had called the nursing sister responsible for Armstrong.

'The boy is still in a coma at present,' she said. 'I would try again later today.'

His melancholy mood was disturbed by the bedside phone ringing. Wearily he picked it up.

'Hello, James?' It was his mother's voice.

With so much else to consider, he had forgotten the need to contact her. 'Hello Mother,' he responded.

'We saw you finish on TV,' she said. 'Well done James, I always knew that you could do it.' There was considerable pride in her voice. He felt lifted by her tone.

'So when are you coming home?' his mother continued.

'I don't know,' he found himself saying. 'There's something I have to attend to here first.'

There was a short, surprised silence. His mother then said: 'Perhaps you should talk to your father. He's right here beside me.'

James could hear the sound of them whispering together, but could not make out the words. His father came on the line. 'James. What's all this about you wanting to stay in Durban?' His voice was gruff.

'I have to.'

'Now look here, don't start getting difficult with me. Just because you managed to complete the Comrades — which I admit has surprised me greatly — that doesn't mean that I owe you anything. I am now, however, prepared to discuss things. But only if you cease this stupid act of yours immediately. Nothing in Durban can be that important to you. So stop your sulking and get yourself home.' He then added pointedly: 'Unless of course you wish to stay away permanently.'

IN THE LONG RUN

James knew that this was his big chance. Despite the gruff tone, his father was obviously weakening. With enough pressure from himself and his mother he could soon be back to his old life. He could not believe the next words that came out of his mouth. 'I'm sorry Dad, I'm not coming,' he said.

Charles Kirkpatrick was speechless for several seconds. When he did finally speak his voice was a mixture of anger and complete astonishment. 'This is your final opportunity James. I'm not fooling around with you any longer.'

James hesitated. He really needed to see this black boy again, if only to make sure that he was out of danger. But how could he explain this to his father without owning up to the cynical use he had made of him? An admission like that would be certain to discredit him forever. His dilemma grew deeper. But was staying in Durban really worth the price? He was now on the verge of regaining everything. No obligation could surely outweigh that?

'You have not answered me yet James.' The tone was impatient.

He wanted to say that he would be on the next flight. His mouth formed the words but nothing came out.

Amazingly his father's voice then softened a shade. 'Very well James, you had better tell me exactly what it is that you consider to be so vital there. Quite frankly your hesitation astounds and intrigues me.'

Normally so adept with the ready and convenient lie, James' mind suddenly went blank. Unwillingly, and to his absolute horror, he found himself relating an accurate account of his experiences with Armstrong. Apart from his fear of HIV infection, nothing was omitted. Not even his desertion of the boy was understated. If anything, the opposite was true.

Quite what made him do all this he couldn't tell. On reflection he realised that he could easily have left out some of the more damning details and presented a sort of cleaned up and edited version. But he hadn't. Every last misdemeanour was related. His father was the priest, and he the repentant sinner.

Purged but fearful, he waited for his father's response.

'You're a bloody disgrace James,' he was told.

His heart sank before the voice added: 'But for all that, there may now finally be some hope for you after all.'

*

Armstrong blinked twice and then fully opened his eyes. Rapidly they widened as he tried to take in his surroundings. Where was he? The last thing he could remember was reaching the top of Polly Shorts. And now he was lying on his back in this strange place with more tubes coming out of him.

He shifted slightly to try and get more comfortable. As he did, he heard someone close by let out a small gasp. He tried to twist his head to see who it was but a painful stiffness in his neck prevented this. The next moment a face appeared. It was looking down at him and smiling. But there were also tears welling up in his visitor's eyes.

'Miss Michelle,' he murmured. 'Where am I?'

She did not reply. Instead she just continued to gaze at him.

Was she in one of her difficult moods, Armstrong wondered? She didn't appear to be. But why didn't she answer him?

Michelle was trying very hard to say something. At that moment though she was almost choking on her joy and relief. All of her family were still with her at the hospital, as were Neil Douglas and both of Armstrong's parents. Throughout the night and most of the day they had sat together either in the waiting room or by the bedside, praying for the boy to show some sign of the recovery that test results now indicated he should make. Eventually, tired and hungry, the group had decided to leave for a short while to get some food.

Michelle refused. 'Just bring me back a cheeseburger,' she said, determined to be there should Armstrong come round during this break. Knowing what his daughter was going through, Piet agreed.

And now Michelle felt that she had been rewarded for her determination. Not only had Armstrong woken up, she would also have him to herself for a short while. There was so much she wanted to say. But with the opportunity here, she found that the words simply would not come.

Still puzzled by her silence, Armstrong repeated his question. 'Where am I Miss Michelle?'

At last the words came out. 'You're back with us Armstrong,' she cried, stroking his head. 'That's where you are.'

*

James heaved an exasperated sigh of relief as he watched the last of Armstrong's visitors leave the boy's bedside. Highly wary of his possible reception, he had not been able to bring himself to approach the youth with such a crowd around the

IN THE LONG RUN

bed. There was no other choice for him but to hang around outside the ward. He had been waiting well over an hour for them to go.

After calling the hospital for a second time late that afternoon he had been told the news. The boy had woken up. Although he would be weak for some time, he was no longer considered to be in any danger. James immediately hired a car and drove to Pietermaritzburg.

His patience was already sorely tested when a formidably large nurse blocked his path to Armstrong's bed. 'I'm sorry sir,' she said, 'Official visiting time is now finished. Anyway I think he's had enough excitement for today. He should be resting now.'

At any other stage of his life James would have sworn at her and demanded that she let him pass. Now, instead of this, he found himself employing tactful diplomacy. 'I'm very sorry,' he said. 'It's just that I've got something very important and private to say. Something I couldn't talk about in front of all those other people.' He even smiled. 'It won't take long, I promise.'

The approach worked. The nurse looked around and then jerked her head in Armstrong's direction. 'Just a couple of minutes then.'

Armstrong watched him come over. Recognition slowly dawned. He remembered them being together at the top of Polly Shorts — but then what? After that everything was a blank.

The boy smiled. 'Hello.'

James found it impossible to meet Armstrong's open gaze. 'How are you feeling?' he asked.

'Tired,' came the brief reply.

There was a short awkward silence. Come on, thought James. Why don't you shout at me? Get angry. Say something for Christ's sake.

'They told me I didn't manage to finish,' Armstrong said at last. 'Did you?'

James found himself looking at the floor as he replied. 'I just made it with a couple of minutes to spare.'

Although Armstrong's voice was weak, it was loaded with relief. 'I'm glad one of us did. After what happened to your father it was right that you were the one. He would have been proud of you.'

Until now this lie had slipped to the back of James' mind. For a moment he wondered why the hell the youth was referring to his father in the past tense. Then he remembered and felt worse than ever. This gullible kid had swallowed every word and taken it to heart. He'd damn near killed himself to make up for something that had never even occurred. And what had he done in return? Called him a black bastard and then deserted him at the first opportunity. With a sudden rush of brutal self-appraisal, James decided that perhaps he did not like himself very much. It was obvious that the kid had no idea what happened after Polly Shorts. He probably believed that they had continued to support each other until his final collapse. Much as he wanted to, James could not give him a true account. Not yet anyway. Whether this was to save his own embarrassment or to spare the boy further anguish, he couldn't tell. All he knew was that now was not the time.

'I just wanted you to know that I'm grateful for all you did,' he said.

It was Armstrong's turn to be embarrassed. He murmured something in Zulu that James did not understand.

'Look, is there somewhere I can get in touch with you when you get out of here?' James asked.

A touch bemused, Armstrong gave him Piet's name and telephone number.

The situation was now getting too much for James. Soul searching was not his strong point. Impulsively he grabbed the boy's hand in a firm grip. 'Maybe you didn't win a medal, but you've got no idea what you achieved yesterday.'

Their eyes meet fully for the first time. A second later the nurse reappeared.

'I'm sorry, but you really do have to leave now,' she said.

James gave her a quick glance. 'That's OK. I've said all there is to say for now.' Without another word he walked quickly away.

*

For two days Ryan drifted between a semi-conscious state and sleep. Even in this ethereal existence there was little peace. An almost constant series of dreams and lifelike visions tormented him. Everything that had taken place over the last week was played out over and over again by grotesque caricatures of those involved. None was more grotesque than Parker. Even in death the man continued to plague him.

On the third day Ryan became more aware of his surroundings. He was in a small but luxurious private ward. A room, he was told, that Manelli had arranged and paid for. He was also told that he had broken three ribs. The pain not only confirmed this, it also severely restricted any movement. Hour after hour was spent flat on his back, staring at the ceiling and trying hard to piece together the disjointed events of that fatal evening.

IN THE LONG RUN

On the positive side, the nurse had been able to assure him that both Gayle and Manelli were unharmed. The sense of relief was overwhelming. She was though, far more evasive when he asked her yet again about the full extent of his own injuries. So far no one had answered this satisfactorily.

'You'll be getting some visitors a little later,' she told him. 'I expect that they will be able to tell you more.'

And so he had continued to lie there. The time dragged interminably.

At last he heard voices. Gayle's was amongst them. He turned his head slightly as the door opened and saw her immediately in the small crowd gathered there. Leaving the others, she hurried over and kissed him gently on the cheek.

'Hello Steve.' Her voice was quiet.

'Is that the best I get?' he tried to joke.

Her response was not what he expected. Instead of smiling she looked at him sadly. A solitary tear dribbled slowly down her face.

He was both puzzled and disappointed. 'What's the matter with you?' he asked. 'Anyone would think I was going to die.'

Before she could reply the rest of the group came over. Nearly everyone was there. Manelli, David, and Kenny. There was also a smartly dressed and distinguished looking man he had never seen before.

Manelli was the first to speak. 'Hi Steve.'

Like Gayle, he did not appear comfortable. 'This is Mr Schoeman,' he continued. 'He's a surgeon.'

Alarm bells began to ring in Ryan's head. 'Surgeon?' he repeated. 'You're not going to operate on me are you?'

Schoeman gave a small, uncertain smile. 'No.' He hesitated before adding softly: 'We already have.'

The alarm bells grew louder. 'What have you done to me?' Ryan breathed, suddenly very afraid.

The general atmosphere of unease increased as the surgeon cleared his throat and began to speak.

As Ryan listened to the man's words a state of deep stupor set in. He could see the surgeon's lips moving, he could hear the sounds coming out, but that was all. He wanted to interrupt. To say something in response. Some kind of awful mistake had been made. He could still feel both of his legs lying there perfectly all right beneath the raised bedclothes. There was no question of one being missing. He tried to lift the covers to prove his point but the surgeon restrained him.

'I wouldn't if I were you,' he told him.

'But you're wrong,' Ryan insisted. He let out a short hollow laugh that seemed to reverberate all around the room. 'Pull back the covers and see for yourself.'

Schoeman let out a deep sigh. Despite years of experience he had never been able to fully come to terms with this aspect of his profession. Nearly all his colleagues were far more hardened than himself. The situation here was being made even worse than normal since he had learned of this young man's athletic prowess. For him to lose a leg must be the greatest blow imaginable.

His voice was soft and compassionate. 'It is quite normal for a patient to initially be unaware of the loss. Certain sensations will suggest that the limb is still there. You could say it is nature's way of compensating.' It was far from being the first time that he had been faced with a disbelieving patient. These were words he had used many times before. For all that, they never seemed to get any easier.

Ryan could not control himself any longer. Anguish and desperation clogged his mind, refusing to accept what he had been told.

'Do you think I wouldn't know if one of my legs were missing,' he shouted out. With a furious motion that sent a violent stab of pain through his rib area, he brushed aside the surgeon's restraining hand and raised the covers.

Gayle and Manelli exchanged distressed glances as Ryan stared down the bed, his eyes wild and desperate to prove Schoeman wrong.

There was total silence as the runner's expression gradually changed from initial disbelief to one of horrified confirmation. Little by little his face began to crumble.

He was right! Oh my God, the man *was* right! This was the only thought that kept repeating itself in Ryan's head. All he could see was a stump where his right leg should be. His head dropped back on the pillows. He closed his eyes as tightly as he knew how. Even through this his could not hold back the tears.

For the following week Ryan did little else other than wish that he too had died with Parker in the crash. His whole aim in causing the Mercedes to skid sideways-on just before impact had been to ensure that Parker in the rear was placed in a more vulnerable position. As it was, the manoeuvre had not only achieved this, it had also saved his own life. It was the rear end of the car that had taken the main force of the collision.

IN THE LONG RUN

Now, full of misery and self-pity, Ryan constantly doubted the wisdom of his actions. At just twenty-five years of age he was finished. His running career, which had promised so much, was now a sick bloody joke. He was doomed to be a cripple for the rest of his life. Paraplegic games were all very well for those who had known no other kind of competition, but they would never do for him. How many people could remember the name of this year's wheelchair winner in the London Marathon? For crying out loud, he couldn't even remember it himself. And it had only taken place a few weeks ago.

On top of all that, what girl would ever look at him now? Sure Gayle still continued to visit every day for the moment, but that was more out of sympathy and sense of duty than any great desire to carry on with their relationship. How could the prospect of pushing him around in a wheelchair for God knows how long possibly appeal to her? Ryan was still brooding on this very point when she arrived. One glance at his face told her that she was in for another difficult session.

Gayle was confused herself. Before the crash she had known that she was falling quite heavily for Ryan. So did the present situation now change anything for her? It shouldn't do, she supposed. Not if you truly cared for someone. It was understandable that for now he was moody and sorry for himself. This would probably pass. But what about her own feelings? Despite what she told herself, how capable was *she* of handling his disability. Time would perhaps tell. One thing was for certain though. He needed her now. She could not even think of letting him down.

She forced a bright smile. 'How are you feeling today?'

'What do you think?' Ryan responded moodily.

He knew that he was being deliberately awkward, but he could not prevent himself. The thought of being patronised soured him even further.

She tried once more. 'I was with David earlier. He sends his best wishes and says that he'll come in to see you tomorrow some time.'

'I see. You two are probably thinking of getting back together I expect.'

As soon as he had said it, Ryan realised just how uncalled for this remark was. There was not the slightest reason for him to suspect that anything was going on between them. Even so, it was a notion he could not get out of his head. 'At least David has two legs,' he added.

For days Gayle had suffered Ryan's bad moods without reacting. This latest snipe was the last straw though. 'That's a lousy thing to say,' she flared.

GEORGE STRATFORD

Although quickly feeling regret, Ryan could not bring himself to express it. He was already at the very bottom of a pit. The only thing that could possibly make matters any worse was if Gayle were to walk out on him.

Go on then, he thought savagely. Why not make it happen? Complete the job. Then I'll have absolutely nothing left to live for. Fate had taken so much from him, it might as well have the whole damn lot. There was a perversely satisfying logic to this reasoning.

Getting no response from him only served to increase Gayle's anger. 'How much longer are you going to just sit around biting people's heads off?' she demanded.

'Don't you think that—' Ryan began.

'I don't know what I think,' she stormed back before he could finish. 'I'll tell you what I do know though. If you don't start improving your attitude, I'm out of here. I want to help — I've been trying hard to understand — but you won't let me near. I might still be able to love a man with one leg, but not one so full of self-pity. For Christ's sake show some fight.'

All the pent-up emotion of days came pouring out. She stood before him, shaking. 'Well, what's it to be?' she finished off.

Ryan tried to look her straight in the eye. 'You could never love a man with one leg,' he said. It came out as half question, half statement.

'I don't know damn you. If it doesn't work out, then so be it. But if we don't even try we'll never know.'

A huge lump grew in Ryan's throat, threatening to strike him dumb. 'I don't want to lose you,' he managed to say.

Gayle moved closer and took his hand. 'You haven't you stupid bugger. Not yet. Let's just try again shall we?'

[C*

It was the third time that the police had visited Ryan. On the first occasion they had taken a detailed statement. The following two visits had been much briefer, mainly to clear up minor points. In spite of his nervous tension while talking to them, he felt reasonably sure that they now accepted his story.

He had stuck as close to the truth as possible, omitting only his connection with Parker who had now been officially identified. As far as they were concerned he had come to South Africa simply to run in the Comrades. After befriending Manelli he had innocently been drawn into events at the restaurant. With both

IN THE LONG RUN

Parker and his henchman dead, it was unlikely that there was anyone else around who would contradict his story.

They tried to make something of the fact that he was inside the getaway car at the time of the shooting. No, he did not know why the occupants had not killed him when he had first gone outside and stumbled across them. Perhaps they planned to use him as a hostage if things became difficult. He had shouted out a warning and had then immediately been knocked unconscious. He had remained in this condition until the change of vehicles took place. It was there he witnessed Parker finish off his injured accomplice. Later on, in a bid to escape, he and Parker had struggled inside the car. This was the cause of the crash. There was nothing else he could add.

At last the police were satisfied. Manelli's story bore out his own, as did minute blood traces found on the butt of the AK47. With the motive behind the attack clearly established, the police investigation appeared to be over. In fact he was now being regarded as a bit of a hero by them.

'This should be the last time we bother you,' the detective remarked, adding that he was very sorry about the leg.

As he left the room, Kenny came in. Ryan was surprised to see the bodyguard without Manelli. He was told that the singer was downstairs and would be up shortly.

'I wanted a quiet word with you first,' Kenny told him.

A tickle of apprehension touched Ryan. 'Sure,' he said. 'Go ahead.'

The American ran a finger up and down his temple. 'When you left the restaurant to go outside, you said you wanted a breath of fresh air – right?'

Ryan nodded warily. 'Yes.'

Kenny's eyes suddenly became very sharp. 'But there was more to it than that, wasn't there?

'What do you mean?' Ryan's heartbeat grew quicker. He had been prepared for the police, but this new, unexpected probing was throwing him off balance.

Kenny sighed. 'Don't take me for a fool Steve. It's my job to notice things. When you walked out of that place there was something real heavy on your mind. It was written all over your face. You were so uptight you nearly bit Gayle's head off when she suggested going with you.' The finger ceased its massage of the temple and pointed accusingly at Ryan. 'You wanted to be on your own for some reason. Why?'

'Hey, what is this?' Ryan blustered. 'I've had enough questions from the police without you starting. In case you haven't noticed, I've got a leg missing.

That's more than enough to be going on with at present. I don't need this sort of hassle from you.'

Kenny was unmoved by his outburst. 'A colleague of mine is murdered. My boss and best friend, not to mention myself, nearly end up the same way. I reckon I'm entitled to ask a few questions of my own. Don't you?'

It was clear to Ryan that the man was not going to be put off. He would have to try and ride this out somehow. 'You forget that if I hadn't shouted out that warning, you and Tony *would* probably be dead by now,' he pointed out.

The first trace of a smile crossed Kenny's face. 'Oh no, I haven't forgotten. That's the only reason why I've said nothing to the cops so far.'

It was impossible for Ryan to conceal a brief look of panic. 'What do you mean, so far?'

'Look Steve,' Kenny's tone became reasonable, cajoling almost, 'all I want you to do is put my mind at rest. Parker's dead, so he's no longer a threat. But my responsibility is to protect Tony from anyone who might have a grudge. Am I safe in assuming that this thing is now over?'

Ryan tried one more bluff. 'I suppose so. How would you expect me to know?'

The minder frowned and shook his head. 'I talked to the medic at the scene of the accident. He reckons you said that you hated Parker — that you started singing when they told you he was dead. Even allowing for the drugs they put in you, that's still a kinda strange way to react about a guy you've only just met. And let's face it, you couldn't have known much of what happened because you were already unconscious before the shooting started. It suggests —just suggests — that you may have known Parker a bit better than you're letting on.'

Ryan's frightened brain refused to work. He had no plausible explanation. He could feel himself colouring up. What could he say apart from continuing to deny any association with Parker? And it was obvious that Kenny strongly doubted his word on that. Yet again he cursed the old man. Dead or alive, he still persisted in making his life hell. Would he never be free from the anguish he brought?

The lengthy silence confirmed Kenny's suspicions. Ryan did know a lot more than he had so far admitted. At the same time he could not visualise the Englishman as a killer. So what was he? An unwilling stooge perhaps? A guy under threat in some way?

Abruptly he spoke. 'That crash. It was no accident, was it?'

'Of course it—'

IN THE LONG RUN

Ryan checked himself. What was the point? He was bound to slip up under this kind of pressure before long. 'No, it wasn't,' he said in a small voice. 'I wanted to kill us both.'

Kenny nodded. 'That's what I figured.'

Ryan's voice then raised. 'You see Parker was—'

The bodyguard held up a hand. 'Stop! I don't want to hear any more.' He knew enough. Whatever part it was Ryan had played, it was more than clear that it had been forced upon him. And even under what must have been huge pressure from a ruthless bastard like Parker, he had still been unable to see it through. He had shouted the warning that had almost certainly saved both his and Tony's lives.

'I'll repeat my earlier question,' Kenny said, his eyes once again probing. 'Can I be certain that this thing is now over? That there is no one else out there waiting to take pot shots at us?'

This time Ryan managed to meet his gaze. 'As far as I know, that's it. You have my word on that. There's no one else.'

Kenny held his searching look for several more seconds before responding. 'OK,' he finally said. 'In that case we'll forget all about this conversation.' He made slowly for the door. 'I better get back,' he said over his shoulder. 'Tony will be wondering where I am. I'll see you again later.'

Ryan called after him. 'So you won't be saying anything to the — the police?'

A smile flickered across the big man's face. 'Why should I? I don't know anything, do I?'

He walked out.

He had only been gone a few seconds when the door opened again.

Ronnie Tyler entered the room.

CHAPTER EIGHTEEN

For a moment Ryan thought that he was hallucinating. He stared at his friend Tyler with a mixture of fear and utter astonishment.

'I'm so sorry Steve,' Tyler began. 'I could never have known that it would turn out like this.'

These words passed completely over Ryan. 'What the hell are you doing here?' he asked, his voice a mere croak. Panic began to rise. Manelli was due up here at any moment. These two must not meet. If they did then the whole thing could still blow up in his face.

As in their university days, Tyler seemed to be one thought ahead of him. 'I've just spoken with your friend Manelli downstairs,' he said. 'He's agreed to leave us alone for a few minutes before coming up.'

Ryan let out a long, unsteady sigh. He could not take much more in the way of shocks or pressure. 'You actually spoke to him?' was all he could say.

'He overheard me enquiring about you at the reception desk. I told him I was a friend of yours come over from England.'

'Is that *all* you told him?'

'Of course.' Tyler appeared so calm and in control. 'The attempt on Manelli's life was in all the newspapers, but there were no real details. I tried phoning you at your hotel to find out what had happened and they told me you were in here. I came over at the first opportunity. I had to. If it hadn't been for me...' He gave an almost imperceptible nod in the direction of the missing limb and placed a hand on Ryan's shoulder. 'You can't begin to know how badly I feel about this.'

IN THE LONG RUN

'I don't feel too bloody good myself.' Ryan could not keep the bitterness from his voice. He paused before speaking again. 'We got it all wrong you know Ronnie.' The bitterness was still there, stronger if anything.

He went on to give a concise account of all that had happened since his arrival in South Africa. For once Tyler said absolutely nothing until he had finished. Only when the truth about Parker's background came out did he display any outward signs of anger. For the large part he just listened with great intensity, his eyes growing colder as the details unfolded.

'So that's it,' Ryan concluded. 'Nothing is as we imagined. We've both been made fools of, especially me.'

'Especially you Steve,' Tyler repeated softly.

There was something in his voice. Ryan looked at his sharply. 'What do you mean?'

Suddenly Tyler seemed different. A cold little smile appeared on his face. 'You were never meant to survive this Steve. I knew that right from the start. Parker said it was the only way, and I was forced to agree with him. You would have become too dangerous a liability.'

'You *knew* Ronnie? You *knew* and you still set me up?' For a while Ryan was too stupefied to be angry.

Tyler nodded. 'I'm afraid so. The thing was Steve, you were so perfectly qualified for the job. If I could have sent someone else, believe me I would have done. I'll admit that I had no idea about Parker's real motives for wanting Manelli dead. The guy fooled me completely. I really thought he was a genuine member of the movement.' He shrugged. 'Now that I think about it though, what does it matter? We both wanted the same thing, it was just for different reasons.'

Real fear was now gripping Ryan. His mouth suddenly became very dry. 'So why have you come here Ronnie? Why are you telling me this now that it's all over?'

'But it's not all over, is it? Things haven't worked out so far. I'm here to see that they do. It's all for the greater good.'

Tyler dipped into his pocket and produced a Czechoslovakian made CZ handgun. 'It's amazing how easy these things are to get hold of over here,' he remarked casually. 'When your friend Manelli arrives in a minute, I'll make sure that there's no mistake this time.'

'You're mad,' Ryan uttered. His heart was now banging away at twice its normal pace.

Tyler laughed. 'Not mad Steve — dedicated. Which, as it's turned out, is more than I can say for you.'

'You'll never get away with it. There's security everywhere.'

The light of fanaticism sprang into Tyler's eyes. 'I've no intentions of trying to get away with it you bloody fool. Martyrdom — that's the name of the game. A hero to the cause.'

'The cause is practically finished you stupid bastard,' Ryan shouted at him. 'South Africa is changing. Apartheid is all but dead. It will be soon. And it's people like Manelli who have helped achieve this. Can't you see that?' He knew as he spoke that his words would make no impact. It was true what he had said; Tyler *was* mad. Totally bloody insane. One look at his wild expression, his crazed eyes, confirmed that. Sure he had always been a bit of a fanatic, even in the early days. They both were. But it was now obvious that somewhere along the way in the ensuing years Ronnie's obsession had pushed him right over the edge.

With great deliberation Tyler picked up a pillow and placed it over the snout of the gun. He then pointed the weapon at Ryan's chest.

'You don't have that belief any more Steve, that's the problem,' he said. 'Since you've been here you've become one of them. Another fucking Manelli. I never thought it possible, that's why I had to see you and hear it from your own mouth. Now I know for sure, there's only one way to fix things.'

Ryan wanted to scream for help, but sheer terror choked back the sounds. Whatever self-pitying thoughts he had imagined during the last few days, he now knew for certain that he *did not* want to die. Not when actually faced with it. And especially since realising that he might still be able to make a go of things with Gayle. The dryness inside his mouth was now so bad that his tongue was stuck firmly to his palate. He had lived through a lifetime of trauma in just one week. Since arriving here it had been one nightmare after another. And now there was this terrible finale to end it all.

A door leading to a small treatment room away to his left burst open. Kenny, arms extended and clutching a large Colt Detective revolver with both hands, stood there poised in the classic position. At the first sound of this interruption Tyler threw aside the pillow and began to raise the CZ toward its new target. His reactions were remarkably quick.

Quick as he was though, he was not a professional. The CZ had lifted no more than a couple of inches when the Colt's heavy slug took him. The force of the round sent him flying backwards and crashing into the wall behind. Kenny's accuracy was deadly. His single shot found the centre of Tyler's heart. Manelli's best friend and chief bodyguard *was* a professional, and a highly skilled one. When

IN THE LONG RUN

faced with a situation like this there was only one way to shoot. To kill!

Facing death himself an instant beforehand, Ryan stared with horrified fascination at the body. Tyler was now slumped against the wall in a half-sitting position. The front of his pale blue shirt was already almost totally red. His lifeless gaze was fixed accusingly on his former friend. Much as he wanted to, Ryan could not look away. His eyes were immovably locked onto Tyler's. Quite suddenly he began to shake. Gently at first, then the spasms increased. Soon he felt he would disintegrate with their violence. His sight, even his thoughts, were now nothing more than a jumbled, unintelligible blur. He was shouting at the top of his voice, but had no idea what he was saying.

He felt restraining hands on him. There was a small prick in his arm. Then sleep overcame him.

*

The first thing Ryan saw when he opened his eyes was Kenny sitting by his bedside. Startled, he looked around, but there was no one else to be seen. Automatically his eyes were drawn to where Tyler had fallen. Everything was clean and in order. Only then did he realise that he had been moved to another room.

'Hi Steve,' said Kenny, as if all were fine in the world. 'You've been out for sixteen hours. I guess you needed the sleep huh.'

Slowly the details filtered through to Ryan's brain. This man had saved his life. 'I suppose I should thank you for what you did,' he said. 'Was I really worth saving?' Kenny shrugged. 'We all make mistakes. At least you tried to put yours right.' Ryan took a deep breath. 'Do you know who he was — the guy you shot I mean?' 'Yeah.'

'And why he was here? What he was planning to do?'
'Yeah.'

This lack of detailed information was getting to Ryan. 'For Christ's sake say something other than "yeah",' he remarked. Then he sighed. 'You must know it all by now.'

'Most of it I reckon.' Kenny shifted in his seat to make himself more comfortable before elaborating. 'I saw this guy Tyler go into your room just as I left. Don't ask me why, instinct I guess, but I felt there was something wrong about him. Anyhow, after our little talk I was curious about who he was and what he wanted. I hadn't seen him around here before.' The American almost succeeded in looking apologetic. 'OK, so I was poking my nose in. But as I said before, that's my job. There's another door in the corridor, which also leads into that treatment room. I just kind of sneaked in there and listened for a while.'

'So you heard the whole conversation?'

'Ninety per cent of it.'

'And then came to the rescue in the nick of time.'

Kenny grinned. 'Just like John Wayne in the movies.'

There was no smile on Ryan's face. 'So what are you going to do about it now you know the truth?' he asked.

Kenny's grin faded. 'After I shot that so-called buddy of yours I was forced to tell the cops what I knew. I'm sorry Steve, but I'd just killed a guy and you have to have a damn good reason for doing something like that. In fact, I'll tell you now, I'll be relying on your evidence to support me at the inquest.'

Ryan's head fell back on the pillow. He let out a deep sigh. 'I'll tell them what happened OK,' he said in a dull voice. 'Although with what everyone knows about me now, I doubt they'll believe a word I say.'

'Why don't you try me first?' Kenny suggested. 'Try telling me about this whole thing right from the start. Just so I can fit the last few pieces together. Then maybe we can work something out.'

Unexpectedly, Ryan felt a huge surge of relief at this opportunity to get things off his chest. Once he started to speak, the words poured out. He omitted nothing. How he had first met Tyler at university, his involvement in the anti-apartheid movement, and complete story from the moment that he received that first phone call from Tyler while in Bournemouth.

'Yea, it's all pretty much as I figured,' Kenny said after Ryan had finished. 'Speaking as a black person myself, I'm not entirely in love with the idea of apartheid either. But there again, as you worked out for yourself eventually, neither is Tony. He came here to help break down some barriers, not reinforce them. And I reckon he's done a damn fine job.'

'He has,' Ryan agreed. 'But it's a bit late to undo some of the damage that's been done in other ways.' He paused before adding in barely audible voice: 'Or give me my leg back.'

There was a short silence while both men pondered the violent and tragic outcome of the last few days.

Kenny spoke first. 'Look,' he stated, 'I know you're not a bad guy Steve. Misguided perhaps — a goddam fool in a lot of ways — but at the end of the day

IN THE LONG RUN

you came good and did the right thing. Tony knows that too.' He rubbed the side of his nose reflectively. 'I've got a small confession to make too. When I spoke with the cops I changed the story a little bit. I told them that, from what I'd overheard, your buddy Tyler had forced you into coming here. That he'd threatened to have your legs broken if you didn't do as he wanted.'

He glanced awkwardly at where Ryan's leg should be. 'In the light of what's happened since that's a pretty lousy choice of words. But for a guy in your position at the time — a promising athlete — it makes a believable reason for playing along for a while.'

Ryan could not bring himself to make any comment.

Kenny continued. 'The story after that is best left as it is. Once you arrived in Durban Parker increased the intimidation by threatening Gayle too. You were tearing yourself apart not knowing what to do, but before things got out of hand you were told it was all off. You imagined Tony was safe, so you decided to keep your mouth shut. Why would you incriminate yourself for no reason? What happened at Hillcrest was out of your hands. In fact what you did there is in your favour. The cops have already told me that.'

'So do you reckon there'll be any charges against me?' It was a question Ryan was afraid to ask. But he had to know the answer.

Kenny gave him a reassuring smile. 'Technically you haven't committed any real crime, so I don't see what they can book you with. Any minor laws you may have broken was only done to protect your girl. The sort of thing any decent guy would do. I'm sure they'll take that into consideration. The same way as the warning you shouted out will be. That took guts Steve. You probably saved two lives.' He continued to relieve Ryan's anxiety. 'You must know that there's nobody left around who's gonna contradict what we say. I reckon the cops will just accept the situation for what it is and not take it any further.'

Hope flickered in Ryan. 'You really believe that? You're not just saying it?'

'That's the way I see it.' There was a confident sound to Kenny's voice. 'Just get your story right and you should be OK.' He winked. 'I reckon that makes us about even huh.'

Ryan was cautious in his optimism. How many times recently had he imagined that he was in the clear? Each time that hope had been destroyed. Now, finally, could it be true? Please God let it be.

'I don't know what to say,' he told Kenny. He was not lying. Gratitude, relief, even a sense of humbleness all contributed to his inability to find the right words.

Kenny grinned. 'Save it for Gayle. You stuck your neck out a long way for that girl and she knows it.'

A look of alarm crossed Ryan's face.

'Take it easy,' Kenny assured him. 'Only Tony and myself will ever know the full story. As far as Gayle's concerned you're still the guy in the white hat, even if it has got a little bit of dirt on it.' He walked to the door before glancing at his watch. 'She should be here soon, so you sure don't want me hanging around any longer.'

Gayle arrived half an hour later. Even Kenny's diluted version of the truth had shocked her. She had spent a long time preparing herself for this meeting. Discovering the lengths to which Ryan had gone to protect her had touched her most poignant emotions. Only now did she fully appreciate the depth of his feelings toward her. It was incredible. Especially considering the short time they had known each other. Looking back, she was horrified at the blunt way she had told him to pull himself together. It was only in the course of protecting her that he'd been reduced to such a condition in the first place.

For all that, she was still reluctant to make hasty promises about their future together. With one broken engagement recently behind her, even under normal circumstances she would have hesitated to commit herself fully again in such a hurry. With a situation as complex as this she still needed a great deal more time.

Brightened by his talk with Kenny, Ryan greeted her with a big smile.

The reception surprised Gayle. She'd expected him to be far tenser given the events of the previous day. Immediately she decided that she would have to be straight with him over her uncertain feelings. There was no point in glossing over things any longer and allowing false hopes to rise. If nothing else, Steve deserved her total honesty.

She pulled up a chair and they began to talk.

*

It was another three weeks before Ryan prepared to fly home. Manelli and Kenny had already left the country a week before. Every one of the singer's concerts had been a huge success and he had departed vowing to return soon.

Before leaving, Manelli had made a point of having a long, confidential talk with Ryan. Although awkward and uneasy at first, the one question Ryan dreaded the most was not raised by the American. Had Parker's plans remained

IN THE LONG RUN

unchanged, even he did not now know for certain if his feelings for Gayle would have continued to prevent him from attempting some desperate, last minute move to save the singer. As the pressure built up, could he really have just stood back and allowed a man he liked and respected so much be murdered in cold blood? He would never know the answer for sure. He suspected Manelli was also aware of his uncertainty over this.

The two men eventually parted on friendly terms. Ryan guessed that it was Kenny's influence that had done much to repair the damage.

Also on the New York bound plane, barely able to believe what was happening, were Tracy and her mother. A four-week holiday in the States courtesy of Manelli lay ahead of them. As a sensitive person appalled by violence, Tracy had suffered considerable shock over the events at Hillcrest. Now, thanks largely to her hero's support, she had managed to put a large part of that night's horror from her mind. Her radiant smile when boarding the aircraft said far more about her recovery than any medical report.

To Ryan's enormous relief, matters with the police had worked out pretty much as Kenny anticipated. There had been endless more questions of course. That was only to be expected. There was also a severe caution as to future conduct. But that was all. No actual charges were to be made. Later, in a more reflective mood, Ryan could not help but wonder if this still would have been the case had he escaped unscathed from the car crash. This was something else he would never know for certain.

He was now sat with Gayle in the cafeteria at Durban airport, trying hard to string out their last few moments together. For a third time his flight was called over the public address, prompting Gayle to hand him his crutches.

'I suppose it's time then,' he said. Reluctantly he raised himself up.

She kissed him. It was not passionate, but there was definite affection there. 'Don't forget to call me as soon as you're home safely,' she said.

He gave her a lopsided grin. 'I'm dreading my phone bill already.'

They stood there looking at each other for a few moments.

'Gayle, I just want—' Ryan began.

She placed a finger quickly on his lips, stopping him in mid-sentence. 'If you come back, you can say it then. I'll still be here.'

A look of fierce determination crossed his face. 'I'll be back all right. And when I do come it'll be without these bloody things.'

He slapped both hands against the crutches.

GEORGE STRATFORD

Another pause followed. There were a hundred more things to be said. There were also a hundred good reasons for not saying them yet. Together they moved on to the final parting point.

Gayle knew that she could not hang around and prolong the issue any longer. It was already difficult enough for both of them. Even at this late stage she felt that he was hoping to hear things from her that she could not yet commit herself to.

'Good luck,' she whispered in his ear before giving him one final kiss.

She then turned and walked rapidly away, hating herself for her inability to accept him as he was now without all this painful soul-searching and indecision. Small tears began to sting her eyes. She stopped and reached into her bag for a tissue to wipe them away. His silver Comrades medal lay there on top.

When she looked back behind her he had disappeared.

Ryan sat in the departure lounge staring through the large window and out across the airfield. He gazed forlornly at the Jumbo Jet that would shortly be taking him back to Britain. Who would have thought it possible, he reflected, remembering his hostile attitude when arriving in Durban? He was another person when he had first set foot here, hating the country and everything that it stood for. Now look at him: in love with a South African girl and minus one leg.

Although deeply hurt to be leaving under such a large cloud of uncertainty, he could finally accept Gayle's need for more time. Sure the wait would be painful, but even this was perhaps better than hearing rash promises made in a moment of emotional obligation. Promises that might prove impossible to keep in the long term.

The question was, how long would she take? She was an attractive girl who would always be a target for men. Able-bodied men who could offer her far more than he ever could. Was he being unfair to her? Did he really have any right to expect the girl to save herself for a cripple living six thousand miles away?

He was still brooding on this when the steward came to assist him aboard.

*

It was the first Saturday that Armstrong had been allowed to return to work in the du Toit's garden. Now fully restored to fitness, he had nonetheless covered the twelve kilometres from home to Blythdale Beach at nothing more than a slow jog. After six weeks of relative inactivity it felt strange to be running once more.

IN THE LONG RUN

So strange that he was not sure if his heart was still in it. Whether or not he competed in the Comrades again remained to be seen.

Piet greeted him warmly, after which Armstrong set about his work in the usual way. A few minutes later a smiling Cecile and Claudine both emerged from the house and came over to welcome him back. Significantly though, there was no sign of Michelle appearing to do the same.

Armstrong thought about her as he worked. She had told him about the laxatives while they were alone at the hospital. At first he had been hurt and angry, but that feeling soon passed. She was only a child, and as the tears of remorse ran down her face he could not help but forgive her. It was easy to understand how she had felt neglected because of all the time and attention the Boss had given to his running. In a funny kind of way her confession had given him a lift. At least there was a reason for his poor performance. Under the circumstances perhaps he did not have too much to be ashamed of after all? There might even be a small cause for pride. He now wondered whether this new, nicer Miss Michelle would continue. Or would she soon go back to her old ways?

His question was soon answered. She appeared suddenly by the garage door. There was no sign of a welcoming smile on her face.

'Armstrong! Come here, I want you.' Her voice was sharp.

He sighed and shook his head. So it had not taken long for her to change back. Reluctantly he approached her.

'Yes Miss Michelle.'

'Come with me,' she ordered, at the same time entering the garage. 'There's something I want you to do.'

Mystified, Armstrong followed her.

An old sheet was spread over something large in the back corner. 'Uncover that,' she snapped, jabbing a finger towards the object.

Armstrong pulled away the sheet. Hidden underneath was a gleaming, brand new bicycle, fully fitted with a host of accessories. It was the very kind he had dreamed of owning ever since his old bike had been stolen. He looked at it with something approaching envy.

'I want you to take that away for me Armstrong,' Michelle continued in the same bossy voice. 'I don't care what you do with it. Just take it away.'

That was as far as the young girl got. Unable to maintain her fierce pretence any longer, she burst into a loud fit of giggling.

GEORGE STRATFORD

The boy looked at her in disbelief and amazement. Then, standing in the garage entrance, he saw the rest of the family gathered. They too began to laugh.

'This is for me,' was all he could manage to say. His eyes grew large.

Piet approached him, grinning. He placed a reassuring hand on the youth's shoulder. 'It's yours Armstrong. A present from Michelle to say how sorry she is for what she did. It was all her own idea, and she's paying me back weekly from her pocket money.'

Michelle stopped giggling long enough to say: 'I didn't really mean to upset you again Armstrong. I just wanted to be nasty to you one last time. You should have seen your face.' The laughter then overcame her once more.

Slowly Armstrong was getting over his surprise. His normal smile returned, now wider than ever. Despite the lump in his throat he felt sure that, for this single moment at least, there was no one in the world happier than himself.

IN THE LONG RUN

EPILOGUE

February 1991

James' efforts to improve his character since returning home from the Comrades had not been easy. Even so, they had not gone unnoticed by either parent.

For six agonising months he had been forced to go about his daily life with the threat of Aids still hanging ominously over his head. It was a hell not made any easier by his own pessimistic outlook. He had learned much more about the virus, and with needle-using drug addicts being such a high risk group, he felt justified in his gloomy thinking. It was like a suspended death sentence. At some low point almost every day he would find himself speculating over what it might be like to slowly waste away, unable at the end to do even the smallest task for himself.

When the all clear finally came it was like being reborn. He had been given a second chance after having come face to face with an early and hideous death. It was during this new beginning that he first discovered just how many of his former values and opinions had now genuinely altered. The seeds of change, subconsciously planted in the aftermath of his Comrades experience, had now taken a firm root.

He had read somewhere a long time ago that the prospect of imminent death causes a man to reassess himself. It was a suggestion that he had scoffed at then. Only now did he fully realise the truth of the statement. For reasons that he did not even fully understand himself, James had concealed his fear of infection from his parents throughout the long wait. Only after the burden was finally lifted did he quietly take his mother aside and tell her what might have been. The look of horrified relief on her face convinced him that he had got it right.

GEORGE STRATFORD

Now, with life opening up before him once more, he was far keener to make something of his opportunities this time around. His delighted father was only too pleased to help him get started. James took a junior position at the stock exchange, and although he was hardly yet blazing a glorious trail through the financial world, he was at least making steady progress. His temper would still flare from time to time, but generally it was now channelled rather than pure blind aggression. Even the timid maid Patience had begun to feel more at ease with him.

As was his habit every evening recently, James was relaxing after dinner for half an hour by sitting quietly on the vast back porch of their house. Earlier that day there had been the state opening of the South African Parliament. During this ceremonial occasion President de Klerk had announced his intention to abolish the remaining few laws of apartheid. It was to be the first step toward elections and majority rule.

The present system had been with James all his life. He pondered deeply on how these changes might affect both himself and the country in general. At one time he would have fought furiously to help preserve white rule. Although still having serious reservations about the proposed speed of such reforms, he could now at least bring himself to positively acknowledge the basic rights of every individual. For him, that was a radical enough switch for the time being. Any further acceptance of a truly equal multi-racial society would only come about when the new system had been fully implemented and sampled. It would, he supposed, require an effort from all sides to make it work.

It was this final consideration that suddenly and uncomfortably brought Armstrong back to mind. Once home from Durban, and with the Aids scare occupying so much of his time, he had all but forgotten about the youth. Now, in this reflective mood, their experience came back in vivid detail. Armstrong was still very much in his thoughts when his father wandered outside to join him.

'A penny for them James,' he remarked, seeing his son's thoughtful expression.

James made a snap decision. 'You remember that Zulu boy I told you about? The one that helped me during the Comrades.'

Charles' face reflected a sudden sharp interest. 'Of course I do. What's made you bring him up all of a sudden?'

'How would you feel if I invited him up here one weekend? You know — as a house guest.'

His father looked taken aback. 'Are you sure that's what you want?'

'I think so,' James replied. 'I still feel that I owe him something.'

IN THE LONG RUN

Charles Kirkpatrick's look of surprise slowly changed to a gratified smile. 'You do indeed James,' he said. 'To tell you the truth, I've been wondering how long it would take for you to finally acknowledge that obligation. Yes, invite him by all means, I'd be delighted to have him here. It's the very least we can do after the insensitive manner in which you repaid him for all his efforts on your behalf.'

A sudden thought then registered with Charles, causing him to regard his son with a humorous smile. 'Don't forget to have a quiet talk with the lad before you introduce us though. After all, I would hate to be mistaken for a ghost.'

James winced at the reminder. 'Oh hell,' he muttered.

*

Moving stiffly but nonetheless unaided, Ryan walked towards the same airport terminal in Durban that he had approached with such different feelings those eight months ago. Given all that had happened since then, it could well have been eight years.

Ever since arriving back in Britain he had been anticipating — had spent hour after hour rehearsing — this very moment. All the time hoping against hope that things would turn out in the way he so longed for. It was this hope, and virtually nothing else, that had kept him going through the endless and painful months of rehabilitation.

Gayle had written to him regularly at least once a week. Encouraged by the tone and frequency of her letters, his optimism had steadily grown. She sounded ever eager for news, and was quick to congratulate him on any little progress he made with the high technology artificial limb that had become an essential part of his life. Even now he was still coming to terms with the thing, but there was no doubt that it got a little easier with practically every day that passed.

Proudly he walked under his own steam into the terminal building. He spotted Gayle immediately. She was stood there just as he had fondly imagined she would be, waving and smiling from the glass-fronted balcony above. Surely, he told himself, she would not appear so happy unless she had good news for him. David was there too, standing alongside her. He also looked pretty pleased with things.

He waved happily back to them both. But then, even as his arm fell to his side, the doubts began to set in. He was doing what he had sworn not to. He was presupposing the outcome of this reunion. He still had no solid proof yet that Gayle had overcome all her doubts and could now happily share her life with a part cripple. For all he knew she might merely be greeting him as a returning friend, not a lover. In fact, now that he looked at her again, that was the impression he got.

While waiting in the queue for passport control, he suddenly found his confidence rapidly draining.

After joining them for a quick drink in the airport bar, David soon took his leave. The manner of his parting led Ryan to believe that this had been prearranged. While genuinely pleased to see David once more, he was still relieved to see him go. Up until now the talk had been just general chatter. All very nice, but it did not provide the answer to his prime concern. Although realising how stupid it would be to rush things, he was already struggling to control his impatience.

Old Martha was waiting faithfully in the airport car park. Her front passenger seat groaned almost as if in welcoming recognition as he climbed inside. Just over twenty minutes later the battered vehicle dutifully delivered them outside Gayle's flat.

Twice during the journey Ryan had been on the point of saying something. On both occasions he had checked himself. Although bursting to know Gayle's feelings, for some silly reason he wanted her to be the one to raise the subject. Surely she must be aware of the terrible suspense he was in?

Much to his continuing dismay, once inside the flat Gayle still showed no inclination to talk. Instead she switched on the TV. A recording of President de Klerk's earlier speech was just beginning.

In spite of his urgent desire to discuss matters, Ryan soon found himself watching closely. This was the first he had heard of the day's news. The announcement had been expected of course, but to hear officially that apartheid was finally finished was a long cherished dream of his. To actually be in the country on the very day this was publicly declared was really something.

The broadcast finished, prompting Gayle to switch the set off immediately. 'I thought you'd be pretty interested in seeing that,' she said, looking directly into his eyes for the first time since David's departure.

Ryan nodded. 'Now that gives some real hope for the future over here.' For a moment his voice was bright with optimism.

Gayle smiled cautiously. 'I hope to God you're right Steve. Time will tell. To be honest, I'm a bit nervous about it all. Not that I don't want the changes to happen — I do. But I know the set up here better than you. Believe me, there'll be a whole stack of different groups and old enemies all demanding different things. How the heck do you please them all? I can't help feeling that there'll be

IN THE LONG RUN

a lot of problems before things are sorted.' She paused briefly to frown. 'We've got to get through it somehow though. It's the only sensible way. Like you say Steve, this is our chance for a great future. I just pray that everyone else eventually gets to see it that way too.'

It was quite a speech for her. There was a lengthy silence as they both reflected on the day's developments and the possible consequences that lay ahead.

Ryan spoke first. Without warning his thoughts turned away from politics and back to more personal matters. He couldn't wait any longer. He had to know how things stood between them right now. This highly significant day suddenly became an ironically suitable time to discover the truth.

'Talking about futures, what about ours? Have we got one?' He shot the question at her. As soon as the words were out he found himself holding his breath.

Gayle did not reply immediately. Instead she walked across the room and placed herself by the window. Her expression was serious.

'I wondered how long it would take you to ask me that,' she said eventually.

'Well what about it?' Ryan pressed. There was now no room for backtracking. 'Can we make some kind of plan together? Surely you must have decided.'

She continued to look serious. 'I'm sorry Steve, but there's something more I need from you first.'

It did not look good. Ryan let out a deep sigh. 'What's that?'

Slowly a large smile formed on Gayle's face. She held up his silver medal. 'I want you to come over here and claim what's yours. And while you're about it you can give me a proper kiss. All I've had from you so far today is a lousy peck on the cheek.'

Even with two good legs Ryan had never been the greatest of sprinters. This fact was now totally belied by the speed with which he somehow managed to cross the room.

Introducing George Stratford – one of the many new authors published by Citron Press, the only publishing house dedicated exclusively to promoting new fiction in this country.

We are determined to give new authors like George Stratford a platform for their writing. We are even more determined to give our growing list of loyal readers access to the freshest, most innovative new fiction – fiction that doesn't bow to the latest fashion or formula.

The face of the future

If you believe that new talent should have a voice and an audience please support Citron Press.

Support New Fiction by Supporting

CITRON
PRESS

Citron Books can be purchased direct from all good book shops, or ordered by phoning **0845 602 2202**. Or you can find us at **www.citronpress.co.uk**

Further Reading
from Citron Press

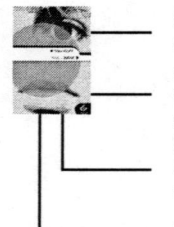

GULLSCLIFF *by* PATRICK BURKE

'An undiscovered literary gem' *Amazon Review*

Cornelius Pardoe's spectacular memorial to the Kentish miners nears completion. Stone carver, lettercutter, fervent admirer of Gill and Morris, Pardoe is an artist obsessed by his craft, working long hours alone in a small studio in Gullscliff, once a fashionable seaside resort, now in slow but inexorable decline.

For six unhappy years, work, alcohol and a small circle of close friends have sustained him following the bizarre and tragic death of his young wife. During a comic, roistering week of heatwave, outside recognition suddenly beckons, whilst the arrival of Sharon promises an end to his long period of mourning.

ORDER NO. D0101

THE FOREIGNER *by* PAUL COX

'Cox's riveting work is more than just a history lesson...it doesn't just tug at the reader's heart strings — it tears them right out' *The Big Issue*

In the post-war climate of change, the foreigner is driven from his native Sudeten Land by Czech Partisans. From internment to employment in the coalfields of Nottinghamshire, Milos is a refugee, a man whose life is a struggle to belong. Handicapped by language and the indelible memory of his past, he finds his own bond of friendship with Peggy, another man's wife. But when he becomes involved in the miners' stand against Thatcher in the 1980s, Milos finds that history repeats itself. Once more in the midst of a divided community, its people at war, he discovers that he is still a foreigner, even to himself.

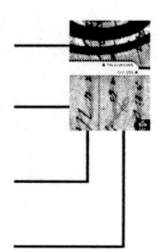

ORDER NO. D0107

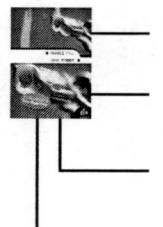

FRAGILE STATE *by* DAVID TURNER

'Absorbing and accomplished New Scottish Noir in the tradition of Irvine Welsh. Could do for booze what Trainspotting did for heroin.' *The Guardian*

When his girlfriend disappears and his best friend commits suicide, Glen McGregor's solution is to get mind-numbingly drunk. But as bad as things are they can always get worse, and soon he's on a reluctant collision course with the truth, his progress hindered by MI5, the Metropolitan Police, various dead bodies and an overwhelming desire to run away and hide.

ORDER NO. T0108

RING OF DEATH *by* JOHN COLLINS

The body of an insurance investigator is found at a prehistoric stone circle in Cornwall. Suicide or murder? Loyal to the end, his best friend's not convinced and his search for evidence begins. High level corruption unearthed, he is led into the dark and sinister world of secret and illicit arms traffic. In this absorbing tale of murder, blackmail and depravity a lethal conspiracy is revealed. But how many victims need there be? And who will finish ahead of the game?

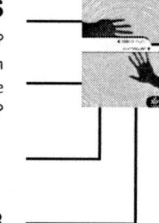

'A vigorous thriller set in the covert world of the illegal arms trade' *Reader's review*

ORDER NO. T2088

Support new fiction

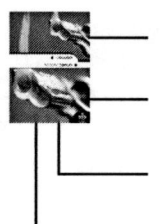

CHINAMEN by ANTHONY FOWLES

Cynical, self-centred thirty-something Alan Prentice, an almost perpetually 'resting' actor, has two interests: adultery and weekend cricket. Then a third preoccupation invades his life — murder. Finding a team mate battered to death, Prentice casts himself as private eye. His discoveries throw an unsettlingly baleful light on both the theatre and coarse cricket, but as increasing bravery and compassion is demanded of him, Prentice grows towards becoming a better man. For all its ingeniously consistent cricket-based resolution, Prentice's ultimate confrontation with the killer satisfyingly confirms that Chinamen is concerned with serious adult values.

ORDER NO. T2163

THE MONDAY LUNCHTIME OF THE LIVING DEAD by JEREMY JEHU

'A terrific read'   Neil Darbyshire, *Daily Telegraph*

Rupert Tranquil sees himself as a clubland hero — hip, smart and ever ready to twist the right screws. When a simple spot of blackmail erupts into a bloody fiasco and old mate Rick begs him to save his life, Rupert's self-deception dissipates. Rick's been dead for twenty years! Rupert should know. He killed him.

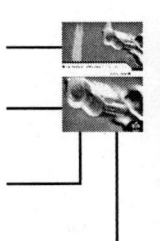

ORDER NO. T0107

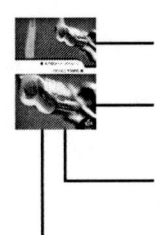

A PATH TO DARKNESS by MICHAEL YOUNG

'Compulsive reading' — a powerful thriller based on the Troubles in Northern Ireland

When international terrorist Emilio Vasquez — loaned to the IRA by Libya — unleashes a massive bomb in Central London, former SAS man Nick Barratt's carefully charted future is violently derailed. Seeking vengeance, he joins the Province Group, a secret organisation waging a covert war against the Provos. Barratt stalks Vasquez through the badlands of South Armagh; through age-old hatreds and betrayals. Meanwhile, both men are hunted by the security forces and the Met's anti-terrorist squad. As the net tightens, and destiny calls, Barratt is pitched into a climactic hand-to-hand fight for survival.

ORDER NO. T2077

THE RIVER THIEF by BARRY ROSS

From the safe lunacy of Soho to the quaint rural pursuits of 'ye olde drugge deale', my decision to 'find myself' in the country gloriously backfired. Seriously threatened and romantically rebuffed, I wanted out... But someone was trying to steal a river and, stupidly, I decided to stop them...

Funny, inventive and sharp, *The River Thief* is a black comedy thriller with teeth, a bizarre cocktail of drugs, heavies and the landed gentry, with a languid hero caught in the fallout. Seldom has country air stunk of such stewed corruption...

ORDER NO. T0109

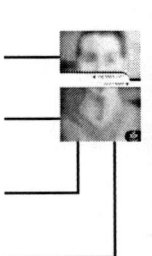

By supporting Citron Press

Further Reading
from Citron Press

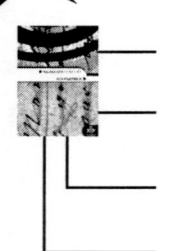

THE KALANISSOS CONTRACT *by* KEN PEARMAIN
Beneath the dazzling light of Kalanissos lies a dark secret

It seemed a simple enough task - to go through St John Beauvoir's unpublished papers to uncover his mysterious past on the Greek island of Kalanissos. But Mark Beauvoir soon finds that he has taken on more than he could ever have expected. After the arrival of Spiros, his Greek lookalike, and a break-in at his home, Mark realises that the truth lies in Greece itself. There, on the island of Kalanissos, he finally confronts sinister forces from the past - and discovers a great deal about himself.

'An intriguing read with a wonderfully strong sense of Greek landscape and light'   *Reader's review*

ORDER NO. R2105

THE MAN WHO SHOT CHE GUEVARA *by* MALCOLM HARRISON

As Latin America descends into the most vicious decade of its turbulent history, Argentina's generals are losing out. The terrorists and the death squad are out of control and Peron's widow is plundering the leavings of a once rich nation. Weak, split and short of cash, no one general is prepared to gamble on winning a civil war. It takes the machinations of Propaganda Due, the Latin world's most secretive and powerful lodge, access to Vatican funds and the ruthlessness of the man who shot Che Guevara to pave the way for a new Junta, whose successors were to stay in power until defeated on the Falklands.

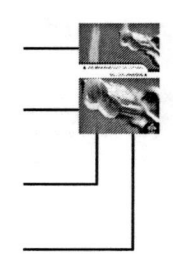

ORDER NO. T1195

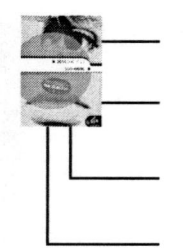

DEAD SANCTITIES *by* SEAN BADAL
'An original thriller which vividly evokes its Indian setting'   *The Guardian*

Journalist Vishnu Kolandra's London upbringing is no preparation for the wonderful yet disturbing dichotomy that is India. Adjusting to frenzied new surroundings, Vishnu finds himself encircled by casual acquaintances and developing interests — that is, until his involvement with a corruption and nepotism scandal jeopardises his new career.

Vishnu is forced to confront a labyrinthine present with the sick realisation that the roads of his past are converging on one surprising location — an old Indo-Saracenic building in downtown Bombay.

ORDER NO. J0107

NIGHTFALL *by* DAVID RICHARDSON

Adam Price has almost achieved his aim of visiting every country in the world — until fate steps in. Stranded in a Middle Eastern airport while Islamic fundamentalists attempt to take control of the country, Price finds himself thrown back into the past. As the clock ticks towards the last days of the millennium, the story of his life is told in flashback — his entry into espionage, his love affair with a terrorist and his passion for danger.

But when you have a guilty secret, the past is just as dangerous as the present.

ORDER NO. T2098

Support new fiction

Order this Fresh Fiction *from* Citron Press

All Citron Press books are available at bookshops nationwide, on-line from amazon.co.uk, the Internet bookseller, or by ordering direct from Citron Press.
To order any of the books detailed above, simply complete the order form below, including the order numbers of your selection in the space provided and post to Citron Press, or phone the Citron Hotline.

Citron Press Hotline: 0845 602 2202

Order No.		£7.99	Order No.		£7.99
Order No.		£7.99	Order No.		£7.99
Order No.		£7.99	Order No.		£7.99

*Please note: postage and packaging are **included** in the above prices*

Name..
Address..
....
....
....Postcode....................................
Telephone...................................E-mail...

Post your order to:
　　　Citron Press, P.O. Box 88, Southampton SO14 0ZA
Please make all cheques payable to: **Citron Press**

　　If you prefer to pay by credit card, please complete the following:
　　Please debit my Visa/Mastercard (delete as applicable) card no:

☐☐☐☐ ☐☐☐☐ ☐☐☐☐ ☐☐☐☐

Signature _____　　Expiry date ___ / ___

Visit our website at www.citronpress.co.uk

By supporting Citron Press

Your nearest bookshop
The most convenient way to purchase innovative new fiction

CITRON PRESS

www.citronpress.co.uk